CW01263080

WHEN DEATH CALLS

HIDDEN NORFOLK
BOOK 16

J M DALGLIESH

First published by Hamilton Press in 2025

Copyright © J M Dalgliesh, 2025

The right of J M Dalgliesh to be identified as the Author of the Work has been asserted by him in accordance with the Copyright, Designs and Patents Act 1988.
All rights reserved. No part of this publication may be reproduced, stored in a retrieval system, or transmitted, in any form or by any means, electronic, mechanical, photocopying, recording, scanning, or otherwise without written permission of the publisher, nor be otherwise circulated in any form of binding or cover other than that in which it is published and without a similar condition being imposed on the subsequent purchaser. It is illegal to copy this book, post it to a website, or distribute it by any other means without permission.

Names, characters, businesses, places, events and incidents are either the products of the author's imagination or used in a purely fictitious manner. Any resemblance to real persons, living or dead, or actual events is purely coincidental.

ISBN (Trade Paperback) 978-1-80080-124-0
ISBN (Hardback) 978-1-80080-948-2
ISBN (Large Print) 978-1-80080-603-0

EXCLUSIVE OFFER

Look out for the link at the end of this book or visit my website at **www.jmdalgliesh.com** to sign up to my no-spam VIP Club and receive a FREE Hidden Norfolk novella plus news and previews of forthcoming works.

Never miss a new release.

No spam, ever, guaranteed. You can unsubscribe at any time.

WHEN DEATH CALLS

PROLOGUE

THE BELL above the door chimes again and I look up expectantly. It's just a little old man, the one who'd been sitting in the far corner taking his sweet time over his pot of tea and a toasted teacake, who is now shuffling out into the street. He draws his coat around him, struggling with the zipper whilst leaning on his walking stick. I think it's far too warm to be wearing a coat that heavy. Maybe that's one of the things that changes as you get older, you need more protection from the elements. That thought sparks something inside me and I remember last night. It's a warm feeling; a sense of longing, excitement and anticipation of it happening again.

Looking up at the clock on the wall, I check my watch to see if they match. The lady behind the counter catches my eye. She saw me check the time. She's thinking along the same lines as me albeit, I suspect, for different reasons. My cup is empty. The hot chocolate is long gone and even the remnants of the frothy whipped cream topping has hardened around the rim. I nursed it for as long as I dared, finishing it when it had already gone cold.

Glancing up towards the counter, she's giving me the stink

eye. There are several people in the queue now and only one free table left, recently vacated by the little chap with the hunchback and walking stick. She wants me to leave. Fair enough, I guess. I've been here for three quarters of an hour, maybe longer. One hot chocolate with cream and mini-marshmallows is hardly going to pay the bills. I pretend not to see her looking but she's staring at me intensely now.

"Fine," I mutter, pushing back my chair. The legs scrape on the wooden floor and I see her smug, satisfied expression as she comes out from behind the counter, gathering up my cup and wiping down the table's surface before I've even stepped away.

She doesn't say anything and I hurry to the door, feeling like everyone's eyes are upon me. They all know. I've been there alone for ages and they all know I was waiting for someone. He didn't show up. I know it. They all know it. I can feel my cheeks flushing as I push the door but it doesn't move. It opens inwards and now I think they can all see I'm also an idiot, unable to read the big red letters on the sticker attached to the glass that spells *PULL*.

Once I'm safely out into the street, I chance a quick look back inside but no one is watching me. Fresh customers are already taking their seats at my table. The sour-faced cow who owns the place is smiling warmly at them. She didn't smile like that at me. Am I invisible or so insignificant that I'm so easily forgettable? Catching my reflection in the window, I feel stupid. The lipstick I'm wearing is a brighter shade of red than is probably best suited to my skin tone and clashes with the frames of my glasses. I'm also wearing far too much foundation and my cheeks are aglow artificially with over-application of my blusher. My embarrassment would probably be enough to achieve the same effect. I look like one of those Russian dolls, the little ones with the painted cheeks.

I wanted to make a good impression. I wanted him to think… I don't know what I wanted him to think. What was all of this about? It's me being silly, isn't it? When all is said and done, what is it that I have to offer him anyway? I'm such a fool.

There's a lady sitting in the soft chair beside the window. Her husband has his back to me but she is watching me, studying me. I turn and hurry away, head down, picking up the pace and pretending that everything is happening exactly as I planned.

A figure stumbles into me on the narrow pavement and instinctively I apologise, knowing I wasn't looking where I was going. I catch his eye and realisation dawns just as he takes a firm grip of my upper arm, steering me into an alleyway off the main road.

"I thought you weren't coming—"

"Shush!" he says, forcibly guiding me forwards.

"Hey!" I say as he pushes me off balance and further into the narrow passage between the old buildings. "You don't have to be so rough—"

"Shut up!" he says firmly, and something in his tone makes me do exactly that. I've always been cowed by authority and I lower my head. His demeanour changes, softening and with his hands gently, but firmly, placed on my shoulders, he turns me to face him, looking down into my eyes. He looks much more serious than usual. Sterner. Older. There's that flutter of anticipation in my chest again, along with the manifestation of the knot in my stomach at the same time but this is very different. I don't see desire in his eyes, passion in his demeanour. His expression is cold.

"I thought you weren't coming," I say again. "I would have waited inside if I'd—"

"Seriously, shut up," he says, his grip tightening on my

bare shoulders, the skin exposed by my choice this morning to wear a sleeveless crop-top.

"Sorry."

"Listen… it's not that I don't… want to see you…"

Why is he speaking to me like this? He's never spoken to me in this way before. I raise my eyes to meet his gaze. He has a hooded sweater on, and the hood is pulled up over his head. He glances back towards the street, people are passing the entrance but none are paying us any attention. *Is he ashamed to be seen with me?*

"I should never have let things get this far," he says, almost apologetically, but I sense there's something else motivating him beyond contrition. He's not had any complaints over the past few weeks. I can't see why anything that's happened should have changed things. But it has changed. All of it. I can see it now, written large in his expression.

"You're… breaking up with me?" The words catch in my throat, and I feel real pain as I say them out loud.

"We were never together," he says, coldly dismissive. "You know that."

"But I thought you said—"

"Forget what I said!" he hisses, startling me. "It never happened."

"But it did happen."

He forcibly squeezes my shoulders and it hurts. I mean, it really hurts. I protest but he pushes me against the wall, the coarseness of the brick scraping the skin of my shoulders.

"It shouldn't have—"

"But it did!" I counter, repeating myself. "You said you loved me—"

"I said all kinds of things! I should have known better. I didn't mean it, any of it." I can feel my eyes tearing and I want to speak but my mouth is dry. He relaxes his grip, if only a little, leaning forward and resting his forehead against mine. He lowers his voice, speaking softly, more like he does usually. "For what it's worth, I am sorry. I never meant to hurt you."

He makes to leave but I reach out, grasping the material of his sweater and trying to pull him back. He shrugs off my hold with ease, increasing the length of his stride.

"No! Wait... please," I shout at him, trying to stop him from leaving me. Running after him, I grab his arm, hauling him back. He spins on his heel, lunges at me and, using both hands, shoves me away from him. I stumble backwards, tripping over my own feet and falling backwards, landing on my backside. He comes to stand over me, jabbing a finger towards me.

"Don't look at me, don't call me... and don't speak of this to anyone... ever," he says, glaring at me. "If you do... so help me girl, I'll make your life a living hell!"

"Please... don't leave me like this!"

But he is already at the end of the passage and, after furtively looking in both directions up and down the street, he moves to his right and disappears from view without looking back. I'm up onto my knees now, sobbing uncontrollably.

Why would he do this to me after everything we've done together, after everything that's been said. I don't understand. How can he be like this, so cold and uncompromising?

What have I done?

CHAPTER ONE

"Come on," Alice said, hauling him forward. Reluctantly, Tom allowed himself to be pulled in the direction of the entrance doors, releasing the backward pressure on his heels. He could have sworn these doors were a different colour back in the day; red if his memory served him correctly. Honestly, so much time had passed that they were probably different doors altogether. "This will be good for you."

"My mum used to say that when we had to go for swimming lessons in the outdoor pool," Tom said, arching his eyebrows at her. "And she was lying too."

"Honestly, I don't know what to do with you," Alice said, scolding him and resuming the action of dragging him up the steps to the doors. They could hear the music playing somewhere inside. The dull rhythmic thud of dance classics blaring out of large speakers. Tom stopped at the top of the stairs, casting an eye over the banner mounted above the doors. *Welcome to the class of...* The year had not been added. Based on the weathering at the edges of the banner it was likely used for every event and the constant reuse, mounting and taking down, was causing it to fray at the corners.

"Do we really need to go in?" Tom asked, a half-hearted question because he already knew his wife's response. She tilted her head in that way she always did when she had no intention of answering the question. The look on her face conveyed her thoughts. "I guess we do then," he said, walking towards her as Alice opened the door, gesturing for him to enter. Tom felt his collar was too tight as he walked inside and he tried to adjust it to be more comfortable.

The music was louder now and if they were in any doubt as to where they should be, then all they had to do was to follow the noise. The corridor approaching the assembly hall was much as Tom remembered it; their footfalls echoing on the polished floors, white walls and a sense of functionality rather than a place that could be described as warm or appealing.

"Bringing back memories?" Alice said, walking beside him.

"Hmm... not happy ones," he replied.

"I find all of this quite amusing," she said, looping her arm through his and giving his a gentle squeeze.

"Amusing? In what way?" He scrutinised her with a fleeting but an enquiring glance.

"This place," Alice said, looking around as they walked, passing a run of offices with opaque glass in the windows and noticeboards mounted in the corridor outside. "The thought that you come from somewhere."

Tom chuckled. "Everyone comes from somewhere."

"Yes, of course but here, this school... I find it hard to imagine a smaller version of you scampering around these corridors getting up to all kinds of mischief."

"I'll have you know that I behaved impeccably during my time at school."

Alice pursed her lips. "Why am I not surprised to hear

that? I sort of hoped you would have been the one setting fire to the table tops in science classes… unscrewing the doors on your classmates' lockers so they fall off. That sort of thing."

"Why on earth would I have done any of those things?"

Alice shrugged. "Because it would add to your dashing, all-round handsomeness. That's why."

"I think I had a detention once," Tom said, optimistically, looking at her. "A lunchtime one."

"Really? Now I am intrigued. What was it for?"

Tom frowned. "Mistaken identity, I'm afraid. Matty D did something daft and when the teacher turned round he saw me first, rather than Matty. He wouldn't listen to reason and I got the blame."

Alice sighed.

"Sorry," Tom said, grinning. "It's the best I can do."

"Well," Alice said, faking a glum expression, "by the time we're through here tonight I am going to have found someone with a story to tell about you."

Tom laughed. "I wouldn't hold your breath. I'll be surprised if most people even remember me."

"Who could forget a gentle giant like you?" Alice asked. The double doors marking the entrance to the assembly hall burst open and they both had to take a step back to avoid being caught by one of the doors. Two men stumbled out, laughing. It was evident they'd been making the most of the beverages available as they struggled to right themselves. The first, a portly man in an ill-fitting brown suit smiled apologetically. It was the second, a slim, balding man who spoke.

"I'm sorry," he said, trying to catch his breath and glancing at his friend. "We didn't mean to catch you." His expression changed and he looked concerned. "We didn't, did we?"

"No, not at all," Alice said. Tom shook his head. The man exhaled heavily.

"Thank God." He made to leave but first took a double take of Tom, sizing him up. His expression brightened and he smiled, snapping his thumb and pointing at Tom. "It's Tim, isn't it?" he said, gleefully. "Tim Johnson."

Tom smiled, cocking his head. "Absolutely. Guilty as charged."

The man stepped forward and threw his arms around Tom in a bear hug. He looked at his companion. "You remember Tim, don't you?" The other man shook his head.

"No, sorry."

"Of course you do! He was captain of the... the..." he looked at Tom. "What were you captain of again?"

"I wasn't," Tom said.

"Oh... I could have sworn you were." He seemed pensive and no one spoke for a moment. "Right, well... it was great to see you."

"You too," Tom said, smiling. "Maybe we could catch up later."

"Sounds good."

The two men resumed their course, wherever they were going and Tom looked at Alice.

"You see. They didn't remember me at all."

Alice took his hands in hers and squeezed them affectionately. "One of them remembered you. And he almost got your name right too."

Tom frowned. "You know, there was a guy we were at school with called Tim."

"Was it you?"

"No."

"Did he captain the something or other team?"

Tom was thoughtful. "Possibly."

Alice shrugged. "Well, if he isn't here tonight, you can be Tim and we can make you captain of something."

"How about the Titanic?"

Alice gently steered Tom towards the doors and pushed him in the small of his back to encourage him to enter.

The assembly hall was large, so large that the number of people present were swallowed up by its scale. Tom cast an eye around the room. Even though the lights were dimmed, disco lights flickering around the room illuminated the faces of those dancing or clustered in small groups chatting. A few people had brought their children with them and these were running around chasing one another or crawling under tables and generally having a whale of a time with the freedom on offer.

Tom could hear laughter and loud voices alongside the music. He already regretted attending, and checked his watch. It had only just gone eight o'clock and the event had started at six. If Alice hadn't pushed it, he would happily have given it a miss. Being here, decades after he graduated, it all seemed the same. Memories, not of specific instances, but more like feelings, came rushing back as if they had happened only days before. The time he spent at secondary school had not been pleasant for him. Memorable, certainly, but for all of the wrong reasons. Alice must have read his mood or seen his expression because she slipped an arm around his waist, bringing him back to the present. She smiled at him and he forced one of his own in response.

"That's better," she said. "Come on, we'll find some of your old friends around here somewhere."

"That's what I'm afraid of," he said allowing her to guide him to the tables where people were serving drinks. He handed Alice a glass of white wine and accepted a glass of orange juice for himself, thanking the lady serving. He didn't recognise her and she showed no sign of knowing him either.

"Tom Janssen!"

He looked round to see who was calling him. At first he didn't recognise her voice, and he studied her face quickly trying to put a name to her. She had shoulder-length blonde hair, styled and presented in a glamorous fashion, sporting an evening dress clinging to her figure. The rims of her glasses were neon green, very visible in the party lighting of the assembly hall. It took a moment but he recognised her.

"Charlotte Sears," Tom said, smiling as she approached. She threw her arms around him and they exchanged a kiss on the cheek before she withdrew from him, looking him up and down.

"You haven't changed a bit, Tom."

"Neither have you," he replied, smiling at her. "You look great!"

"Very kind of you to say so, darling," she said, giving him a twirl in her dress. She spun back to face him and then looked to Alice. "And who have you brought to see us?"

"This is my wife, Alice."

"Shame," Charlotte said, shaking hands with Alice. "All the best ones are taken these days." She arched her eyebrows and sipped from the glass of wine she was holding.

"You're not married then?" Tom asked, before immediately regretting asking. By their age if someone wasn't married it usually meant one of two things, either they couldn't find someone to marry them or, more likely, they had been married and no longer were. Either way, it wasn't a conversation Tom wanted to get into at the first time of asking after several decades.

"I was but, having married a frog, I'm now in need of finding my Prince Charming. And nothing will make me compromise on that mission," Charlotte said. She looked around the room. "But, at this point, the only ones available are someone else's castoffs or those so hopelessly damaged that they were a terrible choice years ago and things tend not to get better for them with age." She looked at Alice and winked. "If you know what I mean?"

"I do," Alice said. "Tom and I only married recently."

"Oh... then forgive me," Charlotte said, grimacing. "I would never mean to suggest that either of you were... damaged or..."

"A castoff?" Alice asked, laughing. Tom knew she wasn't in the least bit offended.

"Perish the thought, young Alice," Charlotte, said, putting her free hand around Alice's shoulder as one would an old and trusted friend. She drew her closer and guided her away from Tom. "Now, you can let me into the secret of how you managed to snare this year group's most dashing prospect." Charlotte glanced back at Tom and winked as the two women walked away. He was powerless to stop them. Alice smiled apologetically at him and Tom angled his head to say he understood. Charlotte Sears was nothing if not a persuasive and powerful force of nature, when she set her mind to it.

"Some people are still the same,' Tom said under his breath. A firm hand clapped him forcibly on the shoulder, so much so that he spilt some of his drink over his hand holding the glass.

"Tom Janssen as I live and breathe," a jovial voice said. Tom looked to his left and it took a brief moment for him to recognise his boyhood friend.

"Aaron," Tom said, smiling. "I heard you were living abroad."

Aaron Bell, not a particularly close friend but one of Tom's teammates on several school sports teams, had come bounding up to him. He looked older, not surprising seeing as it had been years, but he appeared to be in fine shape. Tom didn't recall him being as muscular as he was now and his hairline hadn't moved since their teenage years, nor had he started the greying effect unlike Tom.

The two men shook hands and Tom had to give it to him, the years had been kind. "You're looking well," Tom said. "Really well."

Aaron grinned, revealing a beautiful, dazzling set of white teeth. "You're not looking too bad yourself, Tom."

"I wish that were true," Tom said, glancing about them.

"Are you looking for someone?"

"I was just looking for cover," Tom said. "I think it would be better for my ego if I stood a little bit away from you."

Aaron laughed. "Eat right, get plenty of sleep and live your dreams, Tom. That's all you need."

"Is that all?" Tom said with a wry smile. "Why didn't someone say so. I'm running behind." Even under artificial coloured lighting, Tom could see a bronze tone to Aaron's skin signalling he either spent time abroad or inside a tanning salon. "Have you been somewhere hot recently?"

"I split my time between here and Dubai these days."

"Dubai?" Tom asked, nodding approvingly. "Very nice."

"Have you been?"

Tom shook his head. "No, not my type of place."

"You can get anything you want, at any time of the day or night." Aaron grinned. "The only limit is your own imagination."

Tom winced. "I was thinking more sand, sunshine and oppressively hot leading to far too much sweating."

Aaron cocked his head. "Yeah, that is pretty common too."

"So what is it you do out in Dubai?"

"Whatever I care to," Aaron said. "To be honest, it's a nice place to be to avoid handing over too much to the Treasury, if you know what I mean."

"If only some of us had the chance to."

"What is it you do these days, Tom?"

Tom had been giving a great deal of thought as to how he would answer such a question, anticipating that it was bound to come up this evening. Not that he'd come up with a satisfactory answer and, to be fair, time was not on his side.

A career as a policeman altered your social circle. When he was back in basic training he'd been advised on what actions to take with his friends. A police officer had to avoid placing themselves in compromising situations. It wasn't an option to turn a blind eye to illegal activity, however slight. To do so would compromise not only his own integrity as an officer of the law but could potentially leave him open to manipulation or allegation. Serving officers were advised on friendships, financial status and where they chose to spend their time and alongside whom they spent it with.

Taking care in these matters largely ensured police officers tended to keep within their own circles, often leaving them open to the allegation of being detached from society and not living in the real world. All of this came before any mention of Tom's current predicament, that of being suspended pending the outcome of a misconduct inquiry. The result of that would only be determined as and when the coroner ruled on the death in his last case. The death of a kidnapper and murderer, who died by Tom's hand.

He sighed. "I'm… in between jobs at the moment."

"Ah…" Aaron said, gritting his teeth. "Personal choice or enforced?"

Tom inclined his head. "Definitely enforced."

"That's worse," Aaron said. "Sorry to bring it up."

"It's okay," Tom said. "To be expected." There was no indication in Aaron's expression to signal that he was aware of the case Tom was suspended for. He was confident there would be many in the assembly hall tonight who knew. After all, it was a massive local case in the news even if it had concluded four months ago.

"Who's that?" Aaron said, staring across the hall. "I don't recognise her as a Sheringham graduate."

Tom followed Aaron's gaze. "That's Charlotte."

"No, not Charlie. I know her! I mean the young lady she's speaking with."

Almost as if they heard him talking, Charlotte and Alice came back towards them. Aaron straightened himself up, putting on what Tom considered to be a well-practised winning smile.

"Charlie Sears... please introduce me to your new friend!"

"This is Alice," Charlotte said. Alice slipped away from under Charlotte's arm around the shoulder and slipped her hand around Tom's waist. "She's Mrs Janssen."

Tom looked at Aaron and smiled. He would have told him himself if he'd had the chance to. Aaron looked suitably embarrassed.

"Sorry, old chap," he said. "No offence."

"None taken," Tom said. Alice placed a hand on his chest.

"I'm just going to get another glass of wine. Can I get you—"

"No, no," Aaron said. "Please allow me. A glass of white wine, is it?" Alice nodded. "Charlie?"

"Same for me please, Aaron."

Aaron Bell set off to get the ladies another glass of wine. Charlotte excused herself and went to greet another person who was making a beeline to say hello. Alice turned to Tom.

"How are you bearing up?"

He arched his eyebrows. "All things considered? Okay. Keen to leave though."

"We only just arrived," Alice said. She looked over at Charlotte who now had three people talking to her, almost hanging on every word she said. "She seems nice."

"Charlotte?" Tom asked. "Yes, she is."

"She wasn't in your year though, is that right?"

"No, her sister was though," Tom said.

"She didn't mention her sister," Alice said looking around. "Is she here?"

"No, she passed away."

"That's sad."

"Yes, suicide," Tom said. "It was a real shocker at the time." He pursed his lips. "Even now when I look back on it."

"Was she at school then?"

Tom nodded. "Well, just after graduation I suppose, if I'm to be accurate. In the summer after we left school."

"You and your accuracy. Yes, would have sufficed," Alice said, then lowered her voice. "And she killed herself?"

"Jumped from Sheringham cliffs," Tom said, watching Charlotte. "Her family were devastated. We all were."

"That's awful."

"Isn't it."

Aaron returned with two glasses, passing one to Alice who accepted it gratefully. Aaron looked for Charlotte and, seeing her making her way around the room and not looking like she was coming back, he upended the glass in his hand and drank the contents. Alice raised her eyebrows at Tom, but cleared her expression before Aaron looked at her, smacking his lips.

"Not a bad drop that," he said.

"Steady on," Tom said, amused. "It's still a school night."

Aaron laughed. "Neither of us have to get up for work in the morning though, do we, Tom?"

"No, but *we* do have a rather precocious young madam who will need to get up for school and she will ensure we all do."

"Children?" Aaron asked.

Tom nodded. "Just the one."

"I don't have any myself," Aaron said.

"You don't fancy changing nappies then?" Alice asked him playfully.

"I would happily do so, but the universe saw fit to have me marry a career-minded lady. Children aren't in her plans."

"I'm sorry to hear that," Alice said. "There's still time though. She might change her mind." Alice glanced around the hall. "Is she here with you?"

"No," Aaron said firmly. "She *most certainly* is not."

"Ah…" Alice sipped from her glass, Tom sensing the conversation had somehow turned awkward.

"I need another drink," Aaron said before hastily walking back towards the serving table.

"He seems… nice," Alice said.

"He's all right," Tom replied. "And putting my detective hat back on, for a minute or two, I would guess that all is not well in that particular household." His eye drifted to Charlotte. "It's a good question actually. What is she doing here?"

"Charlotte?" Alice asked. Tom nodded. "She's vice chair of the Parents' Committee." Alice waved her glass in a circular motion in the air before them. "She helped set all of this up, fundraising for the school."

"Ah, that explains it. What are they fundraising for?"

"A new science block or something," Alice said. "She did say, but I was too busy watching you."

"Me?"

"Yes, it's like watching a fish out of water," she said. "If you're not making the world a better place you look like you're struggling to breathe."

"What are you talking about—"

Alice didn't get a chance to answer as raised voices drew

their attention. A gaggle of people around the drinks table appeared to part ways and Aaron stumbled backwards amid more protests from those he bumped into. Undeterred, Aaron righted himself and moved back into the throng. Tom recognised what this could quickly escalate into.

"Excuse me a moment," he said, handing his glass to Alice.

Tom moved across the hall and through the crowd which parted before him. He found Aaron and another man, who Tom recognised as a man called Noah, squaring up to one another. Noah appeared to be the worse for drink and Tom figured that although Aaron carried his alcohol well, he was also likely to be fairly well greased himself. Tom inserted himself between the two men, gently placing his hand in the air in front of their chests but not actually making contact.

"Come on, gents, this isn't the time or the place is it?" He smiled at both of them. The size of Tom's frame made it hard for Noah, who was a great deal smaller and shorter than Tom, to see his would-be adversary clearly. "After all, we're not back at school any more, are we?" Aaron was peering past Tom, staring at Noah with a mixture of bemusement at the smaller man. Aaron wasn't as tall as Tom, but he dwarfed Noah.

"Yes, you should listen to Tom," Aaron said. "You wouldn't want to get yourself into something you can't get yourself out of… again, huh, Noah?"

Tom shot his old friend a stern look and Aaron relented, rocking his head slightly. "Help me out?" Tom asked. Aaron smiled and took a step back. However, Noah glared at him and he didn't seem in the mood to let things slide. Tom waited as Aaron took another backwards step and as long as one of them was willing to back away then the situation would escalate no further. He smiled at Noah, who met Tom's eye briefly before turning and walking away without saying a word.

"Nice to see you again too, Noah," Tom whispered beneath his breath. Those who had been gathered nearby had dissipated, moving off and mingling with others, steering well clear of the confrontation. That was a natural reaction for most people when faced with potential violence. People either froze in situ, unable to react, or moved away. It was a fight or flight response. Very few would choose to intervene or take part when faced with a violent encounter. Tom couldn't blame them. He quickened his pace, falling into step beside Aaron.

"What was all that about?"

Aaron scoffed. "Some people can't let things go, can they?" he said, as if that answered everything. He threw an arm around Tom's shoulder, dragging him off to their right. "Come on, let's get another drink." Tom saw Alice was now back with Charlotte and the latter was keeping a watchful eye on proceedings while Alice seemed concerned. Her demeanour relaxed when he smiled at her, letting her know everything was all right. Charlotte however, pretended not to be observing them but he was confident he was right in his assertion she was paying close attention to proceedings.

And Tom knew why that was.

CHAPTER TWO

THE EVENING WORE ON, or dragged on if you were Tom. It was interesting to him to see what had become of people he'd grown up with. Having largely separated himself from his school peers, not least by moving to London in his early twenties, he did have a curiosity around what people ended up doing. He was surprised to find one boy had gone on to become a world champion in surfing no less. Although a coastal town, Sheringham wasn't revered as a hot spot for the pastime.

With the time approaching ten o'clock, not late by any means, the numbers in attendance had begun to thin. Those with children had already left and Tom was ready to leave. He'd lost sight of Alice though, she'd been seconded into Charlotte's familiar circle and he hadn't seen her for some time. Avoiding the need to deflect any more questions about what he was up to these days, Tom slipped out of the assembly hall and into an adjoining corridor.

The school was very quiet beyond the gathered partygoers, his footfalls echoing on the polished surface as he walked away. During the day this would be a hive of activity and Tom recalled this particular corridor leading past a small cupboard that used to double as a tuck shop offering pupils the opportunity to spend a little money on sweets and chocolates. He wondered whether that was still allowed in school or had the nutrition police intervened? He was fairly sure that the hot meals sold to pupils in the dinner hall these days would not be reheated pies and slices of pizza. That was probably for the best.

Approaching a T-junction in the corridor, Tom hesitated, looking to the left and the right. The lockers used to be sited off to his left, he was fairly sure. For old times' sake, he decided to have a wander in that direction. The school didn't appear to have changed much in the last couple of decades. They must have applied a bit of paint at some point, although he couldn't recall the colour scheme when he'd been there. He could hear sound ahead, and realised he couldn't be the only one to have gone in search of past memories.

However, voices were raised, carrying some distance too by the sound of it. Tom slowed his approach to the end of the corridor, unsure of whether he wanted to continue. If someone else was having a drunken argument then he didn't feel the need to get involved for the second time in one night. His curiosity was piqued though, and as he reached the turn ahead, he stopped to listen. He recognised one of the voices. It was Aaron. Perhaps he and Noah were revisiting their earlier confrontation only this time doing so away from prying eyes.

It was possible. Tom considered leaving them to it. Both men were vocal, both sounding aggressive and equally worse for the alcohol they'd likely consumed. Tom and Alice were in the minority, a significant minority certainly, who were restrained in their drinking this evening. Others, Aaron included, had gone at it like they might have done on a Friday night in their teens.

Tom peered around the corner and spied Aaron, as expected, but the other man wasn't Noah. Tom didn't recognise him. He was heavyset, tattoos visible protruding from both the cuffs of his sleeves onto the back of his hands and from his collar which was undone from the top two buttons. He had a close-cropped beard and his hair was cut short possibly to reduce the impact of his receding hairline. Just as Tom looked, the second man stepped forward and shoved Aaron in the chest and he stumbled back into the lockers, a metal clash sounding along the corridor.

Not to be undone, Aaron responded in kind and the two men began pushing one another but neither seemed willing to throw the first punch. Tom was experienced enough to recognise that this would rapidly escalate into something more unless it was nipped in the bud. He could easily step back, turn away and leave these two to fight over who was the strongest but it wasn't his way.

He rounded the corner and ambled towards them.

"Making friends again, I see, Aaron?" he asked, smiling. Both men hesitated as Tom approached. As he came closer he clocked a tell-tale scar on the other man's upper lip. It was Anthony Slater, although he'd been more of a bean pole when they'd been at school together. Tom would never have recognised him if it weren't for that scar, received when he'd thrown an aerosol can into a small bonfire to see what would happen. The ensuing explosion had injured him, but he'd been lucky not to have lost an eye or worse. He certainly cemented the unofficial pupil's award for the thickest child of that particular year group as a result of the incident, even if it didn't truly reflect Anthony's academic ability which had been fairly strong as Tom remembered.

"Well, you know me," Aaron said, looking unsteady on his

feet and Tom could see the inside of his bottom lip was bleeding. "I'm always keen to get close to people."

"Nothing changes," Tom said, coming to stand a few feet from the two men. Neither of them seemed willing to lower their guard. Tom looked at Anthony. "How have you been, Tony? I've not seen you around."

"I'm all right," he replied but was wary about taking his eyes from Aaron. "How are things with you?"

"I'm doing all right," Tom said.

"That business all taken care of, is it?" Tony asked. "I read about it in the paper, and saw it on the telly."

Tom sighed. "There's still a little bit left to play out, but it'll be okay."

"What's this?" Aaron asked, his stance softening as his shoulders dropped along with his guard. Tony seemed to respond in mind and the two men eased back from one another. "You been on the television or something then?"

"Not for anything I care to talk about," Tom said. He looked between the two men. "Anyway, what are you two arguing about? Who's got the best spot in the sand pit?" Both men looked down, Tony in particular wouldn't meet his gaze, perhaps from embarrassment, Tom wondered. Tony shifted his weight between his feet but Aaron's stance remained unchanged.

"It's nothing," Tony said, his eyes darting momentarily to Aaron who, Tom saw, sported the trace of a smile fleetingly across his lips. "It'll keep."

"That it will, Tony," Aaron said calmly. "Any time you want to revisit this, I'm always ready and willing."

"I guess I'll see you guys around,' Tony said, backing away. He nodded curtly to Tom, but didn't make eye contact with Aaron as he left, walking purposefully back along the corridor the way Tom had come.

"I was thinking," Tom said, frowning.

"What about?" Aaron asked lightly.

"I don't know what you do for a living," he said, looking along the empty corridor now that Tony Slater had rounded the corner and disappeared from view, "but if you fancied a career change…"

"To do what?" Aaron asked.

Tom shrugged. "Relationship therapy, life coaching… that sort of thing."

"I always thought I'd be quite good at motivational speaking," Aaron said, nodding.

"Always worth a punt," Tom said. "You've certainly got a knack with people anyway."

"That's what my wife has always told me."

"Oh, I didn't know you'd brought your wife with you—"

"I didn't," Aaron said. He shrugged. "It's not her sort of thing. You know how it is."

"I suppose," Tom said. "Are you coming back to the hall?"

"Yes, of course," Aaron said, but as he made to fall into step with Tom he stumbled and Tom had to catch his arm to stop him from falling over. He could smell alcohol on him. Aaron was practically oozing it from his pores. "Thanks," Aaron said, as Tom made sure he was upright and stable before releasing his supportive hold on his arm. "I might have had one or two too many sherbets tonight."

"Maybe you should call it a night," Tom said.

"What are you, my dad?" Aaron said, grinning his incredibly bright, winning smile. "Or the fun police or something."

Tom smiled. "Something like that, yes."

They made their way back to the assembly hall and Tom was thankful not to see any sign of Tony or indeed Noah. Aaron didn't strike him as the type to go looking for trouble but, much as it had done when they were at school, trouble did a pretty good job of seeking him out. Alice saw them enter the hall and she came across to them, Tom slipping his arm around her waist.

"I was wondering where you'd got to," she said. Charlotte was alongside her.

"Yes, we wondered whether you'd made a break for freedom when no one was looking."

"Am I that transparent?" Tom asked.

"That you're uncomfortable?" Charlotte asked. "No," she said, smiling. "Only to people with eyes."

"Good," Tom said, exaggerating a release of breath. "I wouldn't want to offend anyone."

"No, that's my job," Aaron said, winking at Charlotte who rolled her eyes.

"Are we leaving?" Alice asked. Tom nodded. Charlotte reached out and placed a hand on Tom's forearm.

"It's been great to see you again, Tom. We should catch up properly over a cup of coffee or something." She glanced at Alice. "After all, now I've met your better half, it'll be fun to see you again. If you have the time, of course."

"Sure," Tom said. The way things were presently, he had nothing but time on his hands.

"Great," Charlotte said. "Alice and I have exchanged numbers."

Tom looked at his wife. "Oh, that's nice." Alice wrinkled her nose.

"Isn't it? Now I can find out everything about what you used to be like—"

"Before you went all serious," Charlotte said and both women grinned at some in-joke they'd clearly already been discussing.

"You'd better get out of here sharpish, Tom," Aaron said.

"Or Taz will sell you down the river like she does everyone else."

The smile left Charlotte's face and she shook her head dismissively. She leaned over and kissed Alice on the cheek. "It was lovely to meet you," she said, the smile returning.

"You too," Alice said as Charlotte offered Tom a little wave before leaving them. Tom noted she didn't say goodbye to Aaron, who acknowledged the slight with a brief shrug.

"Another one to add to your list?" Tom asked. Alice shot him a questioning look but he shook his head slightly. He'd tell her all about it later.

"No change there," Aaron said.

The three of them left the assembly hall and made their way outside. The night air was cool on Tom's skin, and decidedly fresh after being inside with so many people in such close quarters. Alice shivered and Tom took off his jacket and put it around her shoulders.

"Always the gentleman," Aaron said, setting off down the steps. Whether it was the fresh air or simply the alcohol catching up with him, he lost his footing and tumbled down. Alice gasped and Tom hurriedly went after his school friend. Aaron rolled onto his back, and seeing Tom above him, grinned. "I think... I may have overdone it slightly."

"You're not a teenager any more," Tom said. "Are you okay?"

"Never... been better," Aaron said. "If you could help me up and into my car then I'd appreciate—"

"You're not driving home," Tom said, helping him into a sitting position.

"Well I'm not bloody flying home to Blakeney, that's for sure."

"You can't drive," Tom instructed him. Aaron sighed, glaring at him.

"You wouldn't call the police on me, would you?"

"I am the police, you daft sod," Tom said.

Aaron grunted his displeasure as Tom helped him to his feet. He dusted off his knees, then shook his head. "I never would have had you pegged as a killjoy, Tom."

"Whatever I am or am not," Tom said. "You're not driving home. We'll give you a lift back."

"And leave my car here?" Aaron exclaimed. "Overnight? Are you mad?"

"Sheringham is one of the quietest towns in Norfolk. It will be fine—"

"No, not happening," Aaron said, holding both hands aloft. "I'm not leaving it here."

Tom sighed and glanced at Alice.

"I only had the one glass of wine earlier," Alice said. "I didn't touch the second one. I'm okay to drive."

"Are you sure?" Tom asked. She nodded.

"Why don't you drive Aaron home. I need to get back for the babysitter, but I could always wrap Saffy up and could come—"

"No, no, she'll be asleep already," Tom said.

"No she won't," Alice said with a laugh. "You know she won't settle until we're home."

"True. Either way, I'll call a taxi or something and get home that way. There's no need to keep her up later than necessary."

"Sounds like a plan!" Aaron said, clapping Tom's shoulder. "I always knew you were a great guy, Tom. I said to everyone, back in the day, that you were going to succeed."

"Right," Tom said. "You can dispense with the flattery. I've already said I'll drive you home."

"Right, my car's..." Tony looked across the car park, waving his hand in a circular motion in the air. "Somewhere over there. I'll find it. You hang on here." He stumbled away in search of his car. Tom winced, watching Aaron bumble away.

"How do I get myself into these things?"

Alice took his hands in hers, and he turned to face her. "Because you're a decent man, Tom Janssen."

"Oh yes, that's it," Tom said, nodding. "I forgot for a moment." Alice leaned into him and looked up into his face. Tom tilted his head towards her and kissed her.

"Don't ever forget it," she said, smiling up at him. "Your old school friends seem to remember you fondly too."

Although Tom and Alice had been teenage sweethearts prior to Tom leaving for London, rekindling their relationship upon his return to the area, they had never attended the same school and Alice was a year or two younger than Tom. They'd met through shared interests outside of school and college.

"Well... I was a pretty decent chap back in the day too," Tom said, still with his arms round her, swaying them both gently side to side.

"I don't doubt this fact," Alice said. "What was it Aaron called Charlotte?" Tom offered her a quizzical look. "Before, just as we were readying to leave?"

"Oh, Taz?" Tom asked.

"Yes, what's that mean?"

"It was her nickname at school," Tom said. "Short for Tasmanian Devil, after that cartoon character. It's because she always had so much energy on display."

"I got the impression she didn't like it."

"Ah, that's just their history," Tom said. "Aaron dated Charlotte's elder sister at school. It didn't end well between them."

"That's sad. Charlotte is younger, so it's her sister—"

"Who was the one in our year at school, yes," Tom said.

He was interrupted by the sound of a car horn tooting

three times in quick succession and a car accelerated across the car park with a degree of wheel spin, tyres shrieking in protest.

"That's Aaron, I take it," Alice said as Tom ushered her back up onto the steps to give them a little protection by way of the barriers. "He's quite a character, isn't he?"

"He's much like he was when he was at school, only it seems like the volume has been dialled up a bit."

Tom was dismayed as a low-slung Porsche car accelerated towards them from the far end of the school car park, only braking at the last moment. Tom cocked his head and shot Aaron a disapproving look as he opened the driver's door and clambered out unceremoniously.

"It's private land," Aaron said, reading Tom's expression. "Technically, I'm not breaking any laws." Tom pointed to the passenger seat.

"Get in," he said formally. Aaron acquiesced and walked around the front of the car holding his arms out wide as if by way of an apology. Tom glanced at Alice and sighed. She gave him a kiss on the cheek.

"I'll wait up for you."

"There's no need," Tom said.

"There is. I wouldn't be surprised if he tried to whisk you away to some casino in the southern Mediterranean. I want to make sure you come home."

Tom smiled, letting go of her hand and walking over to the car. The car sat very low to the ground and due to his height and frame, Tom found getting in rather awkward. He smiled at Alice as he closed the door, waiting for her to get into their car and leave before he was willing to do the same.

"So," Aaron said, "have you ever driven an electric car before?"

"No," Tom said, looking around at the controls. Everything

seemed very familiar. "But it can't be too hard, after all, you manage it."

"Right, the key thing is that, pickup from the motor is very slow so you have to really push the accelerator pedal hard to the floor to get any response."

Tom glanced obverse at him. "Do you think I'm an idiot?"

Aaron laughed. "Well, it would have been funny if you'd believed me."

Tom shook his head then, seeing Alice leaving the car park, he put the car into drive and eased the accelerator pedal down.

CHAPTER THREE

Aaron Bell's home was on the outskirts of Blakeney, set back from the coast road and directly overlooking the marshland located between his house and the sea. Imposing electric gates opened for them as Tom pulled up revealing a long drive on a gentle incline up to the house. It was an impressive piece of architecture, contemporary design, with a lot of full-height glass lining cantilevered sections hanging out over the drive which wound its way beneath the structure and around to the rear.

"Who on earth do you know in the planning department to get something like this approved?" Tom asked quietly as he drove the car around to a small courtyard in front of a triple cart lodge-style garage.

"It's not always who you know but how much money you have to spend," Aaron said. He had been rather subdued for the duration of the drive back to his house, perhaps entering the next phase of inebriation, that of melancholy. Tom looked towards the house, seeing lights on inside.

"Is your wife waiting for you? What did you say her name was?"

"I didn't," Aaron said, opening his door and hauling himself out. "And she won't be waiting up. She's not even here." Tom sighed, looked around for the off switch to the car and, not seeing one, he just got out. The car seemed to switch itself off when he did so.

"Come inside," Aaron said, beckoning for Tom to follow him.

"Only for a minute," Tom said. "It's getting late and I'm keen to get home."

"That's all it will take," Aaron said, over his shoulder. The rear of the house was built in a U-shape, wrapped around a central courtyard that was lined with raised planters. Between these was a large rectangular swimming pool, enclosed on three sides offering protection to the user from the coastal winds that whipped in off the North Sea. Despite the stiff breeze, Tom felt the benefit from the shelter provided as he approached the house.

Upon closer inspection, Tom saw a mixture of materials used in the construction from masonry and natural stone to sheet metal that was already rusted. He'd seen this approach before but only ever on television programmes of high end, bespoke designs. The name escaped him but he knew it was expensive. The curtain walls of glass were on display here too, and Tom wondered how much this house cost to build. It would be several million, he assumed. He couldn't put a figure on how much it would go on the market for.

Aaron pulled open a sliding patio door. The movement was effortless and Tom noted it had been unlocked. To be fair, this was Blakeney where the chance of being burgled would be slim, but even so it did strike Tom as incredible in a property like this that Aaron didn't bother to secure it. He followed him inside into an open-plan kitchen and dining area. That description didn't do it justice. The square footage of this room alone was probably double that of the entire ground floor of the house he shared with Alice and Saffy.

Aaron went straight to a seating area overlooking the pool and took out two crystal glasses from a cabinet, righting them on the sideboard and reaching for a decanter.

"Not for me, thanks."

"Suit yourself,' Aaron said, removing the stopper and pouring himself a large measure.

"This is quite some place you have here," Tom said, looking around. The interior was clearly well designed but to Tom it felt it was more in line for a studio photo shoot rather than a family home. He looked around for more personal items but didn't see any photographs on display or anything else that gave off the owner's personality.

"It's my wife's vision of perfection," Aaron said and Tom thought he detected a note of bitterness or something similar in his tone.

"You disapprove?"

"Disapprove? No," Aaron said, sinking down onto a velvet-lined sofa and hefting his feet onto a rimless glass coffee table. "It's not my thing... but," he held the glass up to Tom, "it's not my money, so who cares what I think?"

Tom laughed. "Saffy would love this place."

"Saffy?" Aaron asked. "Is that your bit on the side?"

"No, she's my daughter," Tom said firmly. Aaron made a display of mea culpa with an exaggerated downturn at the corners of his mouth.

"Sorry. No offence."

"None taken. Tell me, were you always as popular with people as you were at the reunion earlier, and I've forgotten, or—"

"Have I always been an arse?" Aaron asked. Tom inclined his head. "I suspect I've always had it in me, if I'm honest, but it takes a certain class of person to really draw it out of me," he said making a fist with his free hand and tightening it in the air before him.

"So, where is your wife?"

Aaron sighed. "Hong Kong... Monaco... Skegness? I don't really know," he said, staring into space. "And I don't really care."

Tom arched his eyebrows. "Not going well then?"

Aaron laughed but it was a dry, hollow sound. "I would say I should never have married her but," he said, holding his glass aloft, "I would have missed out on all of this. We're separated, just to be clear." He took a deep breath, then stifled a yawn. Tom felt a little awkward. "Do you remember, back when we were kids, how full of hope and optimism we were?"

"It rings a bell, sure."

"Life certainly kicks that out of you once you get out into the real world, huh?"

"Things get more complicated, definitely." Tom walked over to the window and admired the view. The courtyard was illuminated by recessed feature lighting. "How long have you been living here then?" he asked, turning back to face the room and scanning the interior again. It struck him that maybe this was a holiday home. It had that feel to it.

"I've been here for a month or two," Aaron said, putting his feet down and sitting forward, eyeing Tom earnestly. "But I flit about, here and there, you know?"

"What is it you do?"

"I work – worked – for the family business. Although," he said, frowning, "I'm not sure that I have a place there any more." He sat back again, stifling a yawn. "We'll see."

Tom checked his watch. "I think I should make a move."

"How long have you been in the old bill then?" Aaron

asked, ignoring, or not hearing, Tom's announcement of his desire to leave.

"A long time," Tom said. "I've not really been anything else."

"It didn't sound like it was the case when you said what you said earlier. What was it you said… in between things or something?"

"It's complicated," Tom said.

"It always is. Take all of this," Aaron said, looking around the room, "my name is on the paperwork somewhere but I'll be damned if I know how much of it is mine. Knowing Elena as I do, I probably have a two per cent share of the garden."

"Nice garden though,' Tom said, smiling.

"It is. We've got sea access rights across the far side of the road as well. I can go kayaking whenever I like."

"As I said, this is quite some place. However you've come to be here, your ship has most certainly come in, Aaron."

"Like many ships though, they are always close to sinking."

Tom wasn't sure if he was trying to be funny or was genuinely serious. He checked his watch again. Seeing Aaron's glass almost empty already, and his host getting up to return to the decanter for a refill, he had no desire to settle in and watch him continue drinking or be his sober guardian any longer than necessary. He'd got him safely home, and didn't feel the urge to spend longer with him. "What was all that about earlier, with Tony, I mean?"

"Ah… the guy was always, and still is, full of piss and whinge."

"And Noah?"

"Same," Aaron said without looking at him. Evidently, Aaron wasn't willing to discuss what the confrontations stemmed from. Based on what Tom was reading between the lines, it was quite likely that Aaron had other things going on his life and those stresses simply manifested in the confrontations Tom witnessed.

"It's late. I'm going to call a cab."

"Borrow my car, if you like," Aaron said. "I can always come to you and collect it from you tomorrow." He poured another drink, missing the glass as he swayed ever so slightly to his left. He cursed but persevered.

"Maybe you've had enough?" Tom said.

"Now you're sounding like Elena," Aaron said. "Take the car. Leave me your number and I'll come and get it."

"I can call a cab, it's no trouble."

"Don't be daft, man," Aaron said. "I've had a skinful so I shouldn't be driving until tomorrow afternoon anyway."

"Okay, if you're sure?" Tom spotted a pen on the kitchen island alongside an envelope. He scribbled down his mobile number. Aaron had retaken his seat on the sofa, and was now staring at the glass he held in his lap. For a moment, he wondered if he should leave now after all. There was something in Aaron's expression that unsettled him. "Are you going to be all right?"

"Me?" Aaron half-heartedly waved away Tom's concern. "Don't worry, I'm always winning. I'll be grand."

Tom hesitated but his desire to get home was strong. He picked up the key fob for the car, still wondering if it was a good idea to borrow it but Aaron seemed unconcerned. Tom considered advising his friend, again, to take it easy on the alcohol but thought against it. It wasn't really any of his business. "Okay, well I'll see you tomorrow."

Aaron stood before the large picture window facing out over the rear, watching Tom walk to the car. He looked back and waved as he opened the driver's door but Aaron, glass of brandy nestled in one hand and with his other hand in the pocket of his trousers didn't respond. He simply stood where he was, watching Tom.

Inside the car, Tom started it and glanced back at the house. Aaron was no longer visible.

"Well this hasn't been a completely surreal experience at all," Tom said to himself, putting the car into reverse and carefully turning it around.

The drive home was uneventful and when Tom pulled up in the driveway he could see a light on in Saffy's bedroom. It wasn't unusual for her to sleep with a light on but this was her main light. He got out of the car and saw the curtain of the upstairs window twitch. Saffy was already waiting for him, sitting on the top step of the stairs when he opened the front door. Alice stepped out of the kitchen to greet him, lifting her chin towards Saffy above her.

"She wouldn't settle until you came home," Alice said. Tom could see the frustration etched into her expression and he could picture the little girl's steadfast ability to not yield an inch. He smiled up at the little girl he'd adopted only a few short years ago.

"Go and get into bed," Tom said. "I'll be up to tuck you in, in a few minutes." Saffy smiled and got up, turned away, and hurried back into her bedroom. Tom gave Alice a hug. "I feel your pain, I really do."

"You know what she can get like once she's got herself all worked up."

"I do. Sometimes it's better just to take the easy path."

"But not too often," Alice said, wagging a finger at him.

"Agreed."

"How did you get on with Aaron?"

Tom was already making his way back to the foot of the stairs and he leaned on the newel post, frowning. "There's a lot to unpack there," he said. "And I'm not sure I want to go there."

Alice smiled. "He does seem like a… complex character."

"That's one word for it, yes," Tom said. He looked towards the front door. "He lent me his car, so you'll see him again tomorrow."

"I might be going out," she said, wrinkling her nose.

"And I might join you," he said, setting off upstairs to make sure Saffy got to sleep as soon as possible, thereby minimising the inevitable fallout they would face the following day with an overtired child. Reaching the landing he felt that same uneasy sensation he'd experienced earlier as the image of a watchful Aaron, staring at him through the picture window, came to mind.

CHAPTER FOUR

The imposing entrance gates were already open, a uniformed constable standing guard to ensure no inquisitive local ventured beyond them to see what the commotion was. The officer lowered his head, peering into the cabin and acknowledged both DS Cassie Knight, at the wheel, and DC Eric Collet in the passenger seat alongside her. She drove on, picking her way up the shallow incline of the gravel-lined driveway. A liveried police car was parked at the front of the house, the main door to the inside of the building was also open with a uniformed officer waiting to greet them.

Parked along the side of the house was a small hatchback. Cassie could see a woman was sitting in the passenger seat with the door wide open, a police officer taking notes in a notebook while they conversed with one another. Cassie parked the car and they both got out. She looked over the exterior of the building, then turned to face the coast directly to the north. The house, sited in an elevated position, had a clear view out over the nature reserve to the point where the reserve opened into the North Sea. She was buffeted by the wind gusting in towards them.

"Hell of a spot," she said.

"Isn't it?" Eric agreed, zipping up his thick coat, almost to his jaw. Cassie turned and walked over to the constable standing at the door. PC Marshall nodded.

"Morning, Sarge," he said.

"Morning, David. What do you have for us?"

The constable gestured towards the woman sitting in the car nearby speaking to their colleague. "The cleaner arrived this morning, as usual, and let herself into the property. She found the body, she says it's the owner, deceased. The FME is on her way now, but it looks like he's taken a blow to the head."

Cassie gently bit her bottom lip, listening to him. "Any sign of a break-in?"

PC Marshall shook his head. "No sign, although the doors we checked were all left unlocked so there would have been no need to force entry."

"Signs of a struggle?"

"There's a bit of a mess," Marshall said. "Come on, I'll show you."

Cassie caught Eric's attention and pointed towards the cleaner and Eric nodded, making his way over to speak to her while she followed PC Marshall into the house. The entrance hall was wide, wider than most rooms in a standard detached house. The entrance was clearly designed to offer a maximum indication of opulence. The walls were lined with what Cassie thought was driftwood-style timber but then she realised they were porcelain. It was a bold statement, perhaps reflecting the coastal location of the house.

Marshall led her through the property, plush furniture and high-end chrome switchgear standing out to her as they walked. They dropped to a lower level as they came to the rear and Cassie could see out through a curtain wall of glass to the rear garden, bathed in the early morning sunshine. A set of sliding patio doors on the far side of the room were open, the glazing misted over due to the cool outside air and the warmer interior seeing moisture condense on the expansive panes. Cassie paused, scanning the room.

Cassie dropped to her haunches, inspecting fragments of broken glass both on and beside a large sofa. The contents of whatever had been smashed was pooled on the porcelain floor and had also soaked into a large rug that the coffee table sat upon, with staining of the material visible. The smell of alcohol hung in the air despite the breeze carrying through the house via the open doors. Cassie thought it was scotch or brandy; a strong spirit certainly. She saw an empty glass on a nearby sideboard and what looked like the base of another, this one broken, on the floor.

"Where was the body found?" Cassie asked, standing up.

"Outside, Sarge," Marshall said, standing off to her right between her and the patio door. Cassie moved to join him and they both went outside. The garden area was well sheltered from the sea breeze although Cassie could still taste the salt in the air. Around the pool were raised planters, a mixture of bushes, plants and decorative stone features. There were two seating areas outside, one beside the pool and another covered area that also seemed to house an outdoor kitchen and reception area. There was another building beyond it. PC Marshall saw her looking. "It's an annex," he said. "They rent it out as it's separate to the main property with its own parking and garden area to the rear."

"With sitting tenants?"

"No, holiday lets only. Currently unoccupied."

Cassie nodded, turning her attention back to the pool, as well as the male body lying on its back beside it. He was partially clothed. But for a watch, a Rolex, that was still on his wrist the upper body was stripped naked. He had no visible tattoos or body art nor any injuries that Cassie could see. His lower half was dressed in trousers, black chinos or suit trousers, Cassie couldn't tell. The left leg, bent at the knee, was dangling over the rim of the pool and the foot was underwater, gently swaying as the pump and filtration system moved the water around. He didn't have shoes on but he was still wearing socks.

"Where did you find him?" she asked, moving closer to examine the body.

"We found him face down in the water," Marshall said. He looked over his shoulder, as if able to look through the walls of the house to where their colleagues were standing outside. "The cleaner had tried to get him out of the water but couldn't manage it. The flow of the water through the filter must have eased him away from the edge and back into the centre of the pool. Chloe and me, we had to get hold of a boat hook," he said, pointing to a long pole on the tiled floor nearby, "and haul him back over so we could drag him out just in case there was a chance he was still alive. The paramedics arrived a minute or two after we got him out of the water but there was nothing to be done for him."

Cassie pursed her lips, drawing a deep intake of air through her nose. She dropped to her haunches and looked at the wound to the side of the dead man's head. There was a visible, depressed indentation alongside and above the right eye accompanied by a cut. The wound had long ceased bleeding though. The man's skin was grey and veins were pronounced beneath the surface.

Cassie judged him to be in his early forties and in good physical shape. He was muscular without being too much, well in proportion to his height and body shape. His hair was dark, shot through with flecks of grey but Cassie thought he might artificially colour his hair as well. Lying on his back, his arms were at his side with his palms facing up. Cassie tilted her head to examine his extremities but she couldn't see any damage to fingers, his palms or the backs of his hands, although most of the latter were not visible. She was loathe to touch him until he'd been properly studied by the FME and the forensic team were able to process the scene. If a full forensic analysis was even necessary.

"It's possible there was bit of a scuffle inside and then it continued on out here," PC Marshall said, "before he went into the pool. Possibly unconscious before he hit the water and then he drowned."

"Or it was Colonel Mustard in the cinema room with a piece of lead piping," Cassie said quietly.

"Sorry?"

Cassie glanced up at him, seeing genuine confusion on the constable's face. "Sorry, I forget how young you lot in uniform are these days. I'm suggesting that this might not be anything conspiratorial at all." She looked at the body and then her gaze swept around the pool, eyeing everything nearby. "He could just have easily got himself smashed on booze, stumbled out here and tripped," she said, pointing to a planter where the stems of the plants were recently broken, "and hit his head on the side of the pool on the way in."

"An accident?" Marshall asked.

Cassie shrugged. "Aye. I've seen stranger than this, that's for sure." She rose from her position beside the body. "What do you make of the cleaner?"

"In shock," Marshall said, "but under the circumstances I think she's doing all right."

The sound of movement from within the house made Cassie turn to see Eric approaching with Dr Fiona Williams, the on-call Forensic Medical Examiner, beside him. She stepped away from the body, greeting Dr Williams.

"Sorry I'm a bit behind, Cassie," she said. "The traffic this morning is murder."

"No pun intended."

Dr Williams looked at her quizzically, then realised what she'd said and smiled. "Yes, yes, of course."

Cassie always found comments like that about the traffic in these parts unusual. Where she was from, Newcastle in the north east of England, traffic was far worse than you would ever find in rural Norfolk, aside from peak tourist season anyway. She figured it was just what you became used to and any deviation from that norm stood out.

"No problem," Cassie said, following the doctor's gaze down to the body. "I need to know if this is an accident or something more sinister," Cassie said. Fiona cocked her head. "I don't want to pull out all the stops unless I have to."

"Well, I will do my best to determine that for you, as always, Cassandra," Fiona replied, without taking her eyes off the body. "This is the poor soul then, I take it?"

"It is. He was found this morning, in the pool, when the cleaner arrived for her shift." Fiona opened her kit bag and unpacked a fresh set of nitrile gloves.

"Right, I'd best get cracking then," she said.

"If there's anything you can give me," Cassie said, "cause of and time of death would be nice."

Dr Williams snorted. "You don't want much do you, young lady?"

"Well, I'm not asking you to name his killer," Cassie said by way of concession.

"Leave me to it then, Detective Sergeant."

Cassie indicated for PC Marshall to remain and she gestured for Eric to join her back inside the house. Once they were indoors, Cassie looked around. "Right, although I'm keeping an open mind that this could be a tragic accident, I want you to have a look around the house."

"What am I looking for specifically?" Eric asked.

"Anything that looks out of place," Cassie said, her gaze sweeping the room. "There doesn't look like there's been a break-in or an altercation, other than the broken glass there. If he was absolutely steaming last night then there's every chance he dropped a bottle, had an argument with himself or fell out with the ghost of an ex-girlfriend, and fell into the pool."

"See if there's anything untoward that stands out," Eric said, nodding. "Check." He hesitated. Cassie noticed.

"Problem?"

"It's just… to me, something seems odd here." He looked around. "I know a place like this is so far away from my experience, I mean, it must have cost millions to build this place… but nothing looks right."

Cassie knew what he meant. The house was very cleanly presented, aside from the remnants of what she figured was the result of whatever happened the previous night. It was stylish, dressed to perfection but it looked exactly that, staged for perfection and a far cry from a home. There was no effort seemingly made to personalise it. It was akin to the backdrop of a magazine photoshoot. So far from real life, sterile.

"Well," she said, "just see if anything comes to mind. The cleaner still outside, I take it?"

"Yes, she's had the offer to go to the hospital to get herself checked out but she's passed it off."

"Right, I'll have a word then we can compare notes."

Cassie left Eric to carry out his search of the house and made her way back outside. Approaching the car, the constable, Chloe Bartlett, who was looking after the woman smiled at Cassie.

"This is Carol," PC Bartlett said. Cassie looked at the woman. She was in her late twenties, had red hair which was wavy and would hang to her shoulders if she hadn't tied it back. She had a striking appearance, the pale, freckled skin that came with redheads but she also chose a bright shade of red lipstick which contrasted with her skin tone. Clearly anxious, she sat on the seat wringing her hands slowly in her lap.

"Hello, Carol. My name's Cassandra. I'm with the local CID team. I know all of this has come as quite a shock to you, but do you think you could tell me what happened this morning?"

Carol nodded. Her eyes were bloodshot and the area around them was puffy and swollen. She'd been crying.

"I got here just after seven, about twenty past, I think," Carol said. "I was running a bit late because I was supposed to be here by seven. Aaron – Mr Bell – doesn't like me to be late."

"Aaron is... the owner of the property?" Cassie asked. Carol nodded. "And it was him you found in the pool?"

"Y-Yes, it was," she said. "I let myself in... and I found the mess, the broken glass on the floor..."

"And what did you see?" Cassie asked her.

"What did... when?"

"What did you think had happened?"

She shook her head. "I... I don't know. I thought Aaron had – Mr Bell – had just had an accident. He..." She lowered her head.

"Does Mr Bell often drink?"

"Yes," Carol said. "Most days when I come in he has been drinking the previous night or sometimes during the day too."

"Would you say he had a problem with alcohol?"

"I... wouldn't know," Carol said.

Cassie paused to let the information sink in. She knew what it was like when someone drank every day. It might not seem like a problem to them, or to those around them if that was what they were used to seeing, but Cassie's father was a drinker. He drank every day, be it to excess or simply a few pints or half a bottle of wine, and Cassie had never seen him a day without consuming something. It had never caused an issue because he was an affable drunk, but when he was forced to stop due to health issues, that was when the problems started.

The tragic accident theory was taking shape in her mind.

"What happened next?" Cassie asked.

"I thought the house was cold. Aaron likes to keep it warm indoors, because he's often keen to walk around the house..." she checked herself and left the sentence unfinished. Cassie wondered what she was about to say.

"He keeps the house warm?"

"Yes, he likes it that way." Carol was looking down, averting her eyes from Cassie's.

"Only this morning...?" Cassie prompted her. Carol's head snapped up.

"It was cold. The house was so cold. It made me shiver and then I saw the doors to the garden were open. I went to close them and that was when I saw... Aaron," she said, wincing. "Mr Bell... he was in the pool, face down." She had tears in her eyes now, staring straight ahead with a vacant expression. "I... I tried to get him out of the water but he was too heavy for me. I could only pull him to the side of the pool."

"Could you tell if he was breathing?"

Carol shook her head gently. "He wasn't," she said. "The pool is usually heated but he felt so cold to the touch."

"How is it heated?" Cassie asked. "The pool I mean." She wasn't sure it was relevant, but thought it worth asking.

"There is an air pump or something," Carol said, "but I don't really know."

"Could someone have switched off the heating to the pool?"

Carol shrugged. "I suppose so," she said, before quickly adding, "but I wouldn't know."

Cassie judged it not very interesting and changed tack. "How long have you been working for Aaron?" She deliberately chose to personalise the deceased, using his first name. Carol had used the formal and the informal which Cassie found curious.

"I work out of a local agency. We do the turnarounds for the holiday lets, caravans on the parks over towards Wells… and I've been doing Aaron's for the last six months since we got the contract." She corrected herself. "It's not my contract. I'm just an employee."

"This is a holiday let?" Cassie asked, glancing back at the house.

"It is – was – but Aaron owns it. Him and his wife," she said, lowering her voice.

"Where is his wife?" Cassie had a vision of Eric stumbling in on the deceased's partner whilst exploring the house. "Have you seen her?"

"No, she's not been here." Carol looked up at Cassie. "To be honest, I've never seen her here. Aaron's been staying here alone these past few months. The place hasn't been let in that time."

"But you come here… how often, daily, weekly?"

"Daily," Carol said, looking down again. Cassie had a thought but she chose not to voice it at this time. She looked at

Carol's hands, seeking a wedding or engagement band. She saw a silver ring on her ring finger.

"Mr Bell must be paying handsomely."

"He isn't the domestic type," Carol said. Cassie nodded.

"Tell me, what does he do?"

"Do?" she asked innocently.

"For a living." Cassie arched her eyebrows. "To have a pad like this, he must be worth a fortune."

Carol shrugged. "I don't know. He... doesn't seem to do anything."

Cassie wondered if that was the case. The super rich often looked like they did nothing. "How well do you know him?"

"A little," Carol said quietly. "He's always been very nice to me."

"You liked him?"

She nodded. "I did."

"Do you know if he had anyone around these parts who didn't like him?"

"Like who?"

Cassie shrugged. "I don't know, a partner... a business associate he'd fallen out with." She looked directly at Carol, forcing her to meet her eye. "Maybe a jealous lover who had a bone to pick with him." Carol stared at Cassie and for a moment the DS thought the woman was about to break down but she appeared to steel herself.

"I wouldn't know anything about that. No."

"Fair enough," Cassie said. Eric appeared at the front door, then beckoned for Cassie to come over. She smiled at Carol, then looked at PC Bartlett. "I think we can leave it there for now. If you could finish taking the statement, make sure you have her details but then check with me before we let her head off to wherever she wants to go." PC Bartlett nodded and

Cassie addressed Carol. "I'll leave you with Chloe for now, okay?"

Carol nodded. "I'm sorry I'm not more use to you."

"Nonsense," Cassie said. "You've been very helpful and if anything comes to mind then please do let us know. No matter how small or insignificant it is just—"

"There is one thing," Carol said, her expression changing.

"What's that?"

"Aaron's car, his Porsche. It's not here." Cassie looked around as if expecting to see a car. She inclined her head.

"Okay, thank you. We'll look into it."

Cassie winked at Chloe Bartlett and left the two of them, joining Eric at the front door.

"Anything interesting?" she asked.

"Not really. There's a locked door that I can't find a key to, and it has a vent on the door which suggests it's a hot room."

"A hot room?"

"Yeah, you know with security equipment, plant and that sort of thing. There are cameras around the property and I couldn't find the hard drive unit or master control unit. It has to be here somewhere. Aside from the kitchen room, the only other areas of the house that appear even remotely used are the master bedroom and the ensuite bathroom. They are pretty disgusting too." Cassie looked back at Carol.

"That is interesting."

"Is it?" Eric asked, frowning.

"Aye, the cleaner comes in every day but the most used rooms are in a right state. What does that tell you?"

"That the cleaner isn't very good at their job?" Eric asked.

"Or the service she's providing isn't cleaning."

"Oh," Eric said flatly. Then his eyes widened, and he looked over at Carol sitting in the car nearby. "Oh... right!"

"What was it you needed me for?"

"Dr Williams wants a word," Eric said, still staring past Cassie towards Carol. Another vehicle came through the entrance gates and Cassie noted it was the police forensic officers arriving to process the scene. She'd called them in thinking that she would send them away if the scene didn't look suspect. She would have to make that decision soon.

"Stop staring, Eric. You're starting to drool and if the wind changes your face will stay like that," Cassie said, patting his arm as she went past him and back into the house. Eric shook himself out of his thoughts and followed her into the house.

CHAPTER FIVE

Cassie met Fiona beside the pool, still standing over the body. She came alongside and the doctor greeted her.

"Well, I think I can give you one definitive answer, Detective Sergeant."

"To which question?"

"You have a murder investigation to contend with." Cassie blew out her cheeks as Fiona lowered herself down closer to the body. Cassie did the same and focussed on the wound to the side of the head, located just above Aaron Bell's eye, because Fiona was using the end of her pen to draw attention to it. "You see this indentation, here?"

"Aye," Cassie said, changing her viewing angle to better see. The morning sun was bathing more of the garden in light, and it was making it harder for Cassie to view the detail with it striking her face directly.

"This isn't definitive and the crime scene analysis and post-mortem will need to confirm it, but if he'd hit his head on the fall into the pool, this wound wouldn't be shaped like this. At first, you can see an obvious facial injury here," she made a circular motion in the air above the face. "Then if you look more closely, there is a second injury – or perhaps the most significant part of the injury – here you can make out another indentation in the shape of a sphere or ball." She gestured to the cut stone lining the rim of the pool. "These stones around the pool are bullnose edges, very smooth and rounded. You can see the wound depressing the side of the skull has formed a ball shape, an inch or perhaps a little bit more, in diameter. This is more of a puncture, a large puncture, in the skull rather than a flat edge."

"He was struck then?" Cassie theorised, looking sideways at Fiona.

"Certainly," Fiona said. "Accidentally or with intent, I obviously cannot say, but he was definitely struck and with some force." Cassie looked around, searching for something that would fit the description that could have been used as a weapon. She saw nothing.

"I'm confused," she said. "Are we talking about one strike or two?"

"I'm not sure without the use of an X-ray," Fiona said. "You'll have to wait for the post-mortem results, I'm afraid."

Cassie nodded, thoughtful. "Any idea what the weapon might be?"

Fiona's forehead creased. "Something rounded, spherical maybe, and with some significant weight to it. To crack a human skull, although it can be fragile in places it does do its job of protecting the brain rather well, it would have to be something with a fair bit of mass to it. An object comprised of metal or stone, I would suggest."

Cassie took that on board. "What about defensive wounds on the victim?"

"None that I can see," Dr Williams said. "There is an abrasion on the back of his right hand but it strikes me as an injury likely caused by scraping the skin over a rough surface, a fleeting scrape in passing, rather than anything else."

"When falling into the pool?"

"Yes, that would be possible. The surface of the stone is dressed to avoid slipping as much as possible. The slight texture to the stone would certainly do that."

"Can you see any other injuries?"

"No, I can't. Luckily for me, he saw fit to remove his upper clothes and I can't see any indication of any other injuries. It is always possible that there are some beneath the surface, caused by the fall but he passed away before any bruising would have a chance of beginning to show."

"Time of death?"

Dr Williams breathed in sharply. "Difficult to say. The liver probe suggests death occurred between midnight and two in the morning, however, the cool water in the swimming pool will skew that time frame. The pathologist will have to take into account those temperature variations and give you a more definitive time. He will also be able to confirm the cause of death."

"The head wound or drowning," Cassie said, quietly. "Presumably?"

"Yes, the head wound would have inflicted a significant amount of damage. The bone fragments will have penetrated the brain tissue beneath, undoubtedly. To what extent I can't say at this point, but if that didn't see him off then he will have drowned."

"Would the blow have incapacitated him?"

"I would have thought so. He would have been unconscious or, at best, semi-conscious when he went into the water."

"We're assuming he was struck here and then fell straight in," Cassie said, mentally measuring the distance from the body to the house and pondering whether the assault could have happened away from the pool and the scene was then staged to make it look like an accident.

"That's a good point," Fiona said. "Speculation isn't my thing though. I leave that up to you. Either way, whether he died from the blunt force trauma or drowning, I can't say, but if there's water in the lungs then you'll have your answer."

Cassie nodded. "Would an injury like that," she said, pointing at the head wound, "bleed a lot?"

"A lot is a very subjective term, but certainly nowhere near as much as a wound to the torso, legs or arms. The lack of arterial blood flow through that area of the head would limit it," she cocked her head, wincing momentarily, "when compared to a stab wound or similar to those areas of the body. There will still be blood loss though."

"I'm just thinking that I haven't seen any blood stains inside the house—"

"Which brings into question an attack in there and the body being dragged out here to the pool," Fiona said thoughtfully. Cassie nodded.

"Ah well, we'll figure it out," Cassie said, staring back towards the open patio doors. "Thanks, Fiona. I appreciate your analysis."

Cassie moved away from the body, seeing two forensic technicians waiting to speak to her. They had already donned their white coveralls, and Eric was standing with them. She walked back to join them, circumventing as much of the crime scene as possible now that she was certain they were dealing with more than an accident.

Having set the forensic team to work, Cassie took Eric aside.

"Have Sheriff," she said, referring to PC Marshall by his nickname, "canvass the neighbouring properties. The usual questions, did they see or hear anything unusual. How well did they know... what was his name again?"

"Aaron Bell," Eric said.

"Yeah, see how well they knew him, what he was like. That sort of thing. Maybe they can give us a steer as to the circles he moved in." Cassie glanced around the room. "This seems like the type of place to host large social events. It's an odd place to live in alone."

"It's certainly geared towards it," Eric said, "but it doesn't appear to have been used that way recently. I did find this though." Eric steered her over to the kitchen island where there were some bits of paper, unopened junk mail, in a small pile at one end. In amongst the letters advertising sun blinds, garden furniture and food discounts from local shops, was another flyer. Cassie tilted her head to read it. It was advertising a reunion to be held at Sheringham High School. "It took place last night," Eric said. Cassie noted the date had been circled in red pen. There was a mobile number listed to call for more information and Cassie figured this must be a flyer sent to those who'd registered an interest. No one is crazy enough to list their mobile number on a random public flyer for anyone to see.

"That room," Cassie said, "the one that's locked. Can you see if the cleaner has access to it? There are external cameras all around the building and it would make sense for them to feed back to a central hub."

"In a locked room," Eric said. Cassie nodded. "I'll go and ask her."

The swimming pool complicated matters in Cassie's mind. Not only did it affect the calculations that would determine the time of death, it also dramatically affected forensic trace analysis in a negative way. The chlorine used in the filtration process would destroy any potential DNA evidence that could link the killer to the body. Despite there being no evidence of a struggle, on the deceased's body at least, if there had been then the water in the pool would erase that. Should drowning be the determination of the pathologist following the autopsy, it would also muddy the waters when it came to intent if they were ever able to bring a case to trial. Who could argue murder if the cause of death was drowning, possibly from an accidental fall?

She was hoping the cameras would shed some light on what happened the previous night. Without them, Cassie had to hope that the processing of the crime scene would yield more clues about what occurred. She didn't have much expectation regarding positive results from the door-to-door inquiries. The house sat on a large plot and the neighbouring houses were not close. On the western perimeter there was what appeared to be a storage area for agricultural machinery and the property to the east was at least thirty metres away beyond a mature hedge row that was easily over six feet tall. It would take a gunshot or similar to attract attention, but there was always a chance, no matter how slim, that they might learn something.

She took out her mobile as she walked back outside and into the sunshine, watching as the forensic technicians began setting up their kit to begin their analysis of the scene.

"Morning, boss," she said, but hesitated as she realised the voicemail had kicked in. She had called their commanding officer, DCI Tamara Greave. "I'm sorry to be the bearer of bad news but this is looking like it isn't an accident. Please can you give me a call back when you're free."

Cassie hung up, seeing Eric walking back into the kitchen looking around for her. Upon seeing her, he smiled and raised his hand triumphantly, holding a set of keys. Cassie went with him through the house to the locked door.

"She said she doesn't ever have to access the room but she was told this was a full set of keys to the property," Eric said, examining the keys to try and find one that looked like it might fit the lock. He tried one which didn't work, then another but it was the third key that unlocked the door. Inside they found a relatively large room housing the plant for the property.

There was a large hot water cylinder with its associated pipework, along with several other units that Cassie guessed were related to a heat recovery and ventilation system based on the number of insulated tubes going in and out of them. A large cabinet with a vented metal door was located in the far corner and Cassie could see flickering lights inside. She opened it, revealing multiple data cables. This was the central smart hub for the house. A router sat on the top shelf and on the shelf below were a number of cables that were not connected to anything. Cassie could see the outline of where a small box had once been, visible from a layer of dust that would have settled around it. She sighed.

"It looks like someone else had the same thought as us," she said to Eric beside her.

"We know one thing though," Eric said. Cassie offered him a quizzical look. Eric gestured towards the door. "Whoever came in here had a set of keys."

They stepped out of the room and returned to the kitchen. The forensic technicians were already at work and they gave them a wide berth. Cassie took out her mobile phone, snapped a photograph of the flyer detailing the school reunion and then typed the mobile number listed into her phone.

"It wouldn't hurt to gather a little information," she said to Eric. He inclined his head.

"Not at all."

The number connected and the call was answered swiftly by a female voice.

"Good morning," Cassie said brightly. "I'm sorry to trouble you so early, but I'm looking for a bit of information on the school reunion held at Sheringham—"

"That was last night."

"Yes, yes, I know," Cassie said. "I was just trying to find out if Aaron Bell managed to make it. I know he was planning to go."

"Yes, he did... I'm sorry, who is this?"

"My name is Cassie. I'm a detective sergeant with Norfolk Police. Who am I speaking to?" There was a brief moment of silence which Cassie found unsurprising. After all, it's not every day the police call you out of the blue. "Can I take your name please?"

"Y-Yes, of course. It's Charlotte. Sears, Charlotte Sears. How can I help you?" Cassie glanced at Eric.

"Thank you, Charlotte. Tell me, how well do you know Aaron Bell?"

CHAPTER SIX

Tom felt a tightness in his left leg followed by a short pang of acute pain in his calf. He pulled up but rather than stop completely and allowed himself to walk at a gentle pace, which was very different to the speed he'd managed since he set off. Checking his watch, he read his statistics. He'd managed a little over twelve miles and much of that had been running on sand. This surface was a different proposition to the road running he'd been doing whilst building himself up.

Having spent the first month of his suspension ruminating on what he could, and possibly should, have done differently to avoid winding up in this position he then decided to put the time to more positive use. The internal investigation examining his conduct had been sidelined until after the coroner's ruling on the death of the man by Tom's hand was announced. The coroner's investigation had begun and then immediately adjourned. This was not unusual in and of itself, but it was incredibly frustrating.

The result of all of this was Tom finding himself in limbo with more time on his hands than he'd had in years. At least, since he was a pre-teenager anyway. The ballot for slots to take part in the following year's London Marathon was soon to be announced and that was what he'd been working towards, running to raise money for a charity specialising in making terminally ill children's dreams come true. If he managed to complete the course, raising money for a decent cause along the way, then the year wouldn't be a total write-off.

The pain in his calf had eased a little and he stopped walking to do some stretching, tentatively probing the area with his fingertips. He didn't wish to be sidelined for any length of time. Fitness and stamina gains were hard won, but quickly lost if not maintained. Tom was in decent shape, but this training regimen he'd embarked on was taking him to another level.

Not that this morning was his usual routine. Having returned home from dropping Aaron back at his house, Tom had gone to bed as usual with Alice. Sleep had been elusive though and he'd slipped out of the bedroom and took to the spare bedroom fearing that his tossing and turning was bound to wake Alice. There was no point in both of them getting a poor night's sleep. Insomnia was nothing new for him.

Ever since his suspension he'd been plagued with fitful dreams where he relived the event almost nightly. The counselling service offered by Norfolk Constabulary had proved ineffective for him, but Tom, despite his best efforts, wasn't a man who liked to share his innermost feelings, much to Alice's frustration. Having managed a few hours of restless sleep, he decided to get up and go out for an early run. His route took him across open farmland to the north and up to the coast where he cut east and ran towards the coming dawn. The sensation he felt from watching the sunrise on the horizon was a wonder to behold and this particular morning he'd seen it alone. Often he'd see lone dog walkers or other early birds, but not today. This morning, he had the dawn to himself.

Feeling the chill of the morning air now, his sweat cooling his skin to the point of discomfort, he set off again but at a gentler pace. He wasn't far from home and he'd have enough time to shower and change before taking Saffy to school. That was one benefit to his enforced absence from the office. He was able to spend far more time with his adopted daughter, and it had become the norm for him to both take her to school – although he'd do his best to avoid the other parents at drop-off – and also to collect her at the end of the day. This was something he looked forward to and, based on the size of the hug she gave him every day, he knew Saffy did too.

He left the side of the road, crossing a narrow bridge over a drainage ditch to the side of a farmer's field, Tom skirted the field following the hedge row before cutting left and onto a bridleway leading to the modern estate he lived on. It wasn't a large estate, fewer than twenty properties built primarily to offer accommodation to local people priced out of home ownership by the second home and holiday industry speculators. This was becoming more of a hot-button issue as the cost of living increases in recent years started to put pressure on the local population. Alice's work at the hospital helped her to secure the property, otherwise there was little chance she would have been able to do so with her status as a single parent at the time.

Finally coming within sight of his home, Tom pulled up, breathing heavily despite taking it easier on the final stretch and put his hands on his hips. He saw a familiar car parked in the road in front of their house. It surprised him. He set off again, only this time he walked at a gentle pace, wondering what brought her to his home this early in the morning. It certainly wouldn't be to pass on information regarding his suspension. Tamara hadn't been anywhere near him in months.

Not that he blamed her. She couldn't be perceived as influencing or assisting him in his case. She had to remain objective and detached. It was the way of these things. Not that it didn't hurt him to be effectively ignored by someone he thought of as a close friend. Knowing Tamara, she was here for a specific reason and his curiosity grew as he approached his home.

He went through the gated access along the side of the house, entering the kitchen via the garden to the rear. Tamara was in the dining room, Saffy standing on one of the chairs with her arms draped around Tamara's shoulder. The two of them were sharing a joke, both smiling broadly. Alice was also present, arms casually folded across her chest. She had been less forgiving when it came to his other colleagues, putting distance between them. The only member of the team who'd kept in regular contact had been Cassie; never one to bow to authority.

Tamara turned as Tom opened the back door and walked in. She smiled at him. It was a genuine response, he judged, but he also read a tinge of awkwardness in her expression as their eyes met.

"Hello, Tom."

"Aunty T has come to see you," Saffy said eagerly, hopping down from the chair and running over to meet him. Tom leaned down and she wrapped her arms around his waist. Both Saffy and Alice had been asleep when he left on his morning run.

"I've come to see you," Tamara said to Saffy. "Your dad is just a side project." Saffy beamed at that comment, shooting Tamara a broad grin. She looked back at Tom. "How have you been?" she asked, giving him an appraising look. "You're in good shape."

"Keeping busy," Tom replied, a little more stilted and cool than he'd planned. Tamara's smile faded slightly and she glanced at Alice who looked down at her feet. "It's been a while."

Tamara winced momentarily. "I know. Too long."

"Come on, munchkin," Alice said, stepping forward and holding out her hand to her daughter. "We have to get you dressed for school."

"But I thought daddy was taking me, same as usual," Saffy said, pouting.

"Not today, darling," Alice said. "I think your dad is needed here." Saffy made ready to protest but her mum shot her a stern look and, for once, Saffy thought better of protesting. She lowered her head, resigned to her fate and shuffled past Alice without taking the offered hand. Alice arched her eyebrows. "I'll leave the two of you to it."

"You're okay taking Saffy to school then?" Tom asked, well aware that this was a change to their normal routine these days, but Alice was correct, Tamara would be here for a reason. He was keen to learn what that was.

"Of course," Alice said, looking back at him as she followed Saffy out of the room. She offered Tamara a weak smile and it was reciprocated. Tom picked up a glass and filled it with water, sipping from it while waiting until both Alice and Saffy could be heard on the stairs and were out of earshot.

"So…"

"I'm sorry, Tom," Tamara said before he could speak. "I followed the instructions I was given—"

"You had no choice," he said. Tamara held up a hand, silencing him.

"There's always a choice," she said, frowning. "And I chose to do as I was told rather than what I knew to be right." Tom inclined his head, seeing pain in her expression. "For what it's worth, I'm sorry."

Their eyes met and neither of them blinked, then Tom

smiled. "What's done is done." He inclined his head. "Let's say no more about it, hey?"

Tamara seemed relieved. "I think that's more gracious than I deserve, to be honest."

"I'll keep it in the bank for later."

She laughed. "Now that's more like it."

"Now," Tom said, having finished the glass of water and refilling it, "I'm certain you didn't come by this early to make up."

She grimaced. "No, I didn't. What can you tell me about Aaron Bell?"

"Aaron?" Tom asked, surprised. Tamara nodded. Tom thought for a moment. "I was at school with him back in the day." He laughed momentarily. "I saw him last night as it happens."

"At the school reunion?"

He cocked his head, then nodded. "Yes, that's right. How did you know?"

"We found a flyer or invitation at his house," she said. "When we called the organiser, she said Aaron left with you last night."

"That's right. He'd been drinking heavily, and I didn't want him driving back to Blakeney and so I offered to drive him home. That's his car outside."

"Ah," Tamara said, glancing over her shoulder as if she could see through the wall. "That answers that question then. What time did you leave him?"

"I didn't really look," Tom said, his brow furrowing. "It was pretty late. He was in a bit of a mess. I don't think his life has been going the way he'd hoped recently."

"Oh? In what way?"

"Marital strife... he seemed pretty miserable with his lot," Tom said, recalling the extensive luxury house in Blakeney, "despite outward appearances to the contrary, I think he's unhappy." Tom looked at her. "What's going on? What's he done?"

"I'm afraid there's no easy way to say it, Tom. Your friend passed away at some point during the night," Tamara said flatly. Tom couldn't mask his surprise.

"I... really? What the hell happened?"

"That's what we're trying to find out but it would appear that there was an altercation last night, at his home, and he was found deceased in his swimming pool by his housekeeper first thing this morning."

Tom exhaled heavily. "How did he die?"

"We don't know yet, not conclusively anyway, but he suffered a significant blow to the head. Whether he drowned or not will have to wait for the post-mortem."

Tom leaned back against the counter, setting his glass down beside him and shaking his head. He looked at the clock. "I can't believe it. I was only with him a few hours ago."

"How well do you know him?"

"Two to three decades ago? Very well." He shook his head. "As well as anyone really knows another teenager." Tamara narrowed her eyes. "Let's face it, we hardly know ourselves at that age, do we?"

"True. Although, I was pretty confident that I knew everything back then."

"Didn't we all? The arrogance of youth."

"Aaron Bell," Tamara said. "What do you know about him now?"

"I haven't seen him in years," Tom said, frowning. "Last night was the first time I'd seen or heard from him since we were kids really."

"How was he?"

Tom exhaled heavily. "Troubled, I would say. Outwardly,

he was brash and a bit full of himself. I'm playing it down. He was very full of himself. He was making friends with some of the old gang," he said with a wry smile.

"Not popular then?"

"He was, back when we were at school. He was one of the cool gang, you know? Many people may not have liked him as a result of that, but there was a begrudging respect… no, respect is the wrong word. There were tiers of popularity and those who weren't in the top tier either accepted their place or carried a bit of a chip on their shoulder."

"Was he a ladies' man?"

Tom was thoughtful. "He did okay. Better than most of us, to be fair but that comes with the status as well. There was no shortage of applicants lining up for his attention that's for sure."

"How about you?" Tamara asked.

"Me?"

"Yes, were you… what do you call it, his wing man or something?" Tom laughed. Tamara smiled. "I'll take that as a no."

"You may find this hard to believe but I was quite short even when I was coming up to graduation. Fast, sporty… but not particularly big in comparison to others." Tamara looked him up and down.

"What did your parents do, inject you with growth hormones or something?"

"I grew a lot, in the space of a year." Tom shrugged. "But no, I wasn't one of the in-crowd by any stretch of the imagination."

"You said Aaron was making friends? I presume that is a euphemism?"

"Yes. He had a brief set to with Noah Cook in front of

everyone and then I'm certain I broke up a fight between Aaron and Tony later on."

"Noah Cook?" Tamara asked, making a note.

"You spoke to Charlotte, I take it? She organised the reunion event."

Tamara nodded. "I did. She put me onto you."

"Well, Noah and Charlotte were married for a time. Charlotte's sister dated Aaron when we were at school and, although I said he wasn't a ladies' man, he did treat Kristy – Charlotte's sister – pretty badly. They had a difficult break-up. It was nothing unusual for teenagers, but she… well… ultimately, Kristy took her own life."

Tamara blew out her cheeks. "He treated her that badly?"

"No one really knows what went on. Aaron said Kristy was far too clingy and held onto him too much. He found it claustrophobic." He frowned. "She was fairly highly strung as an individual, looking back, but no one saw it coming. It was a real shock. Not only to her family and Aaron but to the whole town."

"How old was she?"

"Sixteen," Tom said. "Just turned."

"That's awful."

He nodded. "Yes. Charlotte blamed Aaron. At least, she did for a period of time. I think a lot of people did but it was harsh in my mind. It's not like you can stay in a relationship with someone just in case they can't handle a break-up. And, let's not forget, he was also sixteen."

"How was Charlotte with him last night then?"

"Fine," Tom said. "It was all a long time ago and there didn't appear to be any animosity between them."

"But there was with Noah?"

Tom sighed. "Noah… he was always a very reactionary kind of person. He had a quick temper but," Tom added, seeing Tamara's eyes light up, "he was never a violent person. He'd sound off and storm away."

"Maybe he's a bit more willing to fight as an adult."

Tom couldn't disagree. He didn't know the man, not any more. "It's possible."

"And who is this Tony character?"

"Tony Slater. He runs a restaurant along the coast," Tom said. "He took it over from his parents a few years ago. Whether he owns it outright or just manages it on behalf of his folks, I don't know."

"What were they fighting about?"

Tom shook his head. "I don't know."

"You didn't ask?"

"I'm trying not to be a detective at the moment," he said, arching his eyebrows. "Besides, Alice made me go to get me out and about."

"You're not moping are you?"

"I've spent a lot of time on leave, tending to the garden." He pursed his lips. "There are only so many miles I can run each day before I get itchy feet." Tamara fixed him with a stern look.

"Reading between the lines, that sounds like the words of a man who is making decisions."

"Considering the future, yes," he said flatly.

"Tom, this—"

They were interrupted by Saffy running into the room. Dressed in her school uniform with a backpack over her shoulders, she threw her arms around Tamara's legs. "She wanted to see you before she left for school," Alice said, standing in the doorway.

"Well, I'm very pleased that you did," Tamara said, stooping to allow Saffy to put her arms around her neck and kiss her cheek. She detached from Tamara and did the same to

Tom, wrinkling her nose as he hugged her.

"You need a shower," Saffy said softly as she let go of him.

"The next thing on my list," he replied.

"You'll pick me up from school?" Saffy asked and Tom nodded.

"Usual time. I'll be there."

Saffy smiled and, encouraged by her mum, ran out of the room. Alice waved to them both.

"It was nice to see you, Tamara," she said, then smiled at Tom before turning away. Tom waited until he heard the front door close behind them. Tamara looked embarrassed.

"I get the feeling that was insincere," Tamara said.

"You can't blame her. She's had a lot to cope with these past few months," Tom said. "Namely me."

"How are you coping?"

"Bored. I am very bored."

"Please don't make any rash decisions, Tom. This will pass. You'll be back at work in no time."

"Yes," he said, forcing a smile. "I'm sure it will."

Tamara looked down at her notebook. "Do you happen to know where we might find Aaron's next of kin?"

"I don't know if his parents are still around. They talked about retiring to Spain, but I can't say for sure if they ever followed through on that plan. He's married, as I said."

"Do you know where we can find her?"

"No. Not really. From what he told me last night she could be abroad in any number of countries. He's been back here, living in Blakeney for the past few months by himself."

"Was he all right when you left him last night?"

"He was, yes. He'd had a few drinks, and he was… melancholy," Tom said, thinking hard. "Aside from that, he seemed okay. I anticipated he might drink more after I left which did leave me a little concerned but that's all. Not concerned enough to think I shouldn't leave him. He wasn't paralytic or anything like that."

"And you didn't see anyone else at the house when you were there," Tamara asked, "or hanging about outside?"

"No, not at all. It is very quiet out there. Especially when it gets late." Tom looked towards the front window of the house, seeing Aaron's car parked on the road. "I was planning to drive his car back to his place later today." Tamara followed Tom's gaze to the window.

"There's no reason why you shouldn't," she said. "If you still want to."

"Better than leaving it randomly parked here. Someone, maybe his wife, will want it." Tom stared straight ahead at nothing in particular. "I can't believe it. It's so surreal."

"More so when we are familiar with the victim, right?" Tom nodded. "Right, well I think that's it for now," she said, meeting his eye. "You know the drill. If you think of anything—"

"I'll be sure to call. I think I can remember the number," he said, with a wry smile.

"Thanks for the information, Tom. I'll have Eric or Cassie speak to you to take a statement detailing last night. At this time, you're the last person to have seen Aaron alive." Tamara nodded towards him. "It's been good to see you, Tom. I am sorry for not having been in touch—"

He held up his hand. "There's no need. I understand. I really do."

She turned to leave, hesitating before looking back. "There is one thing."

"Anything."

"Saffy's right. You really do need to take that shower."

CHAPTER SEVEN

DS CASSIE KNIGHT eased the unmarked police car around a shallow bend, following the gentle contours of the coastal road. DC Eric Collet sat beside her, flipping through the notes in his pocket-sized notepad. The morning sky was a haphazard patchwork of thin cloud and pale sunlight, typical for this stretch of Norfolk coastline in early spring. A light breeze drifted in off the North Sea, making the tall grasses along the roadside sway as they drove.

They were on their way to speak with Tony Slater, owner of a well-known local restaurant – a place that specialised in hearty seafood dishes, or so the rumour went. Tony was also the man who had argued with Aaron Bell at the school reunion the night before Aaron turned up dead. They'd learned about the confrontation from multiple sources, including a reluctant mention from others who had attended. More importantly, Tom Janssen had confirmed it as well. The details were patchy, but everyone agreed: Tony and Aaron had shared some tense words – or possibly more – just hours before Aaron died.

For Cassie, it was routine procedure to follow up with each

person who'd had any sort of disagreement with the victim. For Eric, still relatively new to plainclothes work, it was a chance to watch and learn. Neither of them was entirely sure what to expect from Tony Slater. He might be completely innocent, or he might be hiding something; maybe even related to that old, half-forgotten grudge from their teenage years. If there was one thing Cassie understood from experience, it was that teenage rivalries could leave a deep mark and sometimes lie dormant for decades.

She guided the car into a small gravel lay-by in front of a modest, whitewashed cottage. Low stone walls bounded a short path leading to a blue-painted door. It might have seemed cosy or charming if not for the restaurant next door: a modern building with large glass windows and sleek signage bearing Tony Slater's name. Both structures shared a broad courtyard with only a slender patch of grass separating them. A slim fence stretched behind the buildings, marking the boundary between Tony's property and a field that gently sloped towards salt marshes off in the distance.

Eric glanced up from his notepad. "Are we sure he'll be at home? Not at the restaurant?"

"His wife picked up when we called," Cassie said, shutting off the engine. "She said Tony was there, but it sounded like she was about to hang up on me. Guess we'll see if that's changed once we knock on the door."

They got out of the car, the crunch of gravel underfoot the only sound besides the distant hush of waves. A gull circled overhead, briefly screeching before gliding away. Cassie took a moment to scan her surroundings. She could see an alley of sorts separating Tony's cottage from the restaurant, presumably for deliveries. Behind the cottage was a small garden, neatly kept, with a winding path and a wooden gate.

At the cottage door, Eric raised a hand and knocked. They

heard a muffled voice, footsteps, then a rattling of a chain. The door eased open to reveal a woman who looked to be in her late twenties, maybe thirty at most. She was tall and graceful, with dark hair pinned loosely at the back of her head and a figure accentuated by well-fitted jeans and a pastel blouse. A faint scent of jasmine perfume drifted out onto the step.

"Hello," she said, eyes moving from Cassie to Eric and back again. "You must be the police officers who called earlier."

Cassie flashed a brief smile and introduced herself. "Detective Sergeant Knight, Norfolk Constabulary. This is DC Collet." She nodded in greeting. "We're here to speak with Tony Slater."

The woman's gaze flickered with apprehension. "I'm Morgan Slater – Tony's wife." She hovered there a moment, uncertain. "He's in the back. Come through."

She led them along a short corridor which opened into a cosy living area. Plush sofas edged a small fireplace, and a thick rug covered most of the polished wooden floor. The décor blended modern touches, like a wall-mounted flat screen TV and minimalist lamp stands, with more rustic elements, such as a driftwood mirror and a basket filled with seashells. Cassie noticed a few paintings featuring local coastal scenes: fishing boats pulled up on the beach, worn groynes battered by the sea.

Morgan paused by a wide archway that led into the kitchen. "I'll just let Tony know you're here."

From Cassie's angle, she could see through the archway: there was a snug, informal dining space centred around a pine table. Beyond it, an open door gave a glimpse of a neat back garden. A cat, ginger and rather plump, prowled along the threshold, investigating something on the stone patio. The smell of freshly brewed coffee lingered in the air.

While they waited, Eric cast his eyes over the tidy living area, evidently in observation mode. He whispered quietly, "Comfy place. Nicer than I expected."

"Not quite the mansion in Blakeney," Cassie said, referencing Aaron Bell's opulent residence, "but it's got a warm, lived-in feel."

Morgan returned, stepping aside so they could pass into the kitchen. "He'll be right out. He's just... finishing something."

The cat wandered in, tail held high, gazing at the visitors with mild curiosity. Morgan bent to scratch it behind the ears, though her eyes remained watchful on Cassie and Eric as if unsure whether to make conversation. There was a polite tension about her, the sort of posture Cassie recognised in people who aren't used to police visits and have no idea what to say.

She took the initiative. "Thank you for letting us in. I hope we're not disturbing you too much this morning."

Morgan shrugged, straightening up. "It's fine. I just—" She paused, looking towards the corridor. "Honestly, I don't know what this is all about, but Tony said you're investigating something that happened at the reunion. I didn't go, so I can't be of much help."

"We just need to talk to him," Cassie said gently. "You may not have attended, but you might be able to help us with a few background details later, if necessary."

Eric offered a friendly, disarming smile. "No reason to worry. This is all pretty standard stuff."

Morgan didn't reply, merely nodding and wrapping her arms loosely around her midsection as if unconsciously trying to comfort herself. Moments later, Tony Slater appeared. He was taller than Cassie had expected – just shy of Tom Janssen's height – but stouter, carrying a bit of extra weight around his midsection. Lines etched at the corners of his eyes suggested a man in his mid-forties. He was wearing dark blue jeans and a short-sleeved collared shirt, revealing tattooed forearms dusted with hair and faint old scars from what might have been long-ago mishaps in the kitchen or the restaurant environment.

"Detective," he said, inclining his head at Cassie, then turning to Eric. "Officer." His tone was guarded but not overtly hostile. "Let's sit, shall we?"

They all moved to the small dining table in the kitchen. Morgan lingered uncertainly, then perched on a barstool by the counter. The cat wove around Tony's ankles and meowed.

"Sorry," Tony said, voice a little gruff. "He's an attention-seeker." He nudged the cat away gently with his foot. "What can I do for you?"

Cassie opened her notebook but did not write yet, preferring to hold his gaze. "We understand you were at Sheringham High School's reunion last night. You had some kind of disagreement with Aaron Bell."

Tony rubbed the back of his neck. "That's right. It was stupid. A drink-fuelled, childish argument. God, the sort of thing that makes you wonder if you ever left school." He dropped his hand onto the table, exhaling loudly. "Do we really need to talk about this?"

"I'm afraid we do," Cassie said, her voice measured. She wanted to establish calm but also not appear too laid back. "Can you walk us through what happened? From the beginning."

Tony shot a glance at Morgan, who lowered her eyes. Then he cleared his throat. "Sure. There's no real big story, though. I'd had a few drinks. Aaron had definitely had a few. We were yapping about old times; who did what back in the day, who went on to do bigger and better things, that sort of nonsense.

Next thing I knew, we were throwing jibes at each other. Aaron liked to show off, bragging about his fancy house, his travelling, the women he'd dated... like we were sixteen years old again."

He paused, working his jaw as though testing how to phrase the next part. "I guess he pushed the right buttons. Back in school, we clashed a bit, always competing for attention or for girls, just silly teenage stuff, but it was real at the time. He was the type who needed to be top dog. And maybe I was resentful, you know? Or maybe just insecure. Whatever it was, he was telling me something about his life in Dubai, or bragging about it, and I told him to shove off. Then we squared up. Some pushing and shoving. That's it."

Cassie took a moment to gauge him. His posture seemed open, honest. If Tony was lying, he was doing a good job, but Cassie's gut said he wasn't. At least, not about the general shape of the argument. "So you were physically pushing each other?"

Tony nodded, a shade of embarrassment colouring his cheeks. "Yes. Like a pair of idiots. One of my old friends broke it up, then I stormed off. I can't remember exactly what time it was, but I left not long after, that's for sure."

Morgan broke in, her voice soft but resolute. "He texted me about half-ten, maybe quarter to eleven, saying he was on his way home."

Cassie glanced her way, making a mental note. "So you didn't stay late. Tony, do you remember seeing Aaron again after that fight?"

"No. As far as I'm aware, Aaron carried on partying, or at least stayed in the hall. I didn't see him once I walked out. Honestly, I should never have let him bait me. I'm not proud of it, but it all felt so... familiar. Like we were back in our teens, still trying to out-do each other. Like I said, it was stupid."

Cassie made a mental note of the approximate timeline. She noticed Eric doing the same from her peripheral vision, writing in his notebook. "That begs the question," she said, scanning Tony's expression, "where did you go after you left?"

A faint scowl creased Tony's forehead, but it seemed more uncertain than defensive. "I drove home, right here. Morgan was waiting up. Well, not exactly waiting up, but she was awake. Is that right, Morgs?" He glanced at his wife.

She shifted uncomfortably on the barstool. "I was awake, yes, but I was in bed watching something on my phone. He came in, and then went straight into the shower because he reeked of beer."

Tony gave a half-smile, perhaps grateful for the mild attempt at humour. "I did. That was it, though. I didn't go anywhere else. We had a quick chat about a few bits and bobs, then we turned in."

"Bits and bobs?" Cassie asked.

"You know, stuff around the day."

"The fight?"

Tony seemed awkward. "Um… no, I didn't really mention it."

"Why not?"

Tony shrugged. "I was a bit embarrassed, I guess."

Cassie tilted her head. "So you came home around…?"

Tony looked to Morgan again. She frowned, trying to recall. "He texted me around half-ten, so maybe it was closer to eleven by the time he got home? I wasn't clock-watching. Something like that."

Eric scribbled the time in his notes. "Was anyone else here

who can confirm that arrival time or that you stayed put?" Cassie asked.

A thin line formed between Tony's eyebrows. "What do you mean? Like a neighbour, friend, or someone who saw me? No, just Morgan. And the cat," he added wryly. "He's the only other witness, I'm afraid. I don't suppose you can interview him?"

Eric, who'd been silent until now, cleared his throat. "Animals are notoriously unhelpful on the record, sir."

Tony snorted a half-laugh, but anxiety was in his eyes. "Look, is there a reason you're asking? If Aaron's gone and made a complaint that I threw the first punch or something then—"

Cassie leaned forward slightly, resting her hands on the table. She caught Morgan's eyes across the way, and the younger woman stiffened, anticipating something bad was coming, Cassie figured. "Aaron Bell is dead," she said simply, letting the words hang in the air.

Tony froze. His face seemed to slacken with shock. "Dead? What do you mean... dead?"

"I mean he's deceased," Cassie said flatly. "Very much dead. Murdered."

Morgan let out a small gasp and stared at her husband. "But...what happened?"

Cassie studied Tony's reaction closely. If he was acting, he was doing a good job. But Cassie saw genuine disbelief in the tension around his eyes and the parted lips that struggled to form words. "He was found early this morning, at his home. I can't go into all the details, but it appears there was a violent confrontation. We have reason to believe it resulted in a fatal injury. The time frame suggests it happened after the reunion."

Morgan's hand flew to her mouth. "Oh, my God."

Tony's gaze fell to the table, his eyebrows drawn. "Are you… are you implying I had something to do with that?"

"We're implying nothing," Cassie clarified. "We need to follow the facts. You and Aaron fought publicly, then parted ways. Our job is to piece together who saw him after that fight and where everyone was during the likely time of death. So far, that puts you near the top of our list of people to speak with."

"I don't believe this," Tony muttered, dragging a hand down his face. "He was in fine shape when I walked away. Yeah, he was hammered, but not falling-over hammered. We'd both drunk too much, that's for certain. When I left, I saw him still in the assembly hall. At least half the old class was still there, some with their wives or partners, whoever. He must have talked to other people. I swear I never saw him again after I left."

Cassie paused, letting him stew in the moment, then gave a subtle nod. "All right. You said you got home around eleven. Then you stayed in?"

"Yes," Tony said. "I told you. We talked for a bit, maybe I had a quick rummage in the fridge after Morgan put her phone away, but I didn't have any more to drink and I was shattered. We were both tired," he looked at his wife, "weren't we, love?" Morgan nodded but to Cassie, she seemed less sure of herself now. "So we headed to bed, right love?" His wife Morgan glanced away, suggesting she might not agree with his timeframe but then she nodded.

"Did you go out again? Any phone calls? Messages that might have seen you go elsewhere later on?"

"Nothing," Tony insisted, though the lines of worry still creased his forehead. "Morgan's phone might have some streaming record, like a show or something if you want to check times. I don't know. She was half-watching something on Netflix while I was in the shower."

Morgan swallowed, nodding. "I can show you the phone, if it helps. But I'm not sure it'll prove Tony got home exactly at eleven. You can see the show I watched started around that time. A half-hour documentary, I think."

"What about?" Eric asked. Morgan looked at him with a blank expression. "What was the documentary about?"

"Oh… I don't know," she said. "It was something on make-up."

"Make up?" Cassie asked, her forehead creasing.

"During Miami Fashion Week," Morgan said. "It's what I do. I'm a make-up artist."

Cassie nodded. Streaming logs, although useful, were hardly conclusive evidence. People could leave a programme running while they were out, but at least it was something. She pivoted to another line of questioning. "When you were talking to him, prior to the fight… I assume you had some conversation beforehand and you didn't just launch into one another?"

"No, we did talk, yes."

"Did Aaron ever mention any issues he was having? Was there anything in your conversation that led you to think he might be in trouble at all?"

Tony shook his head in disbelief. "Not at all. Why would he say anything to me? The only problem was me wanting to deck him because he was bragging. But, for the record, I didn't deck him. I just shoved him. He shoved back, a bit more verbal abuse, and that was that. It was all a bit of handbags, you know?"

"You mentioned old grudges from your school days," Eric put in quietly. "Would you say there was a genuine hatred between you two, or was it typical teenage rivalry that never fully disappeared?"

Tony sighed, considering. "More the latter, I guess. I never truly hated him. And I doubt he truly hated me. We were just… both proud, both impulsive sometimes. We wanted the same girls back then, and it often caused friction. He was always a show-off, wearing fancy clothes, and always sporting that cocky grin. I was the type who'd let it get under my skin. Just typical teenage nonsense."

"But you're not a teenager now," Cassie said.

"I suppose last night proved we haven't outgrown all of it."

"What specifically was last night's fight about?" Cassie pressed. "Same old territory?"

He paused, ruffling the hair on the back of his head. "It was basically that. Which of us had done better in life, who was still the same loser from when we were kids. He brought up the fancy house in Blakeney. I knew he'd come back here every now and again. He's been into the restaurant with his wife once or twice. There was never an issue between us." Tony frowned. "Everyone knows his house is worth a fortune. I made a crack last night about how it was probably his wife's money that bought it. Then he got personal, and I did the same and… I lost my rag."

"Personal in what way?" Cassie asked.

Tony waved a dismissive hand. "He said something about my place here being a pitiful little restaurant, told me I was an also-ran punching above my weight." His eyes flicked to his wife, and Cassie wondered if having a younger partner was part of the punching that Aaron had referred to. "He said that I'd never really made it. Classic teenage jab, isn't it, only we're not teenagers any more, so it stings all the more."

"Sounds unpleasant," Cassie said gently, "but nothing out

of the ordinary. Did you see anyone else join him or overhear any mention of anyone with future plans with Aaron? Maybe he told someone to meet him after the party?"

"Not that I noticed. He was with Tom when I left him." Tony looked at Cassie and then Eric. "Tom Janssen. Has anyone mentioned that? Tom will tell you."

"We'll be sure to speak to him," Cassie said.

"Yes, well... it's all a blur after that, really."

Cassie made a note, then checked her watch. "All right, Mr Slater. Let me summarise. You admit there was a drunken fight, you left around 10:45 PM or so, and you were home by eleven. You stayed here all night. No one else can confirm your whereabouts."

Morgan bristled again, defensively. "I can confirm his whereabouts. I was here."

"Yes, of course," Cassie said, softly. "I only mean an independent witness, aside from your spouse. Standard procedure in a murder investigation. We check every angle."

Morgan's cheeks took on a faint flush. "Right. I understand."

Eric cleared his throat. "We'll need to keep in touch, Mr Slater, Mrs Slater. If any new information comes up, or if you remember anything else – people you saw at the reunion, or if you overheard something about Aaron's later plans – give us a ring." He passed over a card with the station's number and his direct line.

Tony accepted it. Cassie could see the wheels turning behind his eyes, the shock still rippling through him at Aaron's death. For all Tony's bluster, it looked as if guilt or alarm was settling on him. When he spoke, his voice was subdued. "I can't believe he's dead. If I'd known, I'd have... I wouldn't have left it like that. Even though he was a pain in the backside, I never wished something like this to happen to him."

Cassie sighed. "Sometimes these things come out of nowhere. That's exactly why we're thorough, so if something suspicious happened, then we can figure it out."

A silence fell among them, broken only by the quiet hum of the refrigerator and the rustle of the cat's tail against a chair leg. The creature was completely oblivious to the severity of the conversation. He just wanted attention. Eventually, Cassie nodded to Eric who closed his notebook. "We appreciate your help. If we have more questions, we'll be in touch. We will need to document a formal statement soon."

She and Eric made to leave. Morgan got down from the bar stool, smoothing a hand over her blouse. Tony stayed where he was sitting, shoulders hunched, his expression distant. Cassie offered a simple nod of respect and turned to head back through the way they'd come, escorted by Morgan.

Morgan took the lead, walking to the front door. Before she opened it, she ventured in a hushed voice, "I know this is… perhaps something I shouldn't ask, but do you think Tony is really a suspect in this? I mean, he's not the sort."

Cassie considered her words carefully. "Everyone who had recent contact with Aaron is a person of interest until we can place them clearly. That's how murder investigations go. We haven't arrested your husband, and we may never do so. It's just a process we follow. As long as he's been honest with us, and you have been honest with us, then I'm sure all will be well."

Morgan exhaled, a tremor in her shoulders. "I see. Sorry… I'm just worried."

"I understand," Cassie said gently. "You have been honest though, right? Because, if you haven't been truthful then you both could be in a lot of trouble."

Morgan glanced back down the hall. Tony was still seated at the table, absently stroking the cat now. She nodded. "I've told you the truth."

Cassie and Eric stepped outside. Morgan followed them onto the little stoop, closing the door quietly behind her. The wind whipped Cassie's hair across her eyes, and she brushed it away.

"Take care," Morgan said softly. Then, as if she'd already said too much, she swiftly retreated back inside, leaving them alone on the gravel path.

CHAPTER EIGHT

THEY WALKED BACK to the car. Eric circled around to the passenger side, scanning the courtyard. One or two staff members were visible through the large windows of Slater's restaurant, apparently prepping for lunch service. There was no sign that anything was amiss there. Cassie paused by the driver's door, her lips pressed together in thought.

"What do you think?" Eric asked. He stepped closer, voice low.

Cassie shrugged as Eric slipped his notebook into his coat pocket. "They say it was a quick argument. He left. That's his story. Certainly no direct evidence says he's lying... but it doesn't mean he's telling the whole truth either. Tony definitely had reason to resent Aaron."

Eric drummed his fingers briefly against the roof of the car. "Yeah, and from the timeline, it's plausible he could have driven to Aaron's house after leaving here. That'd be a fifteen-minute drive, if the roads were empty, maybe less."

"Possible," Cassie agreed. "And he could have followed Aaron home. Streaming logs don't prove he came home when he said he did. But I sense genuine shock from him. If he's acting, he's pretty good at it. Also, let's not discount that there might be other conflicts in Aaron's life that overshadow Tony's spat last night. We just don't know yet. I went to school with some arseholes myself, and I might even like some of them to feel a bit of pain, but murdering them? That's something different."

Eric nodded. "I get the feeling Tony's telling the truth about not seeing Aaron again, but we'll see if forensics or witness statements back that up. What's our next move?"

Cassie opened the car door, sinking into the driver's seat. "We'll compare Tony's timeline with any CCTV from the roads, if we can find any. These roads along the coast pass by pubs and shops. Someone might have recorded some footage of passing vehicles. We'd better find out what the Slaters own vehicle-wise."

She started the engine, and Eric climbed in on the passenger side. The air inside the car felt warmer, a welcome shift from the cool breeze outside. As Cassie checked the rear view mirror, she saw Tony's silhouette in one of the front windows, half-concealed behind the curtain. He was watching them leave, or so it seemed.

She guided the car down the gravel drive and back onto the coastal road. The day was still young, and there was plenty of investigating yet to be done: collecting more statements from the former classmates who attended the reunion, re-checking the timeline, and waiting on the forensics report from Aaron's house. A murder inquiry often turned into a puzzle, with each piece needing to fit or be discarded. For now, Tony Slater's piece sat somewhere in the middle, uncertain.

Eric broke the silence as they drove. "So we have Tony confirming the narrative, teenage rivalry, a clash of personalities."

Cassie nodded, eyes scanning the quiet road ahead. "It sounds like Aaron Bell ruffled more than a few feathers at school and people around here have long memories, it seems. If Tony's to be believed, they parted ways, and that was that. We need to see if anyone else saw Aaron after the party. Somebody might have gone with him or met him. Or maybe he picked an argument with someone else entirely."

Eric scribbled a note in his notebook, then flipped it shut. "What about Aaron's wife? I heard from the DCI that she's probably overseas, but does that help us at all? If their marriage was on the rocks, maybe she or a representative was in town?"

"Could be. Tamara has Danny working on tracking the wife's whereabouts," Cassie replied. "And the forensic boys and girls are rummaging through all that fancy tech in Aaron's place, even though the main recorder was missing. With any luck, we'll find a clue."

They continued in silence, Cassie mulling over everything Tony and Morgan said, in case she'd missed anything. They passed fields of swaying crops on one side and glimpses of the sea on the other. Cassie's mind played over Tony's expression of disbelief when he learned of Aaron's death. She'd seen that look before in other cases: a mixture of shock, regret, and a dawning understanding that an insignificant argument could suddenly look like a motive for murder. Was Tony simply an unlucky bystander, a person with zero knowledge of the events that had truly killed Aaron? Or was he reeling from guilt, wrestling with the knowledge that he'd done something far worse and concerned that he was about to be nicked for it?

A buzz from Eric's phone cut the peace. He answered quickly. "Yes, DC Collet?" A moment passed, and he turned to Cassie. "CSI team's started a closer sweep inside the Blakeney property. They want us to know they've found an interesting partial print on a piece of broken glass near the pool. It doesn't match Aaron's. They're running it now. Could be one of the staff, or the cleaner, or a guest from the holiday let, I suppose."

Cassie raised an eyebrow. "Might be nothing. Might be everything. Let's keep on it."

Eric ended the call. "Looks like we have more than a few leads in play."

"Then we'd better keep up the pace," Cassie said, exhaling as she shifted gears. The tyres hummed against the road, the sea just a pale line in the near distance. "Let's head back to the station, collate everything, and see if any of Tony's story can be corroborated. After that, we'll go down the line of everyone else who might have had a grudge, new or old, with Aaron Bell."

Eric closed his eyes briefly, as if mentally bracing for a day of phone calls, computer searches, cross-referencing, and possibly more interviews. "All right, Sarge. Let's do it."

Cassie accelerated, the wind from the open window ruffling the notes in the console. As they rejoined a larger road leading inland, the lunch hour traffic began to pick up; cars of locals, a few early spring tourists. The reflection of the watery sun glinted across the car's bonnet, and Cassie felt that familiar surge of drive that always came when a case was in motion.

Somewhere out there, among old classmates, new acquaintances, or hidden enemies, lay the truth about Aaron Bell's last hours. They'd stripped away the easy explanation of a tragic accident and were confronted with something darker. Had Tony Slater left his boyhood rival behind in that school assembly hall, or had he followed him home to settle an old score once and for all?

A call came through to the car, Tamara's name flashing up on the display. Cassie answered it.

"Yes, boss."

"How did you get on with Tony Slater?" Tamara asked.

"Interesting," Cassie said, concentrating as the road narrowed as they entered Thornham and the Coastliner bus was coming towards her. "I'm not sure he and his wife are telling us everything, but he seemed genuinely shocked about Aaron's death."

"Did he mention Noah Cook?"

"Noah who?"

"Cook," Tamara said. "I spoke to Tom and he said Aaron Bell had a falling out with Noah Cook prior to the altercation with Tony Slater. He didn't mention it then?"

Cassie glanced at Eric for confirmation and he shook his head. "No, the name didn't come up. The organiser we spoke to… what was her name?" Cassie asked.

"Charlotte," Eric said.

"Aye, Charlotte. She didn't mention him."

"Well, Tom says she was married to Noah," Tamara said. "They have a child. Maybe she doesn't want to get him into trouble."

"That gives us someone else to speak to then. Did Tom say where we could find him?"

"No, but he won't be too hard to locate."

"I'll get on it as soon as we are back in the station," Cassie said. "How… er… how is he?"

"Tom?"

"Aye," Cassie said.

"He's well," Tamara said. "We're all looking forward to having him back on the team."

Cassie said goodbye and hung up. She glanced at Eric. "I'm not sure he'll be back you know?"

"Why not?" Eric asked. "You can't think he did what they—"

"No, not at all," Cassie said. "But, let's face it, he's been put through the wringer, hasn't he?"

"Yes… but he'll come back. He has to." Eric turned to look out of the window. "It won't be the same without him. And you might get made up to DI."

"Every cloud," Cassie said, smiling.

"Has a nightmare of a lining," Eric said. Cassie snorted a laugh. She pressed her foot a little harder on the accelerator, keen to get back to the station. The investigation was just beginning.

CHAPTER NINE

Tom Janssen was halfway through loading the dishwasher with the breakfast crockery when his phone rang. The sharp buzz cut into the quiet of the house, shaking him out of his thoughts. The morning sunlight slanted in through the kitchen window, and the hush of a nearly empty home – Alice at work, Saffy at school – made the sudden interruption feel louder than it was.

He wiped his hands, checked the caller ID, and felt a small jolt of unease. It was Charlotte Sears. She'd gleaned his number from Alice at the reunion and she did say she'd be *in touch soon*. He hadn't expected *soon* to be the following day. After Aaron's death, Tom was in no mood to endure more awkward encounters with old classmates. Yet some part of him also felt compelled to answer.

He pressed Accept.

"Tom?" came Charlotte's voice, breathy but businesslike. "It's Charlotte. You busy?"

Tom swallowed. Busy? He had absolutely nothing on his calendar aside from picking up Saffy from school mid-afternoon. Even that felt like a blessing, a daily anchor preventing him from drifting aimlessly. Once he'd got his run complete, his day was empty. "I'm... mostly free," he said. It wasn't untrue.

"Great," Charlotte replied with a tone too bright for the morning. "Remember when I said we should get a coffee sometime? Maybe talk about old times and have a proper catch up?"

He did remember, though he'd been determined to avoid it. "Ah... well..."

She rolled right over his hesitation. "I'm actually in Sheringham this morning. I have a free hour or two – scheduling fiasco with some parent committee business – and I thought, why not see if we can meet? We could have a natter over that cup of coffee."

Tom's mind raced for a plausible excuse. He considered Saffy's school run, but that was hours away. He could claim errands, but Charlotte might just propose a briefer meeting. If he stalled too long, he'd look rude or suspicious. Or he could just face it.

"All right," he said, forcing a polite tone. "Where do you want to meet?"

Charlotte gave a delighted hum. "Café Romano on the high street? I'm sure you remember it. It used to be that tacky tourist tearoom, but it's changed hands. They do a decent cappuccino now."

Tom wasn't sure he remembered the place at all, given how many businesses had shuffled in and out of Sheringham's high street in recent years. "Sure," he said, already bracing himself. "See you in about twenty minutes?"

"Perfect," she replied. "I'll grab us a table and see you there."

She ended the call with a breezy farewell, leaving Tom to stare at his phone. He realised the dishwasher was still ajar, half-loaded, the last few plates perched precariously next to the sink. With a sigh, he finished the task and turned it on. He considered changing out of his casual sweater and jeans into something more formal, but that felt silly. After all this was just coffee, not a job interview, and he wasn't looking to impress.

Still, he felt a twinge of anxiety. He and Charlotte had parted on friendly enough terms at the reunion, but there'd always been something about her – some vibrant energy, a kind of pushiness veiled in breezy charm. She was the type who drew you in with a laugh, then hammered you with candid questions. After last night's news of Aaron's death, he expected she might press him for details seeing as she was the one who put his colleagues onto him in the first place as having left with Aaron. Or maybe she just wanted a gossip session.

As Tom headed out, locking up behind him, he felt a dull ache of guilt at how normal the routine was. Meanwhile, Aaron Bell, someone he'd driven home only the previous night, lay dead on a pathologist's slab. The sense of unreality clung to Tom like a thin mist. He reminded himself that investigating was no longer his job. At least, not for now.

A short walk later, Tom preferred walking these days, he found himself on the high street, which bustled with mid-morning shoppers. Bright awnings, a handful of tourist-trinket shops, and a newsagent's sign proclaiming *LOCAL MURDER SHOCK*, written in chalk on an A-frame outside gave him a blast of subdued energy. The sign unsettled him. Tom's heart fluttered at the starkness of seeing it written large before him.

He found Café Romano easily enough: a glass-fronted

coffee house with a modern sign and a row of rattan chairs outside. Inside, large windows let in abundant light, and the décor was a mix of sea-themed prints and pastel walls with natural wood lining them to waist height. The aroma of espresso pulled at him gently, reminding him he hadn't eaten much breakfast.

Charlotte was already there, perched at a corner table beneath a wide-screen TV mounted on the adjacent wall. Another reminder of the creep of modern interiors. There were few pubs, contemporary cafés or even doctors' surgeries that didn't have a wall-mounted display these days. Charlotte wore a deep-blue blouse with a stylish cut that set off her blonde hair and neon-green glasses. She caught sight of him and waved, a bright grin on her face. He forced a smile in return.

"Tom!" she said as he approached, standing to give him a light hug. "I already ordered coffees. I hope that's okay? I got you a flat white. You were never one for anything fancy or overcomplicated. Is that still true?"

He was momentarily touched she recalled his tastes, uncertain though it was. "A flat white's fine," he said, sitting opposite her. The table was small, but that only heightened the sense of intimacy. The café wasn't large as many of the older buildings in the town had once catered for fishermen. Functional and without hospitality in mind.

She sat, crossing her legs. "So, how are you?"

Tom rubbed the back of his neck, conscious that it had been a standard question from so many well-meaning acquaintances. "I'm... taking things day by day," he managed. It was the best summary of his suspended-limbo life.

Before Charlotte could respond, a barista arrived with two steaming mugs. One was indeed a flat white for Tom, the other presumably a latte for Charlotte. Tom thanked her, noticing the faint shape of a leaf in the foam.

"Lovely," Charlotte sighed, taking a quick sip. "Anyway, I was thinking about last night. The reunion was… interesting, was it not?"

He gave a short, humourless laugh. "I imagine you'd call it that."

She nodded. "Certainly not short of drama. Some old grudges rearing their heads. It's funny how the school dynamic never truly dies." She said it lightly, but Tom detected tension swirling beneath her casual tone.

"People have a way of slipping back into old roles," he admitted. "But some can change."

"Some can," Charlotte conceded. "Others, not so much."

She stirred a packet of brown sugar into her latte. He took a tentative sip of his flat white. It was quite good, with a pleasant bitterness from the espresso. For a moment, an awkward hush reigned as they both oriented themselves in the conversation. A flicker of movement drew Tom's eye to the overhead TV. It was muted, but the subtitles ran at the bottom. The BBC news channel displayed a bright, stylised banner reading: *BREAKING: MAN FOUND DEAD IN SEASIDE NORFOLK TOWN*. A reporter stood near a police cordon that Tom recognised as Aaron Bell's driveway. His stomach tightened.

He stared. The subtitles scrolled… body discovered early… investigating as suspicious… name withheld until relatives can be informed … formal identification. Then the anchor reappeared in the studio, and the segment pivoted to a traffic update. Tom inhaled slowly, forcing his gaze away from the screen. Charlotte, noticing the sudden tension in him, arched an eyebrow. "What is it?"

He shook his head, letting out a tight breath. "Just... the news." He gestured slightly at the screen. She twisted around to follow his gaze, just in time to see the tail-end of the rolling news feed along the bottom of the screen.

Though the segment had changed, the banner offered more detail, *Man Found Dead in Blakeney*, was still visible in the news ticker. Charlotte's lips parted, a flicker of curiosity on her face. "Wait, that's not...?"

Tom exhaled, keeping his voice low. "It's Aaron."

Her eyes widened. "Aaron? Are you sure?"

"They haven't named him on there," Tom said, nodding at the TV, "but trust me. I know it's him."

She set her latte down abruptly. "Oh my God. Is that why... the police called and asked me about him, and the reunion last night?" Tom nodded. "What... happened?"

Tom bit his lip, struggling to maintain composure. He still wasn't sure how much he should say, or how much he wanted to. Officially, Tamara had only told him the bare outlines. "I'm not entirely sure," Tom lied, trying to keep it vague. "I only found out he'd... died, last night or early this morning."

A swirl of emotions crossed Charlotte's face, shock, a trace of something like fear, and perhaps a flash of guilt. "I can't believe it. He was... at the reunion. He was alive and kicking. I only spoke to him once or twice in the hall, but he looked... well, lively, if a bit too lively."

Tom mustered a wry grimace. "He was definitely in a partying mood. That's true."

She leaned in. "I heard from some of the other guests that you left together. I mean, that you took him home. I told the police. I hope that's okay?"

Tom's pulse quickened. So, the rumour mill was already spinning. "He was too drunk to drive, so I offered. I dropped him off, late."

"And he seemed... normal?"

Tom paused, meeting her gaze across the small table. "He was a bit subdued, but yes, mostly normal. He was upset about a few things, or maybe just moody. I didn't really pry. It's not my business, you know?"

Charlotte put a hand to her chest, voice trembling. "It's so surreal. He was in my year, well, no, I was younger than him by a bit, but we overlapped enough. I knew him through Kristy, my sister... Kristy... well, you knew her."

Tom nodded softly, sensing her emotions. Even decades later, the memory of Kristy's death – a tragedy that overshadowed their entire year group – had never fully settled. "I'm sorry," he murmured. "This must bring back all sorts of difficult feelings."

She gave a half-smile. "It does, yes. Being at the school, seeing the places where I always saw her. This town," she said, glancing out of the window, "has memories of her on every corner."

"Seeing Aaron again must have been hard," Tom said.

"Yes. I know that's uncharitable, especially now," she said, looking briefly up at the television, "but he reminded me of a lot of pain."

Tom reached for his coffee, letting the subject rest for a moment. The café around them buzzed with low chatter, clinking cups, a hiss of the espresso machine. He realised this was the first time they'd been alone together since school. At the reunion, Charlotte was always drifting from one group to another, ever the social butterfly. Now, she was quiet, subdued, her eyes staring down at her latte.

After a moment, she took a breath. "He was married, you know, some wealthy woman from a foreign family, I heard." She glanced at Tom with a conspiratorial arch to her brow.

"Apparently they own a big hotel chain? Something about property here in town, too."

Tom recalled Aaron's hints of a complicated marital situation, though specifics had been vague. "He mentioned he wasn't sure about his place in the family business."

Charlotte huffed. "Probably wise. Word around Sheringham is that his wife's family sank a lot of money into certain developments, maybe some questionable expansions. Nothing proven, just gossip. You know how it is."

He tilted his head, curiosity piqued. "Questionable how?"

She shrugged. "Oh, you know how small towns are. People see big money coming in from overseas and suspect shady dealings. Maybe it's all above board, maybe it's not. I only know the rumours."

Tom studied her. "You seem well-informed. Doesn't that make you just as much a gossip as the rest of them?" His tone was gentle, but the question was sincere.

A quick flash of a smile curved her lips. "I suppose so. I have a child in the local school, I serve on the parents' committee, I do some volunteer stuff. People talk, Tom. You know what this town is like. And I have ears."

His mind flicked back to something she'd said at the reunion: it's still a small town, Tom. You've been away too long. The words hovered, unspoken, as if she'd read his thoughts.

"I guess you're right," he admitted, a faint sigh in his voice. "I was away a long time. Maybe I lost touch with the… the heartbeat, so to speak."

Charlotte sipped her latte. "I never left," she said quietly, as though in answer to an unasked question. "Never wanted to, I suppose. Where would I go? My parents, my sister… everything was here. I was foolish enough to think that I could fix my life by staying put."

Tom studied the slight tension in her shoulders. He contemplated the different paths they'd taken. He had left for London, become a police officer. She had remained in Sheringham, married young, to her childhood sweetheart, Noah Cook, of all people, and now was... what exactly? A single mother, from the sound of it, involved in local committees. There was nothing wrong with that but he sensed she wanted more.

"Do you regret not leaving?" Tom asked softly.

She let out a laugh, a bit forced. "Regret is a strong word. I've thought about it. But any time I do, I think about how Kristy left. In a manner of speaking, she left everything behind. And I never wanted to... to vanish that way." She winced. "I know that probably sounds daft." Tom shook his head. "Then I got married, thought it was the solution. Turned out it was just a new problem."

Tom opened his mouth to ask about Noah, but Charlotte pre-empted him with a wave of her manicured hand. "Marriage to Noah was good, for a time at least. He was charming for about a week." She smiled. She was joking, at least a little. "Then real life set in. I fell pregnant the last year of school." Her eyes darted to Tom's. "You remember the fall out of my scandalous pregnancy?"

He nodded. "I do. It was a long time ago."

"We had the child, Dean. He's eighteen now, but God help me, he's more trouble than ever. Noah and I divorced years ago, and Dean is basically a grown man who still calls me for every little thing. Seriously."

As if on cue, a shrill ring from Charlotte's phone interrupted her. She rolled her eyes, rummaging in her handbag. "Speak of the devil," she muttered. She glanced at the screen. "Yep. Dean."

She answered, turning partially away to murmur in hushed

tones. Tom sipped his coffee, feeling momentarily like he was intruding on her personal life. He gleaned bits and pieces without meaning to eavesdrop. Dean needed money or help with something trivial. Charlotte made vague exasperated replies. "Well, I'm in town... yes, I'll be done soon... no, I can't do that... Dean, for goodness' sake... all right, all right, bye."

She hung up, exhaling in frustration. "I thought the early teenage years were the worst, but evidently at eighteen, they can still be entirely hopeless."

Tom managed a sympathetic smile. "That's men for you. You should speak to Alice."

"That's true. Without us, you lot wither quickly."

Tom smiled. "Maybe he's not as grown up or as self-assured as you think he should be."

Charlotte gave him a quick, assessing look. "Oh, so you're on Dean's side now, are you?" Her tone was teasing, not truly accusatory.

Tom raised both hands. "I just remember how clueless I was at eighteen. We never really stop needing our mothers, do we?"

The line triggered a subtle shift in her expression. Something gentler, a memory perhaps. "You're right," she said after a beat. "I guess we all hold on in some way."

A lull settled between them, not quite awkward but laced with mutual introspection. Charlotte broke it by clearing her throat. "Anyway, how about you? You left, joined the Met, or so I heard, and now you're back with the local force. Married with a daughter. Actually, you said at the reunion you'd... well, people were saying you'd been married before. So which is it, once or twice?"

Tom's lips tightened. He never liked discussing personal matters, but Charlotte had a knack for extracting information.

"Twice. My first marriage... it didn't work out. Then I came back here, reconnected with Alice, and I adopted her daughter, Saffy."

Charlotte's brow furrowed in concern. "That's a lot. You're happy now, though, right?"

The suspension from duty, the unresolved inquiry into his last case, along with the nights of broken sleep haunted by regrets. But in the bigger picture, yes, he had love and stability. "I have a family I care about deeply," he said at length. "That's enough for me."

She studied him carefully, as though reading between the lines. Then she offered a small nod. "Well, maybe we all have complicated stories, but at least you have that, Tom. Not everyone does."

He wasn't sure how to respond, so he sipped the last of his coffee. After a moment, Charlotte glanced at the TV again, another news item had replaced the previous story. "I still can't believe Aaron is gone. I mean, yes, he was a pain, but that's... that's no reason for him to end up dead. I wonder what happened."

Tom felt the question like a spotlight turning on him. He recalled Tamara's instruction to keep a low profile, not to muddy the waters of the official investigation. "I really don't know," he said, truthful in part. "The police are investigating. I'm out of the loop these days."

She nodded slowly, expression pensive. "He was bragging about that wife of his, so I'm told. When he visited home on occasion. Did he mention her to you?"

"Briefly. He said they were on shaky ground. He implied she wasn't around, maybe travelling. He was pretty hammered, though."

Charlotte frowned. "We'll see what comes out, I suppose. If

there's a big inheritance or some messy business, it'll end up in the papers."

Tom didn't like the cynicism but couldn't exactly refute it. The tabloids loved a scandal with wealthy families. Charlotte wrapped her hands around her latte cup, which must have been lukewarm now. She stared into it, froth drying on the edges. "We never do know what's going on behind the scenes, do we? The secrets people keep."

He wondered if she was thinking about Kristy. Aaron's entangled history with her sister, and that heartbreak that ended in tragedy. Sometimes secrets had lethal consequences.

"Speaking of... I hope you don't mind me bringing this up," Charlotte said, not meeting his eye at first, "but this week is the anniversary of Kristy's death. Some of us hold a small vigil every year up on the cliffs. It's not a big thing, just a handful of us gathering to remember her. We light candles, say a few words. It would mean a lot to me if you could come."

Tom's eyebrows shot up. He felt his chest tighten. He hadn't expected her to invite him. He hadn't even known about this annual event. "I... Charlotte, that's... I'm honoured you'd ask, but are you sure?"

She gave a sad smile. "Kristy used to talk about you sometimes, how you were a nice guy. She said you'd always wave if you saw her in the corridor. I mean, you weren't close friends, but you were kind to her. And that means something to me. Those memories... and the vigil... are about remembering who she was, even if it's only once a year where we come together."

Tom recalled Kristy, along with her bright but, ultimately, fragile nature. She'd once asked him for directions around the school when they first arrived at the high school, and he'd teased her gently. The memory felt distant, fleeting. "I'd love to come," he said softly. Charlotte's eyes lit up.

"Thank you. We'll get together at the top of the cliffs above the old harbour around sunset. I'll send you a text with the details, if you like?"

Tom nodded, swallowing the lump in his throat. Another date in his otherwise empty schedule. Saffy would be at home with Alice, presumably, so he'd be free to go. "I'll make sure I'm there," he said, meeting her gaze. "It'll be good to remember your sister."

"Thank you," she repeated, a hush in her voice. "It'll mean a lot to me and to my parents, though they rarely come out nowadays." She seemed to falter, drifting into her own thoughts for a moment. Then, as if shaking off a spell, she glanced at her phone. "I'd better see to Dean's demands before he stages a rebellion and makes matters worse."

Tom checked the time on his watch. He still had a good few hours before picking up Saffy. "Is there anything I can help with?" he asked.

"No," she said curtly. Tom was taken aback. Charlotte winced and her expression softened. "Sorry, I didn't mean to snap. Dean is just… a bit trying at times."

"Children often are," Tom said, "but we love them."

They both rose. Tom offered to pay for the coffee but Charlotte pointedly refused. "No, it's my treat. I invited you, remember?"

"I'll get them next time then," he said and she smiled.

"Next time," Charlotte said. They both headed for the door, weaving among other patrons. Outside, they were hit by the wind channelling up the high street from the shore. The bright sunshine of earlier had been replaced by grey clouds above, threatening drizzle. Tom zipped his jacket. Charlotte pulled on a light cardigan. She gave him a sideways glance. "Thank you for meeting me, Tom. I needed… someone who kind of knows the old days, but isn't mired in all that drama."

He shrugged. "Not sure how free of drama I am, but you're welcome."

She nodded, hesitated a moment, then took a small step closer, dropping her voice. "If you hear anything about Aaron's case… I'd appreciate a heads-up. I know it's not your job any more, but I can't help being curious. Kristy, me, Noah… we're all tied together in this town."

Tom considered how to respond. He couldn't promise to feed her inside information. In fact he would do no such thing and he found it odd that she'd even ask him. He simply nodded but didn't offer to do anything.

"I'll be discreet," she said. "I just… want to know the truth."

He met her eye. "So do I."

Then she turned, heading off down the street towards a small row of shops, presumably heading to meet Dean somewhere. Tom watched her go. After a moment, he walked in the opposite direction, navigating the narrow pavements of the high street, weaving between passers-by. Tom replayed Charlotte's words about Aaron's wealthy in-laws. He remembered how Aaron had tried to present an image of control, but Tom had the sense he'd been left in a precarious position after the separation.

Tom mentally pushed aside the detective puzzle. It wasn't his case. Yet he couldn't help feeling the prickle of curiosity, or the pang of regret that he'd left his school friend alone and he'd wound up dead. It wasn't Tom's fault, he knew that. But the feeling was there nonetheless. He cut through a small lane behind the post office, then turned away from the town centre making for the quiet road where he and Alice lived. The breeze carried the faint cry of seagulls overhead, a reminder of the coastline just a few minutes' walk away. Usually, the sound was comforting. Today, it felt tinged with sorrow.

As he walked, Tom pictured what Kristy's vigil might be like. Who would attend? What would people say? A handful of candles flickering in the sea wind as the sunset, a cluster of middle-aged mourners remembering a sixteen-year-old girl who never got to see adulthood. A wave of old sadness crept into him.

He remembered, vividly, the day the news spread of Kristy Sears's suicide. He'd felt sick, helpless, and outraged that someone so young could see no better path. Many had pointed fingers at Aaron, who'd broken up with her around that time. Others whispered about mental health issues or family problems. The truth was never entirely pinned down. Like so many of these types of cases, it was multifaceted. But he remembered Charlotte's devastation. He recalled how she vanished from school for weeks, returning haunted and cold-eyed.

Tom stopped for a moment as he stood on an incline. From here he could see the water. He pressed his palms to his eyes. He was part of this situation, like it or not. If he were still an active detective, he'd be on the case, but now he was consigned to watching from the sidelines. Yet Charlotte's invitation to the vigil, the mention of Aaron's shady in-laws, the whispered regrets... it all felt like a silent call for him to dig deeper.

Once back at home, he was surprised to see Alice's car in the drive. He heard Alice's voice call from the kitchen as he entered.

"Hello? Tom?"

"Hey, you're home early. I thought you weren't going to finish until later."

"We had a machine failure, and so most of my appointments were cancelled and I got off a bit sooner as a result. I thought we could pick Saffy up together?"

Tom felt relief at her presence, a grounding calm. "I'd like that."

She glanced at him curiously. "You all right? You look a bit... pensive."

"I had coffee with Charlotte."

"Oh? You two used to be old acquaintances, right?"

"Sort of," Tom said. "She wanted to talk. She's... well, still hung up about her sister, Kristy."

Alice nodded softly. "I remember you mentioning it. She died. Suicide, wasn't it?"

"Yes, just after we left school" He thought on it. "Is that nineteen or twenty years? Not sure. Charlotte invited me to a vigil for Kristy."

Alice frowned, stepping closer to rest a hand on his forearm. "That's nice of her, I think. Are you going?"

He hesitated, then nodded. "I said I would."

"Do you want me to come along? Or is it...?"

Tom considered. He realised Charlotte hadn't said anything about it being invite-only to old school friends. But he had the impression she kept a tight circle. He wasn't sure if Alice would feel comfortable there. "Let me find out if it's okay first," he said gently. "It sounded personal. But I'd love your support."

She gave him a warm smile. "Always."

They shared a quick embrace, then parted. Alice glanced around the living room. "So, coffee with Charlotte. How was it? She seemed... flamboyant at the reunion."

Tom let out a soft breath. "She was. She still is. But she's also carrying a lot of sadness. And, well... hearing about Aaron's death didn't help. The news media is all over it."

Alice's face fell. "Oh, yes. That's all over the hospital chatter too. Are you okay? You were the last one to see him, right? That's why Tamara came by earlier, I guess."

Tom recalled how that had already spread. The entire town might know soon enough. "I'm fine. Just… uneasy. It's surreal. I'd say intriguing, if it wasn't so close to home."

"It sounds like you're taking an interest," Alice said, eyeing him warily. "A professional interest."

He scoffed. "Of course I'm not. I couldn't."

"You couldn't," Alice said with a knowing smile. "Of course not."

CHAPTER TEN

CASSIE KNIGHT STOOD JUST inside the cold, tiled corridor of the mortuary, arms folded across her chest as she kept an eye on the double doors at the far end. The hum of fluorescent lights overhead and the faint chemical tang in the air brought back memories of countless identifications she'd overseen. No two were quite the same, yet there was always that same tension: a loved one gone, a spouse or relative forced to confirm the worst.

DC Eric Collet, leaned against the wall nearby. "You think she'll show?" he asked quietly.

"She confirmed an hour ago," Cassie said. "She'll show. Remember though, she's Elena Novak, not Bell."

"Changed her name back already?" Eric asked.

"If she was ever a Bell in the first place."

Eric exhaled, about to speak, but the double doors at the far end swung open. A uniformed officer escorted a striking blonde woman in a white belted coat and sleek black heels. Even in the utilitarian gloom, her attire was immaculate: designer scarf, matching handbag. Not exactly how most people dressed when they came to view a body, let alone that of a spouse, estranged or not.

Cassie unclasped her arms and approached, extending a polite but subdued greeting. "Mrs Novak?"

Elena Novak's cool, appraising stare took in Cassie and Eric in a single sweep. "Yes. I was told you needed me for a formal identification. Let's get it over with, shall we?" Her accent was mostly British with a faint European undercurrent. It was difficult to pin down precisely, but it certainly suggested an international background.

Cassie introduced herself and Eric. "Thank you for coming so promptly," she said. The corridor's silence felt heavier around them. "This won't take long, but please know we're sorry for your loss."

Elena's gaze flicked to the closed mortuary doors, then back to Cassie. "Loss implies you care about what's gone. Let's just see him and confirm, shall we?"

Cassie exchanged a glance with Eric. He kept his features neutral, but Cassie could sense his surprise. She was certainly not sentimental, that was for sure. Gesturing for Elena to follow, Cassie pushed open the door into the viewing suite. It was a small, clinical room where the body waited beneath a simple white cotton sheet under subdued lighting.

A staff member, clad in a white gown, already had the table prepared. The sheet was folded back to reveal Aaron Bell's face. Elena took two steps forward, a single neat click of her heels on the tiled floor. She looked down at her husband's still features. No flicker of shock, no tears. Simply a slight purse of her lips, as though she were assessing an unremarkable item. "Yes," she murmured, barely audible. "That's him. This is Aaron."

Cassie inclined her head at the mortuary attendant, who made a note on the paperwork. Then, with a gentle nod, the attendant covered the face once more. Elena stepped back, folding her arms. "I can't say this comes as a total surprise," she said evenly.

Cassie's eyebrows rose, but she kept her tone professional. "You're certain of the identification?"

"Absolutely," Elena replied. She glanced around, as though the smell of antiseptic annoyed her. "Can I go now, or is there more?"

Cassie drew in a breath. "We appreciate you confirming. We do have a few questions. If you'll follow us to a private room, we won't keep you long."

Without protest, Elena followed Cassie and Eric into a small side office. Once they'd settled, Elena standing rigid, arms still folded across her chest, Cassie began. "First, I'm sorry again for the circumstances, Mrs Novak."

"It's Miss Novak," she corrected with pointed coolness. "Aaron and I were separated, pending a formal divorce. You can drop the niceties, Detective Sergeant Knight. My husband and I fell out of love a long time ago. I couldn't wait to be rid of him from my life. I know that sounds harsh, but if you knew him like I did, you'd understand."

Eric darted a quick glance at Cassie. They couldn't help but note Elena's directness. Cassie steeled herself and remained calm. "We appreciate your... candidness. Were you and Aaron in much contact recently?"

"Only through our lawyers," Elena said dismissively, letting her bag dangle from one hand. "Dividing property, ensuring the settlement was... equitable."

"Did he have any ongoing disputes or issues we should be aware of?" Cassie asked. "Anyone who held a grievance against him?"

Elena gave a short, icy laugh. "There are too many to count, including myself. Aaron could be charming, but it was a veneer. He had a knack for stepping on people. I suspect you'll uncover that soon enough. I would take less issue with him if it were not for the backward nature of laws in your country."

Cassie frowned. "Please… er… could you elaborate on that for me?"

"Prenuptial agreements are not automatically enforceable within your legal system as they are in other jurisdictions. This element of doubt allows for the… charlatan, the fraudster to take advantage in matters of the heart."

Cassie and Eric exchanged a look. "Are you implying that Aaron was a fraudster?" Cassie asked.

"There are three reasons a person marries, Detective Sergeant," Elena said. "For power, money or for love."

"The three don't need to be mutually exclusive though," Cassie countered.

"Aaron married for two of the three." She looked between Eric and Cassie. "I will let you decide which one to discount."

"Could you narrow down the list of people who had grievances with Aaron?" Cassie asked.

"He had business partners he swindled, old so-called friends he offended, mistresses he lied to…" Elena shrugged. "I've already given the broad picture to you on the telephone. If you want a complete list of names, you'll have to rummage through the pathetic existence that passed for the life he left behind. Believe me, I have no interest in playing detective."

Cassie acknowledged that with a nod. "Understood."

"Is it, Detective Sergeant?" Elena asked. "Is it understood?"

"Crystal clear," Cassie replied with a slight smile. "It would be in your interests for you to assist us in this case."

"Is that so?"

"Yes," Cassie said with a curt nod. "We need to resolve

what happened to your husband before we can close the case. If there is any doubt as to who profited from his death, then it could slow down the closure of his estate. Do you understand?"

Elena shot Cassie an almost contemptuous smile. "I understand. I assume you have something you wish to ask me?"

"Can you confirm your whereabouts last night?"

Elena's expression remained impassive. "I was in London, at our penthouse apartment in Knightsbridge."

"Alone?" Eric interjected.

She arched a perfectly shaped eyebrow. "I have staff. Building security, housekeeping. Any of them can verify I was in the apartment from mid-afternoon until this morning, when you contacted me. If you need a written statement, I'll provide it. I'm sure the building's CCTV will confirm it too."

"Thank you," Cassie said. "It's standard procedure for us to ask. If we need the footage or further statements, then we know where to come. Where are you staying while you're in Sheringham, in case we need to follow up?"

Elena brushed an invisible speck of lint from her sleeve. "I own a small boutique hotel off the esplanade. The Aurora. I'll be there, presumably for a day or two, to finalise… whatever needs finalising with Aaron's remains. You or your officers can find me there."

"The body will not be released for a funeral until the cause of death, and possibly the case, is resolved."

Elena held Cassie's gaze. She shrugged. "So be it. Is that all?"

Cassie sensed Elena's impatience. "Yes, for now. We may have additional questions as the investigation continues."

"Fine." Elena's tone was clipped. She turned on her heel and headed to the door, casting one last look over her shoulder. "Believe me, Detective Sergeant, I have no tears to shed for Aaron. Not any more." With that, she slipped out.

For a moment, the office felt oddly colder than the mortuary corridor. Cassie and Eric stood in silence, absorbing the encounter. Finally, Eric broke it. "That was… definitely not the grieving widow I expected to meet."

Cassie let out a slow breath, leaning back against the small desk. "No tears, no trembling voice. She barely blinked at his body." Her gaze lingered on the door Elena had just used. "You'd think she was signing off a property sale."

Eric nodded. "Or returning a broken hairbrush for a refund. Could just be her nature, I suppose, or the relationship was dead and buried long before Aaron ended up in that pool. Still, it's a bit eerie. She's frosty as you like."

Cassie pushed off the desk and straightened her jacket. "Frosty is right, but that doesn't make her guilty of anything except having no love lost for her estranged husband. Personally, her view of the incompetence and general untrustworthiness of men… chimes with my personal experience."

"Thank you very much," Eric said.

"Not you, Eric," Cassie said, placing a gentle hand on his forearm. Eric smiled. "I mean proper men."

"Again… thanks," Eric said.

Cassie ignored the comment. "She says she was in London; we'll confirm it. If that pans out, we move on."

Eric stuffed his hands into his pockets. "What do you think the odds are she's telling the truth about last night? She could have easily popped over here and then gone back."

Cassie shrugged. "It's possible, but Knightsbridge to Sheringham is a fair haul. It would take half the night, and she didn't look tired, did she?"

"She could have got someone else to do it. What did she

say, she had building security, staff… and she doesn't look the sort to get her hands dirty."

"True," Cassie said. "We can't rule it out. But let's not forget: She's obviously well-off. She'd have the resources to cover her tracks if she wanted to, but that also means multiple staff who can confirm her presence. We'll request the building's CCTV and see what it shows us about her movements. Otherwise, we'll just have to see if any of her connections turn up during the investigation."

"If she's right," Eric said, "and Aaron had a lot of pissed off people hating him. How are we going to find the killer?"

"By being bloody marvellous at our jobs, Eric," Cassie said, winking at him. "Luckily for us, we're quite good at what we do."

They headed for the corridor, the quiet footsteps echoing on the tiles. Cassie mulled the conversation. Elena Novak was an enigma. An outwardly immaculate and wealthy woman who radiated cold disdain for the man she once married. Cassie couldn't entirely blame her if what she said was true. Perhaps Aaron had been a philanderer, or worse. Plenty of plausible reasons for bitterness. Too many grudges to count, Elena had said. Long-held personal grief derived from a failed marriage or was she simply being truthful about the type of man Aaron was? Time would tell.

At the double doors, Eric paused. "She said she'll only be around for a day or two. Do you think we'll have enough time to glean more from her?"

"We'll see," Cassie said. "If her story checks out, she'll likely take off back to London in a couple of days. Earlier, if we won't release the body which we won't because it's a piece of evidence in a murder. And if we need more from her, a day or two before she goes will plenty of time for more interviews.

She doesn't seem shy about stating her opinions. I don't think she'll do the dance, do you?"

Eric gave a snort. "No, that's for sure."

Cassie glanced back at the viewing room, where the mortuary attendant was already tidying up. She couldn't shake the image of Elena's calm, almost bored face as she gazed at Aaron's body. Some people cry inside, Cassie reminded herself. But something about her manner was unsettling to say the least.

"Come on," she said to Eric, stepping forward. "Let's follow up on her alibi. We'll request the footage from that Knightsbridge penthouse. Then we keep piecing this puzzle together."

They pushed through the doors, leaving the mortuary's stillness behind and, somewhere within its walls, the body of Aaron Bell, identified at last by the wife who barely acknowledged his passing with anything more than a raised eyebrow.

CHAPTER ELEVEN

Tom Janssen stood at the edge of the clifftop, gazing out over the wide sweep of the North Sea. The breeze up here always carried an unmistakable tang of salt, and though the setting sun hung low in the sky, the gusts still felt brisk against his skin. The tide rolled in below, its rhythmic crash against the dilapidated, battered old wooden sea defences at the base of the cliff sounding oddly comforting. Tom tried to settle the flutter of nerves in his stomach. He wasn't even sure why he was nervous, but something about returning to these cliffs stirred old memories in a way that felt heavier than he'd anticipated.

A simple wooden bench lay a few paces away, perched just off the path. As Tom approached, he saw the small, engraved plaque affixed to the backrest:

In Loving Memory of Kristy Sears
    May your spirit soar as free as the sea breeze.

TOM EXHALED GENTLY. He recalled the initial shock of Kristy's death reverberating through the town. Now, with the prospect of a vigil, Tom felt both awkward and oddly responsible. Charlotte had invited him, sure, but what did he truly have to contribute?

He ran his fingertips over the brass plaque, finding it cool to the touch. A tightness spread through his chest, and he wondered if he had any right to be here. He was never as close to Kristy as Charlotte implied. They were passing acquaintances. Just a friendly face in the corridors of the school they shared. But that seemed to matter to Charlotte. Maybe that was enough.

A scraping sound drifted across the short stretch of grass. Tom turned to see a man kneeling at the edges of the cliff path, raking away encroaching brambles that he had just cut back. His petrol-powered strimmer lay on the ground near to where he was working. He wore a dark-green jacket and heavy boots, his hair cut neat but dusted with flecks of grey. A white pick-up style van sat parked nearby. Tom recognised the man. Noah Cook, Charlotte's ex-husband.

Noah noticed Tom at about the same time, pausing his work to straighten. He lifted his chin in acknowledgement. Tom raised a hand in return, picking his way carefully over.

"Didn't expect to see you up here, Tom," Noah said, his tone somewhat curt but not overtly hostile. "Funny how the past drags us back to the same spots, eh?"

Tom dipped his head. "Yeah… it is."

The two men stood in a short silence, the wind rattling the leaves of the scraggly shrubs. Noah sighed, bracing the rake against the line of fencing keeping people away from the cliff edge. The coastal erosion was real here, and the path was now much closer to the edge than Tom remembered. The local authority shifts the fencing back every few years to maintain safety on the route.

"Strange how someone from our old days can bring back all these memories," Noah said absently. "First the reunion, then Aaron... and now all of us turning up on the cliffs again to remember Kristy. Makes you think about how nothing stays buried forever."

Tom nodded, uncertain how to respond without prying. "Charlotte mentioned she sometimes comes up here. I didn't realise you'd be around, too."

Noah's expression softened slightly. "Charlotte and I used to come up here twice a year. Kristy's birthday, and the anniversary of her death. I still do it on my own from time to time, but I try to leave Charlotte to her own grief, you know?"

"Why do you keep coming?" Tom asked.

Noah shrugged. "Habit, I suppose." He looked past Tom towards the bench. "Charlotte wanted a small vigil tonight. She roped me into tidying the pathway and the approach from the hotel up the hill. It's not like I could say no. Even if we're not... together any more."

"That's kind of you," Tom said quietly. He turned, taking in the route Noah had cleared: a short strip of wild grass leading towards a footpath that wound to the hotel's rear lawns and further along the coastal path. "It's a nice gesture. Charlotte told me a few people from school would be here?"

Noah shrugged. "She said it's a bigger crowd than usual. Somewhere around fifteen, counting old classmates and neighbours who remember Kristy. Usually, it's just a handful. This year, maybe because of Aaron's... you know." He swallowed. "Strange how a fresh tragedy can remind us of another one. She wanted to make it a joint memorial. Fitting, I suppose, seeing as they were together. Kristy and Aaron, I mean."

"A long time ago," Tom whispered. He grimaced. The past few days had been a whirlwind of uneasy revelations. Aaron murdered, suspicion swirling among their old crowd, and he remembered the gossip about Charlotte's sister. Aaron was now likely receiving the same treatment, after a fashion. "I feel like the reunion's forced all these old feelings to the surface," he murmured, echoing Noah's sentiment. "We're all remembering things we thought we'd left behind."

Noah gave a short laugh, though it lacked real humour. "Yeah, well. Life has a way of digging up ghosts." He stepped to one side, gathering the last of the cuttings he'd just raked up and stuffing them into a large garden waste bag. "Anyway, what about you? Why are you here, Tom?"

Tom glanced at the plaque on the bench, then back at Noah. "Charlotte invited me. I guess... the same reasons as you. To pay respects. I wasn't close to Kristy, but I remember how it shook us all up. It's weird, now I think about it, it feels like it was yesterday and not twenty years ago."

"I know. Time flies, huh. Where did it all go?" Noah said. Tom looked over at him. Noah reflexively looked away, making himself busy. Tom found something pricking his subconscious, but he couldn't place what it was that had triggered him. He pushed the thought aside. Noah didn't add anything.

"I suppose I'm also curious," Tom said. "Maybe I'm looking for answers... about Kristy, Aaron, about everything." He hesitated. "I'm sorry if that seems intrusive."

"No, not intrusive." Noah's eyebrows rose slightly. "It's a free world. You're... in the police, aren't you? It must come with the territory, a curious nature."

Tom paused, uncertain how much to divulge. "I'm with

the Norfolk Constabulary," he conceded, "at the moment. Who knows about the future. Anyway, uh… I'm not active at the moment. I'm on a sort of enforced leave."

Noah gave him a quizzical glance. "So, you're not investigating Aaron's death, or anything like that?"

"Not officially," Tom said, voice taut. "Just trying to keep my head down. But it's complicated. Old habits and all of that."

"Bet it is," Noah replied. He began to gather up his tools. "I'm just a gardener. It's a simple life. I like it. Less drama. Less stress. Just me, the outdoors," he lifted his head and faced the sea breeze, "and the salt air."

Tom offered a tentative smile, remembering that Noah used to be easily riled at school. "Seems like you found your niche. That's good."

"Sometimes I think so," Noah said, "but Charlotte… she's got a different vision for life." He let out a sigh, resting a hand on his hips.

"Oh?"

Noah raised his eyebrows. "She wants our son, Dean, to go to university. Of course, you've probably heard that from her."

Tom shook his head slightly. "She mentioned Dean, but nothing specific."

Noah made a noise half between a scoff and a laugh. "She thinks he's bound for some big academic future. But he's like me. He's good with his hands. Mechanical stuff. Landscaping, carpentry… that's his real knack. I've tried telling Charlotte, but she won't hear reason. She claims we're holding him back if he doesn't get a degree…" He shrugged. "Not all kids need that route. It's not for everyone."

"They say education broadens the mind," Tom said, playing devil's advocate.

"The boy has a mind of his own," Noah snapped. "He doesn't need it filling with nonsense."

Tom sympathised. "I only have the one child, but yeah, I get it. Sometimes parents have different ideas about what's best. Different to each other, and perhaps different to the child."

"Just one, huh?" Noah said. "Boy? Girl?"

"A girl," Tom replied, smiling a bit. "Her name's Saffy."

"That's nice." Noah paused, a flicker of something crossing his expression. "I always said Charlotte invests too much into her kids. Not that it's bad to care, but… it's like they're rolled into her entire identity now, especially since Kristy died. Her parents put a lot of pressure on Charlotte. After all, she was all they had left. Charlotte… seems to have picked up their copybook, you know? And since the divorce, she's doubled down. Dean…" He shook his head. "It's the same with her daughter too, although that one isn't mine."

Tom remembered Charlotte vaguely referencing a child at the school now. That must have been who she was referring to because Dean had left school and must be in college or he's considering university.

"Right," Tom said. "Charlotte mentioned another child, the little girl, but not the father," he said delicately. "I must admit I assumed it was also yours."

Noah gave a brisk nod. "Not mine, no. And no one knows who he is either. At least, Charlotte's never told a soul. I just know it's not me." He grabbed the bag of clippings. "I guess it doesn't matter as long as the kid's healthy. But it's typical Charlotte, closed off in some ways, unstoppable in others."

Their conversation drifted into silence, the wind rustling overhead. Tom looked out at the horizon, steeling himself for the vigil. "Are you staying for it?" he asked.

"Yeah," Noah said. "Might as well. I'm not exactly dressed

for it, but I doubt Kristy will care. I told Charlotte I'd stick around, keep an eye on the path, make sure no one trips in the dark. People should start arriving soon." He hesitated, glancing at Tom. "You came alone?"

"Alice, my wife, offered to join me but it's awkward with the little one," Tom said. "So yes, it's just me." Tom's gaze slid to the plaque again. Noah gave a small grunt of approval.

"Fair enough," Noah said, picking up his strimmer and looping the strap over his shoulder. He then grasped the bag.

"Do you need a hand with that?" Tom asked.

"No, you're 'right," Noah said, hauling it towards his van parked in the nearby car park of the hotel overlooking the sea. Tom looked at the business name. It would appear that Noah had plans of his own for what his son should do next. The van was a little banged up with damage to the rear quarter panel and he thought he could see the rear bumper was hanging off slightly, away from the body. The vehicle had seen better days. The stencilling on the side panel read *Cook & Son Landscaping*. Clearly, Noah's plans for his son involved staying in Sheringham and not moving away.

WITHIN THE HOUR, the small group of old classmates gathered near the bench. The sky had begun to soften into twilight, the sun a molten strip on the horizon as it sank from view. The darkness across the North Sea heralded the onset of night. An inky blackness in stark contrast to what was on view to the west. Tom counted about fifteen people in total, some faces from school he recognised and had seen at the reunion. A couple of Charlotte's old friends, one or two neighbours who'd known Kristy as a child were also present. They formed a half-circle around the bench, some holding small candles in paper cups to shield the flames from the breeze.

Charlotte arrived last, walking slowly towards them. Her blonde hair was brushed back beneath a stylish scarf. She wore a simple black coat and cradled a plastic bin of candles under one arm. Her neon-green glasses caught the dusky light. Noah hovered off to one side, having spruced himself up a little despite saying he wasn't bothered earlier. Several people nodded in greeting to Charlotte, offering murmurings of *Good to see you* and the like.

Tom stood near the bench, holding a candle Charlotte had pressed into his hands. He felt that anxious flutter again, uncertain what to say or do. Charlotte glanced around the group, her expression tight with emotion. She cleared her throat.

"Thank you for coming," she said quietly, looking from face to face. "I know this was short notice for some of you, but… today is the anniversary of Kristy's death, and I wanted to mark it, together. Some of you remember her well, others might only recall her as the quiet one in your year. But she was… she was my sister. Our daughter, our friend." She blinked hard. "We usually do this vigil in private, but… we all lost someone else recently and I thought it right to remember him also."

A sombre shift went through the group. A few people nodded, recognising the reference to Aaron. The wind picked up, and Charlotte rubbed her arms against the chill.

"I don't want to turn this into a big speech," Charlotte said, voice unsteady. "But Kristy's passing was a tragedy we've carried for years. And now, losing Aaron so abruptly… I know some of us had mixed feelings about him, but he was part of our lives once too. I think we should remember him as well. His good points, at least. Life can be short and cruel." She paused, swallowing. "So, if it's okay, I'd like this to be a combined memorial. We'll keep it short. Just a few words, then maybe we can have a moment of silence with our thoughts to remember them."

No one voiced an objection. In the dimming light, people bowed their heads as Charlotte opened a lighter and passed the flame to the nearest candle. One by one, small points of light bloomed around the circle. Tom lit his own, the flicker dancing along the rim of the paper cup. The breeze rustled the tall grass on the other side of the nearby fence, carrying the slight hiss of the sea below. For a long moment, no one spoke at all. It was a hush steeped in mourning.

Tom found himself wondering what was in everyone's thoughts. Were they contemplating Kristy's heartbreak, Aaron's abrupt end, or for some other unnamed regret. As for Tom, he found images from the school reunion evening coming to mind; Aaron's brash grin, the hour spent chatting in that luxurious Blakeney home, the uneasy guilt that Tom was the last to see him alive and questioning what he could have done differently that might have changed the outcome.

A man near the back whispered a quiet memory of Kristy: how she used to keep a notebook of poems. Another mentioned that Aaron once gifted him a set of sports gear in school. These were pleasant recollections. Charlotte closed her eyes, tears tracking down her cheeks as she listened.

After the murmurs stilled, the small circle let the silence stretch, candle flames dipping and flickering in the wind. Tom felt his throat tighten, uncertain if he should speak. He chose to remain quiet, letting the stillness stand. Eventually, Charlotte raised her chin, blinking away tears.

She whispered, "Thank you," to the group, then carefully blew out her candle, signalling the end. One by one, others followed, dousing the tiny flames until twilight reclaimed them. The group broke apart into smaller clusters, hushed conversations and subdued nods of goodbye. A few wandered towards nearby parked cars, pulling coats tighter against the rising wind.

Tom was turning to place his half-spent candle in a small metal box someone had brought for disposal when he felt a light touch on his arm. He turned to see Charlotte, her eyes red-rimmed but determined. She tilted her head, indicating she wanted a private word. Tom nodded and followed her a short distance from the bench, near an overgrown section of brush that provided some shelter from the gusts coming in off the sea.

"I'm glad you came," she said softly, arms folded across her chest for warmth. "It meant a lot to me. To all of us, really."

Tom shrugged modestly. "I'm just sorry I wasn't closer to Kristy. But I wanted to support you... especially after everything that's happened."

Charlotte managed a thin smile. "You've always been a decent man, Tom. And I've taken advantage of that decency, I think." Her voice dropped. "Which is why I wanted to apologise."

He tilted his head, confused. "Apologise? For what?"

She glanced around to ensure no one was within earshot. Noah was off by his van, tidying supplies, and the others were dispersing. Charlotte lowered her voice. "I shouldn't have asked you to keep me informed about Aaron's case. It was inappropriate. I realise that now."

Tom hesitated. "I understand why you did," he said gently. "He was someone you knew well, once, and there's all this history between you. Emotions can make us do that kind of thing."

"Still." She bit her lip. "I put you in a corner. You said

you're not active in the investigation anyway, but it was wrong of me to even ask. It's not my place. I'm sorry, Tom. I thought I should say so."

He studied her expression: genuine remorse, yes, but also an undercurrent of anxiety. "I accept your apology," he said finally, giving her a kind look. "But... can I ask why you were so determined to find out more? I know there's curiosity, but it felt like more than that."

She hesitated, looking out at the dim coastline. "Aaron was part of Kristy's story, at least, that's what I tell myself. Even after all these years, I question what really happened back then. And with him dying like this, in suspicious circumstances, I worried there might be secrets about Kristy I never learned." Her voice caught. "It's irrational, maybe, but part of me wonders if it's all connected. Or if I'm just conflating two tragedies because I can't let go." She shook her head. "You must think I'm a real head case or something."

Tom felt sympathetic. He touched her shoulder gently. "Sometimes these things can get tangled in our heads," he said. "Like you say, these two people are at the heart of something traumatic for you. It's only natural for you to draw them together."

"Natural, but mental," she said, forcing a smile.

"Maybe a little," Tom said, holding up his thumb and forefinger. She smiled and then nodded, blinking back fresh tears.

"Thank you. And sorry if I dragged you into my confusion."

Tom squeezed her shoulder once, then let his hand drop. "You didn't drag me anywhere. I came on my own. If you ever need to talk, I can listen, but I won't do anything behind the backs of my old colleagues."

"That's fair," she whispered. She inhaled deeply, then let out a deep breath. "Anyway, I'm grateful you were here tonight. Kristy deserves to be remembered, and... so did Aaron, in a sense. Even if that might be controversial to some."

Tom offered a slight nod, thinking back to the group that had just gathered. Not everyone had liked Aaron. In truth, many had harboured ill feelings towards him. Still, he was part of their youth, their shared memories. "I understand."

Charlotte caught sight of Noah heading towards them. She wiped her cheeks discreetly. "I should gather myself. My parents left early, so I'd better catch them tomorrow."

"Oh, I didn't realise they were here," Tom said, looking around as if to see them.

Charlotte glanced at Tom once more. "They do these things, but they find it painful. I think they only do it for me. They'd much prefer to keep their grief private. Always have." She reached out and took Tom's hand, squeezing it softly. "Thank you again, for coming, Tom. Really."

He offered a slight smile. "Take care, Charlotte. I'll see you around."

She turned away, walking off towards the path that led away from the hotel and back towards the town. Noah approached Tom, carrying a small torch.

"All good?" Noah asked, flicking his gaze after Charlotte.

Tom nodded. "We're all set. I'll head off in a minute."

Noah inclined his head, scanning the empty path. A few stragglers lingered near the bench, quietly chatting. Tom didn't know them, but soon they also set off. "Good seeing you, Tom. Even if the circumstances are... well." He trailed off. "You know?"

"Yes," Tom said quietly. "They are what they are."

Without more words, they parted ways. Tom took one final look at the plaque on the bench, its etched letters now barely visible in the growing darkness, then made his way down the sloping path. The hush that followed him felt thick with unspoken questions – about Kristy, about Aaron, about the uncertain puzzle that still loomed. Yet there was also a strange sense of relief. They'd at least acknowledged the past, instead of pretending it didn't exist.

As he climbed into his car and started the engine, Tom's thoughts lingered on Charlotte's apology and the flicker of fear in her eyes. She was sorry for trying to pull him into the investigation but, at the same time, she'd clearly not let go of the idea that Aaron's death might unlock secrets about Kristy. Tom wondered if her motivations ran deeper than she admitted.

Regardless, he had no formal role in the inquiry. He was just a suspended officer with too much time on his hands and too many ghosts in his head. Yet he couldn't deny that he cared. For Kristy's memory, for the truth of Aaron's final hours, for Charlotte's grief. Maybe it was none of his business, but maybe it wouldn't leave him alone until the questions were resolved. Could Aaron's death be related to Kristy's? It wasn't really plausible. Charlotte had unresolved grief, that was all.

Tom drove away, the memory of candle flames dancing in the wind etched in his mind. A small, solemn vigil for a girl gone almost twenty years and a man who died barely hours before. Two tragedies befalling the same group of friends. Both leaving unanswered questions behind them. He pressed the accelerator gently, the road winding ahead through darkening farmland.

Whatever the future held, Tom felt certain the past was far from finished with him. One way or another.

CHAPTER TWELVE

THE DRIVE back from Kristy's vigil at the cliffs left Tom feeling strangely drained, though he couldn't decide whether it was from the fresh air of the coast or the overwhelming emotions. Darkness had fully settled by the time he reached the outskirts of Sheringham, headlights illuminating the winding country lanes. Flicking on his turn signal, he slowed to navigate a narrow bend. It felt like it had been a long day.

His phone rang, a sharp vibration in the cup holder. Tom glanced at the screen, expecting Alice, perhaps checking to see if he was nearly home. Instead, the display read *Unknown Number*. He swallowed, let out a breath, and tapped the hands-free button on the steering wheel.

"Hello?"

A crisp, cultured female voice came through. "Is this Tom Janssen?"

Tom frowned. "Yes. Who's calling?"

A brief pause. "Elena Novak." The name registered instantly. Aaron Bell's estranged wife. "I understand you were with my husband, Aaron, last night."

Tom wondered how she had got his number. He didn't

pass it around and this was his personal mobile. He hadn't switched his work phone on since he was suspended. "Yes, I was. I'm... sorry for your loss."

"I'm at my family hotel in Sheringham. We should speak. Tonight, if possible."

Tom's knuckles tightened on the steering wheel. He glanced at the clock. Past nine. "I'm not sure we have much to discuss. Certainly nothing that we couldn't talk about over the phone."

"Oh, you will find we do." There was a cutting edge to her tone. She was direct, with no hint of apology. "I'm staying at The Aurora. Are you familiar with it?"

He vaguely recalled a boutique place, fairly new, just off the esplanade. "I know where it is, yes."

"Good. Come to the reception. I've already told them to expect you."

Before Tom could object, she ended the call. He exhaled, eyebrows lifted. The day that wouldn't end just took another turn. He considered ignoring her summons, but curiosity – along with some sense of caution – nagged him. Elena Novak. The way Aaron had briefly spoken of her made him think she was quite a strong character. This brief conversation seemed only to firm up that reputation. She was wealthy, or at least well-connected, and evidently unafraid to make it clear what she wanted... expected, even. Perhaps she had answers, or perhaps she simply wanted an audience for some other reason. The question Tom had to consider was whether he wanted to find out?

The streets of Sheringham were quiet at this time. The shops were closed and only the restaurants and pubs were seeing any footfall but midweek was a quiet time. He debated calling Alice to let her know he'd be late. Instead, he sent a quick text at the next traffic light. *Change of plan. I'm meeting someone regarding Aaron's death. I shouldn't be late but don't wait up. Love you & Saffy.*

He drove around the roundabout housing the war memorial and garden and then pulled onto the esplanade, the dark sea straight in front of him. The Aurora rose up three storeys, tastefully lit and built in a style in keeping with the seafront. Tom pulled into the small car park to the side of the hotel and found an empty space near the entrance. He got out of the car, zipping his coat up against the chill. The strength of the sea breeze reflected in the sound of the waves crashing upon the sea defences below. The sound carried up to where he walked across to the hotel reception.

He wondered again how Elena had obtained his number. Perhaps from Tamara, but he doubted that, or some other back channel which he found more likely. Wealthy people had networks of acquaintances who could provide a favour. It was also possible that it came from Charlotte rather than some other Machiavellian route. He had no clue.

Inside, The Aurora's reception area was all polished marble floors, tall floral arrangements, and a faint scent of citrus cleaning agent. A desk clerk looked up from behind a sleek counter crafted from a wood that he didn't recognise. It was high end, without a doubt. Tom introduced himself, explaining he was meeting Elena Novak, and the clerk nodded as if this were common knowledge.

"Yes, Mr Janssen. Ms Novak is in the private lounge through there." He gestured to a frosted glass door to the left.

Tom offered a polite thanks. The lounge was small and modern, low sofas, bright abstract art on the walls with a contemporary take on an art deco theme. The hotel couldn't be very busy. There was only one person in the lounge beyond the bartender who was busy wiping down the counter off to one side. Elena Novak stood near a window, arms folded as she studied the view of the twinkling lights away to the right. She wore a black turtleneck and fitted trousers, her blonde hair pinned neatly. She exuded a calm, poised confidence at odds with the circumstances. As Tom approached, she turned.

"Tom Janssen." She said his name as though trying it out for the first time. "Thank you for coming."

"I was on my way home," he replied, voice even. "Your call was unexpected."

She studied him appraisingly. "Yes, well. I prefer to do things directly." She waved a hand, inviting him to take a seat on a low sofa before a huge fireplace with a classic surround. She settled opposite him, crossing her legs. Even in her posture, Tom sensed she was used to control and a degree of formality.

Elena motioned to the door, and the bartender quietly disappeared, leaving them alone in the lounge.

"You were with Aaron," she began, "last night, prior to his death."

Tom nodded. "Yes, I drove him home from the school reunion. He was too intoxicated to drive himself." He paused, then added, "I didn't expect to talk to you about it, I must be honest."

She pursed her lips. "Aaron and I were separated, as I'm almost certain he will have told you. Good riddance, if I can also be honest with you. But… he was still my husband and personal feelings don't simply vanish when a relationship ends. Especially when money is involved." She eyed him. "And money always is."

"Money," Tom repeated, uncertain. "Your priority today is… money? I'll be direct as well. That sounds callous."

Elena gave a dismissive shrug. "Callous? What is the meaning of this word?"

"Insensitive," Tom said. "A cruel disregard for—"

"Yes, yes," she said. "I understand. Forgive me, but do you believe Aaron will care?"

"No," Tom said. "I suppose not."

"You may think… in fact, I'm sure you do, that I am… a callous person but Aaron had a roving eye, you see. A womaniser, some might say worse. My father warned me not to marry him, but I was naïve. I thought I knew best. I was… swept off my feet, I suppose." She almost rolled her eyes. "I loved him. He had that skill so very rare in most people, the ability to make a person feel special. To feel like you were the only person who counted in his world."

"That does sound… a lot like Aaron." Tom shifted slightly. "So you've been separated how long?"

"Officially? Six months," she said. "Six long months. The final settlement drags on. He wouldn't accept any of my offers, always wanting more." Her tone was contemptuous. "That's the man you drove home. Unquenchable greed. And I assume he took advantage of your generosity that night, too."

"Well, I just didn't want him on the roads drunk. There was nothing to take advantage of."

"Generous indeed," she murmured, sounding unimpressed. "My father told me not to trust him from the start. But I married him anyway." She brushed an invisible fleck of lint off her sleeve. "It's tiresome, regret. Reliving the mistakes of youth."

Tom cleared his throat, deciding directness might work best. "Elena – may I call you Elena? – I'm not sure what you hope to gain from me here. I only saw him that evening—"

"You are a policeman are you not?"

Tom inclined his head. "Yes, but I'm not part of this investigation."

She smiled thinly. "Yes, I'm aware you're suspended from duty." She let the word hang in the air, gauging his reaction.

She had been doing her homework. "I make it my business to learn about those around me, Tom." She made a pointed note of using his first name. "You remain a police officer, though. Even if you're temporarily sidelined. And from what I gather, you're a conscientious detective. I'm told your moral compass is… well calibrated."

He bristled slightly at the mention of his suspension but he was more interested in who was passing judgement on him, to her. "I'm not sure who told you all this."

She spread her palms, elegantly dismissive. "I have my own resources. Let us not waste time dancing around the matter. I will not explain. You were the last person to see my husband alive. This interests me. And yes, I know you're on forced leave… or something. However that works in your line of work."

Tom tried to rein in his impatience. Curiosity brought him here, but the novelty factor was wearing thin now. "What exactly do you want from me?"

"I want to know who killed him," she said bluntly. "And why."

Tom exhaled. "It's a murder investigation. I don't know how familiar you are with police around the world, but here in England we are pretty good at finding killers."

She flicked her gaze away, unimpressed. "I do not have faith in the local constabulary, no offence to your colleagues, Tom. My husband was a cunning man. If there's any complexity to this, I suspect the regular course of these things might stall. Aaron had ways of clouding his world, ensuring no one really knew what he was up to. He was… resourceful. That is one reason why our marriage survived as long as it did."

Tom folded his arms. "I'm not sure it's a good idea for me to get involved. Even if I wanted to, I have no official standing. Me poking around could compromise the ongoing case."

Elena's eyes narrowed. "Compromise? If you won't do it, I will find someone else who will. Perhaps a private investigator with fewer scruples. If you prefer me to do that, then we're done talking tonight and you may leave."

He studied her. Despite her outward projection of calm, there was tension in her shoulders, her jaw was set. Beneath the crafted exterior, she was clearly rattled or at least determined. "Tell me more about why you think you need your own investigation."

She leaned forward a fraction. "Forgive me, but I have less faith in the police than you do. And... because there's something bigger here. My estranged husband has been haemorrhaging money from our UK bank account. My money, in effect. Do you know a man by the name of Shaun Whale?"

Tom frowned. "Shaun Whale? No, never heard of him. Who is he?"

She let out a sharp breath. "Aaron's been spending thousands of pounds on him. Thousands. Possibly north of ten thousand. My lawyers discovered suspicious transfers from accounts that are, nominally, family accounts. Aaron had partial access, courtesy of our marriage, of course." A bitterness etched her words. "It wasn't strictly his personal money to give away. That's the settlement fiasco in a nutshell. But he ignored me, funnelling large sums of money to this man, Whale. I want to know what my husband was paying for and if that has anything to do with his death."

Tom watched her carefully. "So you believe your husband's murder might be connected to these transactions? Or that he was dabbling in something... dangerous?"

"It's plausible. If these funds were paying for illegal services or hush money, that could come back to bite him.

Maybe this Whale character decided it was easier to remove Aaron than keep cooperating." She huffed softly. "I don't know. But what I do know is Aaron never cared about honest deals. Everything he did was done with a motive in mind, be it personal profit or leverage. It's quite possible there is another angle entirely. Maybe he was working to undermine my father's business interests. He might've even been stupid enough to cross the wrong people."

Tom resisted the reflex to defend Aaron, but it wasn't his place. "What are your father's – your family's – business interests? What is it Aaron could do to undermine you?"

"Our affairs are complex, Tom," Elena said. "If Aaron saw an opportunity to leverage his position in our settlement discussions, then I'm sure he would take it."

"I can see why you're concerned. But it's a big leap to think someone in your family or this Whale character murdered him. Let the police do their job. They'll figure it out. I can assure you that you can have confidence in them."

Elena's lips curved wryly. "You're suspended, and yet you still talk like a policeman. Do you plan to return to the force?"

He hesitated. "I... haven't decided. Everything's up in the air at the moment."

"There are companies," she said, "who could use a man with your experience. Security, investigative know-how. Even corporations needing risk assessments. I'm sure you'd find your skill set is in high demand in the private sector, and also of significant value."

He gave her an unsure look. "That's not the path I planned. Why do you mention it?"

"Because I want to hire you," she said flatly, as if it were obvious.

"You are very direct."

"It pays for me to be. I want you to find out who killed

Aaron and why. Consider it a private contract. I pay your fee. You investigate. No red tape, no departmental politics. And if you reach the same conclusion as your colleagues in the police eventually do then... fine. But I want it done thoroughly, discreetly and, above all, quickly. I'm not someone who enjoys waiting for official processes to take place."

Tom was silent for a moment, absorbing her pitch. "Even if I agreed, which I'm not sure about, it could complicate things. My colleagues might see it as interference, or I might run afoul of certain laws. Investigations aren't a free-for-all."

"And that is why your country is, how do you say it, on the slide? Too many rules and regulations. It stifles progress and innovation." Tom made no comment. She lifted her chin. "If you prefer, you can do it quietly. I'll ensure you have the resources you need: digital forensics, financial data. And if you run into trouble, you can pass the leads to your colleagues. You won't be alone. But the impetus will be entirely yours."

Tom rubbed the back of his neck, mentally replaying all the reasons why stepping into this would be ill-advised. Yet a persistent part of him was intrigued and, admittedly, he was unsettled by leaving the case in others' hands. He couldn't deny that the question of who'd killed Aaron loomed large. Old ties, old regrets... maybe this was an opportunity to do something good. Or it could be a disastrous mistake. His gut reaction was to steer well clear, and he had no intention of making this a paid job. At least, not right now.

Elena intrigued him as well. He'd met many people over the years who thought the rules everyone else lived by did not apply to them. Her motivation seemed plausible enough. She was clearly used to getting her own way. Maybe it would be better for him to play a role, at least for the time being. It may even help Tamara and the others. He tried changing tack.

"Let's say I consider it." He wouldn't, but he could feel the itch that needed scratching. The pull of an investigation. He was already embedded into it one way or another anyway. "Tell me more about these finances?"

She cocked her head. "My father's property empire stands behind me. Aaron's tastes were champagne and caviar, but it was all financed by me or my family. He used that access well, negotiating payments from others for influence within my family, introductions… impromptu meetings. That kind of thing. He did this until we separated, and even afterwards too while it worked. Then he found ways to keep draining money despite my best efforts to curb his appetites. I severed any business ties we had, allowed him access to a joint account with suitable balances. I am not a vindictive woman, Tom. I was fair. Aaron though… it was never enough and he was a resourceful man, as I said."

"No children," Tom repeated quietly, reflecting on what Aaron told him. A flicker of pain crossed her face.

"We tried," she said. "For children, but with no success. The reasons are irrelevant now. On reflection, it is probably for the best allowing for a clean break. That is, before these events came to pass. As for the accounts he was accessing to draw money, yes, they are Novak family accounts. A portion was set aside in a bridging account under both our names, pending the final settlement. He exploited that to fund these questionable outgoings. Possibly to Shaun Whale or who knows who else? I need to know why. Did he intend to destabilise my father's business from within? What was he doing with the money? As a business, we need to be ahead of any negative press or actions that could harm us. I want answers."

Tom wondered what these people might be involved in. Did every business, above a certain level of wealth anyway, need to worry about such things or was there more she wasn't letting him in on? Tom let out a measured breath. "As I said, I understand your concerns. But you must see the legal and moral issues with me investigating behind the scenes. Especially while the police are actively building a murder case."

She offered a thin, humourless smile. "Morals? Legality? I'm not forcing you to do anything, Tom. But if you refuse, I'll find someone else but I'd rather have a man with a conscience. I trust you'd be more… careful, shall we say."

He felt himself waver. Maybe it was pride, or maybe a desire for the truth. "I need time to think about it."

Elena inclined her head, apparently satisfied with that small concession. "Time is short, but do think quickly. I'll be in Sheringham for another couple of days, at least. After that, I may return to London. Keep me advised." She reached into her handbag, removed a small business card, and handed it to him. "My mobile is on there. Message me when you've decided to help."

"You are confident."

"I get what I want, Tom," she said and he didn't doubt it for a moment. Tom placed the card in his jacket pocket.

"Okay. I'll… let you know."

She stood, an implicit dismissal. "Thank you for coming. I assume you can find your own way out."

He rose, feeling the tension of the abrupt meeting. "Yes. Good night, Elena." He paused. "Again, I'm sorry for your loss. Even if the two of you weren't on good terms. Losing someone is still a shock."

Her lips curved in a wry, joyless smile. "Thank you, but truly, I feel no sorrow. If anything, I feel relief that my father's warnings have at last proven correct. The only regret is how much trouble and money has been wasted in between. Now… all that's left is to see if Aaron has threatened my family's interests."

Tom could think of no gentle response. He smiled, nodded and walked out, the lounge door closing behind him. The reception was silent, the marble floors reflecting the light from a large chandelier hanging in the entrance lobby. As he passed the reception desk, the clerk glanced up politely but said nothing.

Outside, the wind stung his cheeks. Tom pulled in a long breath of the cold air. He felt... unsteady, as if the ground beneath him had shifted. Elena Novak's proposition was bold, manipulative even. Yet she'd pitched a puzzle he couldn't entirely dismiss. The concerns surrounding the mysterious financial dealings, suspicious payoffs, and the possibility Aaron was entangled with some other unknown players. Could it explain who killed him and why?

He reached his car but hesitated before unlocking it. He considered the position of this unknown figure, Shaun Whale. Was he some shady contact receiving large sums from Aaron. What was it for? Extortion? Money laundering, or some partnership that needed uncovering? Even if he didn't take Elena's job, Tom found his curiosity piqued.

You're suspended, Tom, he reminded himself. Don't do anything reckless. Yet the memory of Aaron's grin came to mind. That last glass of brandy at the house in Blakeney and the uneasy sensation he felt when he left him. It wouldn't let go of him. Aaron had died a few hours after Tom had left. If there was a hidden reason, a hidden killer, and Tom was in a position to help unveil them, then he had to be involved. As long as he was careful.

"Damn it," he muttered under his breath before getting into the car and starting the engine. The headlights flared, catching the hotel's sign in a pale glow. He pulled onto the road, heading home to Alice and Saffy who should be asleep by now. As he drove through the deserted streets, Elena's business card pressed lightly in his jacket pocket. It felt as though it weighed a ton. She had given him a choice, accept her job offer or she would find someone else. Tom knew he wasn't compelled to do anything, but also that he intended to.

He signalled onto the main road towards home. A wave of doubt and possibility washed over him. He pictured the investigations that might tangle him further, the potential conflict with the official inquiry, the strain it could put on his relationship with Alice. And yet... he also pictured that battered bench at the cliff's edge, Kristy's plaque shining in the final glow of day, Charlotte's tears, Noah's quiet anger, and now Elena's single-minded push for answers. One way or another, the threads were pulling him back into the mystery of Aaron Bell's final hours.

His phone buzzed once, a text from Alice checking when he was coming home. Tom cleared his throat, mentally composing a reply. Yes, nearly there. I'm fine. Even though, deep down, he wasn't sure that he was. As he took the final turn onto his street, Tom caught sight of the reflection of his own eyes in the rear view mirror. If he doubted continuing as a policeman, he now knew for certain that he didn't want to leave. Suspended or not, he was a detective. And perhaps Elena's proposition was only the beginning of something deeper, and maybe a whole lot darker.

CHAPTER THIRTEEN

THE NEXT MORNING, Tom parked Aaron Bell's Porsche just inside the open gates of the Blakeney property. He'd intended to drive in further, nearer to the front door, but he stopped short on the long gravel driveway under the watchful eye of PC Marshall who was on duty at the gated driveway's entrance standing beside his liveried police car, parked on the verge.

For a moment, Tom stayed in the driver's seat, the electric vehicle's motor silent. The car itself felt oddly quiet for such a high-performance car. He exhaled, remembering how he'd first brought the car back to his own place a couple of nights ago, thinking Aaron would swing by to reclaim it the next day or he'd bring it back. Instead, Aaron was dead, and Tom was returning the Porsche to an empty, cordoned-off house.

Tom cracked open the door which was enough to shut the vehicle down. He rested his hands on the steering wheel, absorbing the strangeness of it all. Just days ago, he had helped Aaron stagger out of the reunion, driven him home, left the man sitting on a plush sofa, surrounded by opulence. Now the only signs of life were the uniformed constable stationed near the front door and a small knot of forensic staff wrapping up their scene analysis by the side entrance.

The forensic team's van was parked in plain view, its reflective stripes catching the morning light. He glanced in the rear view mirror at his own face, slightly worn from another restless night. In truth, he'd been awake well past midnight, brooding over Elena Novak's unexpected proposal. He repeatedly told himself he hadn't decided anything, but the seed was planted. He was just lying to himself. Better that then accept he was planning to meddle in something he wasn't supposed to. As long as he was cautious it would be all right. Aaron's death had unsettled him more than he cared to admit and leaving it alone just wasn't something he would countenance.

There were lines that he wasn't going to cross though.

Finally, Tom unclipped his seatbelt and got out. A gust of the cool, morning air whipped across him. As he stepped onto the gravel, he caught a glimpse of Detective Sergeant Cassie Knight walking across the rear of the property, heading in from the direction of the second property on the far side of the courtyard. She wore a navy jacket zipped high around her neck, and her breath fogged faintly in the chilly air.

She spotted him at once. Her eyebrows rose, and she offered a small wave. Tom lifted a hand in return, walking around the Porsche to meet her halfway as she hastened down the side of the property. The uniformed officer nearby also acknowledged him with a nod but said nothing.

"I heard you were going to drop the car off," Cassie said by way of greeting. A breeze ruffled her dark hair. "This is... I'd forgotten just how fancy these Porsches look in person."

Tom glanced back at the car. "It's certainly not a Volvo, that's for certain. It's a bit more than I care to drive if I'm honest. I'd rather not keep it at my place any longer. It doesn't belong to me, and I'm sure at some point someone in Aaron's circle, or his other half, will want it back."

Cassie nodded, folding her arms. An awkward pause lingered between them. She gestured towards the driveway. "I'll have Sheriff pull it round to the garage at the rear," she said. "For now, the keys will just go into evidence storage, I imagine."

Tom caught a glimpse of the triple-bay garage at the rear of the house, the wide doors sealed shut. Cassie paused, then flicked her gaze back to the house having clocked Tom doing the same. "Did you come hoping for a guided tour of the crime scene, by any chance?"

He let out a short laugh, albeit self-conscious. "Thought I'd ask. Any chance I could take a look? Might satisfy my curiosity."

Cassie laughed outright, shaking her head. "You? A suspended copper? Wandering through an active murder investigation site? Absolutely not." Her mock-serious tone made them both smile.

"You're quite right," Tom said, lifting both palms in surrender. "Just testing you, DS Knight."

She smirked. "I'm a test all right, sir. Don't you forget it."

They stood there a moment, the sense of easy camaraderie tempered by the knowledge that Tom was no longer part of the job. Another silence settled, until Cassie rubbed her hands for warmth and said, "So, Aaron Bell. Did you know him well? You were at school together, right?"

Tom shrugged, remembering his discussion with Elena and wondering about how much he really knew him. "Not as well as I thought I did. Back in school, he was the star. Popular, sporty, charming. Everyone assumed he'd go on to do big things. It was nailed on." His voice turned wry. "He did seem to live life large, but it's dawning on me now that I never had a clue what was actually beneath the surface. From what I hear... he's not quite who I thought he was."

Cassie nodded. "Maybe he changed rather than you misread him? We keep learning new facts. For starters, this house isn't even in his own name. Belongs to a shell corporation based in the British Virgin Islands." She eyed him curiously. "Any idea why that might be?"

Tom pursed his lips. "No, not for certain. Aaron's father-in-law is quite a player in property investing, or so I'm told. The family firm seems vague about real estate. But I suspect it's bigger and more complicated than that, especially if shell companies are involved."

"Sounds about right." Cassie's gaze wandered over the property's sleek lines, the glass walls, the rusted steel architectural elements. "From what I've gleaned so far, the Novak family are property and tech entrepreneurs, with fingers in lots of pies. They are listed as large investors in big developments in Asia, rumoured government contracts in India and Singapore, plus connections around Europe. They're not short on money."

Tom recalled Elena's crisp voice, her lavish hotel. "I imagine they're not, no. You've met Elena, right, Aaron's wife?"

A half-smile came to Cassie's lips. "Oh yeah, I have. She's... not the typical widow. Very matter-of-fact. Kind of weird, if you ask me. Then again, rich people usually are. They don't live in the same world as the rest of us."

Tom slid his hands into his coat pockets. "I can't argue with that." He knew Cassie wasn't aware of his private conversation with Elena, but the memory of Elena's gaze made him uneasy. "Did she mention anything to you about what she thinks brought all of this on?"

Cassie's mouth tightened. "She gave us a few hints about

business associates, potential enemies. Nothing concrete. Frankly, we've got more questions than answers. I'd love to see the full results from the lab. But I can't share too many details with you, not officially. You know how it is."

Tom shrugged, feigning a casual manner. "Understood. I was just curious. Speaking of details though... have you heard how he actually died? The cause, I mean." He tried to keep the question light, though the answer mattered to him more than he cared to show.

Cassie hesitated, caution flashing in her eyes. "We won't have the official pathology results until later today. Preliminary findings suggest a blow to the head or possibly drowning... or both." She exhaled. "Off the record, I suspect he was knocked unconscious and fell into the pool. Something like that."

A brief silence, and Tom nodded. "Grim."

She offered a tight smile, then ventured, "We've also picked up some evidence that he may have been... let's say intimately involved with the housekeeper, Carol. We suspect it wasn't strictly an employer-employee arrangement. From what his wife said, Aaron apparently had a love of women. I guess the hired help keeps it close to home, saves venturing out."

Tom recalled Elena's remark that Aaron often had extra-marital affairs. "Elena told me the same thing. That he was cheating on her left, right, and centre. Didn't get into specifics, but if that's true, it's definitely a potential lead. An angry husband or boyfriend out for revenge, maybe."

"Could be," Cassie agreed. "We'll look into it. There are a lot of angles." She glanced back at the front door where the forensic team was loading equipment into a marked van. "Anyway... I should probably be getting on with my day. But let's stop ignoring the elephant..." she glanced around them, "in the driveway and start being honest."

"What are you talking about?" Tom asked.

"Why are you really here, Tom?" Her voice was softer, less teasing.

Tom ran a hand over the back of his neck. "Honestly? Partly to drop off the car. Partly... I guess I'm restless, still suspended, I can't do my job. Feels like there's something I should be doing, but I'm sidelined."

Cassie studied him a moment. "How's that process going, the inquiry? Any chance it might wrap up soon?"

He looked away, his gaze drifting across the wetlands towards Blakeney Point. "I'm the last one who'd know. The coroner's verdict from that case was adjourned, as you know, and the subsequent internal misconduct hearing is in limbo until the coroner makes her call. I'm stuck. And I've been thinking a lot lately... maybe it's not worth going back. The job. The stress."

She cocked her head. "But you know it is. C'mon, you're a better copper than most. If you walk away, who's going to catch Norfolk's bad guys?"

Tom managed a faint smile. "You, Cassie Knight. You, Eric and the DCI can handle it just fine."

Her laugh was short, a gust of amusement that caught in the wind. "I note you didn't mention Danny Wilson."

"No, I didn't," Tom said, smiling.

"And don't count on me. I'm missing the north-east. It rains there. I like the drama. Here, it's just tractors, tourists and coastline with not a drop of decent downpour when you need it."

Tom cracked a broader grin. "I never knew you loved the rain so much."

"Hey, we all have our quirks. At least it's not about extra-marital affairs." She sobered then, and stuffed her hands in her jacket pockets. "Anyway, we all miss you in the office. Even the boss."

"How has she been getting on?" Tom asked.

"She's coping, you know, but... we could do with your size-thirteen shoes back around the place. Honestly, come to think of it," Cassie said thoughtfully, "I reckon she's enjoying being in charge without you. She gets to do all the fun stuff... paperwork, listening to me bitching and moaning, babysitting Eric and Danny." She rolled her eyes playfully. "What's not to love?"

Tom chuckled, more at the mental image of Tamara fielding Eric Collet's endless questions and Danny's occasional flights of fancy. But the laughter faded. He took a breath, lowering his voice. "Cass... have you come across anything untoward in Aaron's finances? Something about big payments going astray, maybe to people you haven't identified yet?"

Her eyes narrowed. "That's oddly specific. Why do you ask?"

Tom's heart thumped. He was dangerously close to revealing Elena's confidences about suspicious money transfers. He shrugged, trying for a nonchalant air. "Just a rumour I overheard. You know me, I can't help hearing things. I was curious if it tied into the case at all."

Cassie's suspicion was evident in her expression. "Are you dipping your toes into this investigation, Tom Janssen? That's not exactly your place right now."

He let out a soft laugh. "I told you. I'm restless. Let's just say if you do come across anything along those lines, you know where I am. And you can always call me if you need an extra perspective, unofficially. Otherwise... I'm just going to keep my head down."

She eyed him, trying to read whether there was more

behind the question. "Uh-huh," she said slowly. Then her expression softened. "A quick question."

"Ask it."

"Since when were you speaking to Elena?"

Tom arched his eyebrows in query. "Say again?"

"You just said that Elena told you the same thing," Cassie said, "about Aaron playing away."

"Oh yeah," Tom said, his face reddening. "I did. I met her last night, briefly."

"What did she want?"

"Who says she wanted anything?"

"Elena Novak isn't someone who strikes me as flippant or breezy. If she was talking to you then there would be a purpose."

Tom nodded. "Yes. She has… concerns about the motives of whoever killed Aaron, and she's curious to know."

"Aren't we all," Cassie said. "I'll keep it in mind. Honestly, I think we'd all be much happier if we had you back on the team. Personally, I think you're a great boss regardless of what everyone else says about you."

Tom grinned. "I can't wait to write your performance review, Cassandra."

"Then you'll need to come back to work to write it," she said with a wink. "As for all of this," she said thumbing towards the house. "Don't worry. I have it covered."

Tom nodded. "I know you do. And thanks."

They held one another's gaze, an unspoken camaraderie passing between them, colleagues who understood each other's frustrations. Then Cassie looked at the house. "Guess I should get back inside, see if forensics missed anything. We're wrapping up soon, but there's a few places we need to re-check now that the furniture's been moved for deeper examination."

"Sure. Do you want this?" Tom held up the key fob. Cassie took it from him.

"Do you need a lift home?" Cassie asked, looking towards PC Marshall. Tom shook his head.

"No, I'm going to take a walk along the coast. I don't have a pressing need to be anywhere just now."

"Okay… well, take care of yourself, sir."

They parted ways, Cassie heading towards the front door while Tom made his way back down the gentle slope of the drive to the entrance gates.

"See you soon, sir," PC Marshall said as Tom passed by him.

"You can count on it, Dave," Tom said to him, turning and walking backwards. He took one last lingering look at the house's modern façade. It loomed over him, a monument to Aaron's complicated and, possibly, shady life. He paused by the roadside waiting for a gap in the light traffic to cross where he'd cut to the footpath through the marsh on the other side of the road which would lead him down to the old harbour front at Blakeney. From there he'd cut across to Cley before reaching the beach and heading east.

He wanted to help Cassie, to help solve Aaron's murder, if for no other reason than his own sense of justice and maybe a lingering feeling of guilt. Officially, he had no business snooping around a murder case. Still, Elena's cryptic references to missing money, Cassie's mention of shell companies, and the talk of multiple lovers were all pieces of a puzzle. And Tom, detective or not, couldn't stop himself from assembling them, at least in his head.

Was he dipping his toes in? Maybe. Maybe more than just toes. If the connection to Shaun Whale was in any way suspicious then he shouldn't keep quiet about it. Or was that doing Cassie and the team a disservice? The lines were blurred.

CHAPTER FOURTEEN

DCI Tamara Greave stood at the head of a long table in the Hunstanton CID operations room, tapping her pen lightly against the whiteboard behind her as the team took their seats. This was day two in the investigation, and a little more since someone murdered Aaron Bell. Turning to face the room, she quickly cast a glance around the team. She could see that everyone looked tired. The overhead fluorescent lights cast an almost clinical glow over the room. On the board behind her, pinned photos and case details along with potential leads were populating swiftly now.

Cassie and Eric Collet sat side by side, each with notebooks open, while DC Danny Wilson hovered near the back, chewing the end of a pen. Tamara's gaze swept across them.

"All right, let's come to order," she said. Her voice had a clipped efficiency, honed by years of running major investigations. "We've got a lot of ground to cover, so let's not waste time. Everyone ready?" There was a chorus of nods. Tamara took a breath and started systematically. "First, the main points from forensics at Aaron Bell's property in Blakeney. The damage to the scene is minimal. We do have shards of broken glass, tumblers based on what's left of them, and nothing else significantly smashed. There is nothing to indicate a wild struggle that trashed the place which is what we might expect bearing in mind the age and physical shape of the victim. Aaron Bell was in good physical shape and, even if he'd had a few drinks, his blood alcohol content was not high enough to judge him as incapacitated."

"He would have put up a fight," Cassie said. Tamara agreed.

"There's no sign of burglary ransack either. The contents of drawers and cupboards have not been rifled through. Likewise, locked cupboards and drawers have not been forced." Tamara pointed to photos taken at the crime scene by the forensic officers. "If this was a burglary, in and out in less than five minutes and making a hell of a mess along the way. That's how it works."

"Next we have the missing hard drive. The CCTV system is decent, the set up and positioning of the cameras is very well done. Professional. The cameras will have picked up most points of entry onto the grounds and certainly into the house itself. The hard drive is missing from the locked technical room. The entire area around where the unit was located has been wiped clean. No fingerprints. Not one. It's likely that the room was targeted by the killer. Did they stumble across it by accident or were they always planning to cover their tracks?"

"That would be a pro if that's the case," Cassie ventured. "Your average burglar is looking for quick cash, tech they can knock out on marketplace or down the pub."

"Good point, Cassie. Let's assume, for now, that someone knew about the surveillance set-up and understood what would be required to either circumvent it or simply to hide their presence. There is a suspicion the CCTV might have been backed up to a central server, so someone needs to chase that with whichever security or cloud service Aaron was using at the address. Let's find out who provided that service. Maybe we'll get lucky."

She glanced at DC Danny Wilson, who was already scribbling. "That's you, Danny. I want you on it immediately. Find the company, get a hold of them, check if there's a remote back up or any third-party data centre that might have Aaron's camera footage."

Danny nodded. "Yes, boss. I'll have an answer by the end of the day, or at least a lead on who the service provider is."

Tamara nodded. "The results of the post-mortem are in—"

"Doctor Death working fast then," Cassie said drawing a murmur of amusement from Eric and Danny.

Tamara smiled. "He did ask me to send you his best, Cassie."

Cassie shuddered, exaggerating the action as if she was uncomfortable. "The feeling is not mutual." Eric glanced sideways at her. "He gives me the creeps. What else can I say?"

"The cause of death," Tamara said, continuing with the briefing, and lifting a forensics report from the table in front of her, "is confirmed as drowning. The pathologist—" Cassie silently mimicked retching, "says that, significantly, Aaron was still alive, though likely unconscious, when he went into the water. The blow to his head came first."

She scanned the faces around the table. Eric shifted uncomfortably in his chair, Cassie's brow furrowed.

"The head trauma was apparently inflicted with a hammer," Tamara went on. "Specifically a ball-peen hammer or something similar with a spherical head." She pointed to comparable images of the suspected murder weapon that she'd pinned on the board before the team assembled for the briefing. "The fracture was massive; it left a depression consistent with a 'ball' shaped impact. There was substantial subcutaneous bleeding on the brain."

"That means we're definitely looking at murder, right?" Danny asked. "He was struck, then left to drown. Not an accident."

"No question," Tamara said firmly, then tapped her pen again on the table in front of her. "Even if he fell into the water by accident, it would have been as a result of this injury. The killer could just have easily dragged him to the poolside and pushed or rolled him in for all we know. What we are certain of is that no such hammer or tool that matches the victim's wound has been found at the property. The killer must have taken the weapon with them and either has it now or disposed of it elsewhere."

She turned back to the board, scanning the contents.

"Entry and exit," she said, frowning. "Consistent with no sign of a burglary, there is no indication of a forced entry on doors or windows. The forensic team says some windows were open, which might have let a prowler or burglar in, but we also know from the housekeeper that Aaron tended to leave doors unlocked when he was at home. So the door being unlocked doesn't necessarily indicate an intruder."

"He felt safe in his home," Eric said. "Suggesting he didn't feel under threat at all."

"Unless," Cassie said, "someone exploited that carelessness to sneak in and confront him, and then it turned violent."

"Precisely." Tamara inclined her head. "We also have footprints in the mud outside the living room window. These impressions don't match the footwear Aaron was wearing the night he died or any of those found in the house. Different size, different tread pattern. There are plaster casts which are now with the lab, but no match to anything so far. It is possible, with time, that a tread match can be found to a manufacturer but there are no logos or marketing stamped in the cast. It's more likely that if we can find a suspect then we can try to match the footwear. Otherwise it's—"

"A needle in a haystack," Cassie said glumly.

"The location of the footprints, positioned standing at the window, suggest a prowler, a stalker, or just someone lurking around rather than a gardener at work. Bear in mind that if the person came inside, we still don't know their motive. Snooping, robbery… revenge… we are still guessing."

"Is there any useful evidence of someone inside?" Danny asked, looking up from his notebook.

"Thanks, Danny," Tamara said. "That's my next point." He nodded, wincing slightly at jumping in on the presentation. "There is trace evidence in the master bedroom. Forensics found hair, fibres in the bed that don't match Aaron Bell. We suspect it belongs to an intimate partner. Possibly the housekeeper, Carol, since you and Eric," she said to Cassie, "think Aaron was intimate with her. We can't confirm it yet, but we need to rule that in or out. If it's not her then he has another partner we're not aware of. We'll need to interview her, be candid and direct. She might be a witness or have knowledge of who else was around that night."

Cassie raised her hand slightly. "I can take the lead on that conversation with Carol if you want. I've already spoken to her once, but it was cursory. Woman to woman, she might be a bit more open."

Tamara nodded. "Yes, do that. We need to see if she'll admit to a relationship and whether she was actually at the property at a different time to when she claimed. If she's lying, that's suspicious. If she isn't, maybe she knows who else we should be looking at in Aaron's orbit."

"On it," Cassie said, making a note.

"Next, the possible burglar," Tamara said. "We should also

look at the possibility that the footprints belong to a burglar. Maybe they got in through an unlocked door or window and Aaron disturbed them. As you said, a brief fight ensued but due to Aaron's intoxication, the fight was short hence the lack of destruction. The burglar could have panicked, disregarded the robbery and simply looked to clear their tracks and put as much distance between themself and the body as quickly as possible."

"It would have to be someone who knew what they were doing," Cassie said.

"Yes, I agree," Tamara said. "The location of the house, as well as the level of security, probably rule out an opportunistic criminal. This would be someone who's targeting high-end properties. Someone who knows how to handle CCTV. Wiping out the footage and removing the hard drive is quite sophisticated and not done by your average thief. Danny," Tamara looked at the detective constable, "once you're done chasing the server lead, coordinate with the local intel unit. See if we have any burglaries in the region matching this M.O. The fact that Aaron was hammered and left to drown might be an escalation, an unfortunate mistake on the criminal's part, but we can't rule it out."

"Got it," Danny murmured.

Tamara paused, letting all that sink in before switching tack. She flipped to another page in her notes. "That's the forensics side. Now let's move on to the last big item. This one casts an altogether different shadow over the case which is why I've left it until last. During the sweep of the house, we found a folder among Aaron's belongings. Hard copies of old news articles about a teenage suicide from nearly twenty years ago."

Cassie cleared her throat. "That's Kristy Sears, boss. Charlotte Sears' sister. Kristy took her own life after an alleged break-up with Aaron shortly after they graduated from high school."

Tamara flicked her gaze around. "Yes, Tom confirmed as much to me. The puzzle is, why did Aaron have this? They were newly printed articles, not faded old clippings that he kept as a keepsake or something darker. So, he's been looking into it recently. Otherwise why would he have them? Perhaps he could have felt guilty about Kristy's death? Or was he, for some reason, investigating something about that incident? We don't know. It's odd though."

Eric spoke up. "We know Charlotte Sears was at the reunion. She saw Aaron there. Maybe something about that old tragedy came up. If he'd been trying to patch old wounds or dig for answers, it might connect."

Tamara tapped the pen lightly on the table, tension in her shoulders. "Agreed. But there's no way he searched for these articles, printed them off and put them in a folder after the reunion. He already had these. We can't ignore the possibility that this teen suicide is relevant. Maybe not directly as a motive to kill Aaron now, but it's suspicious that he was looking at it. Could be blackmail, guilt, or something else entirely. Look into it."

"Charlotte Sears hasn't said anything to us about Aaron's renewed interest in Kristy," Cassie said. "If she knew he was revisiting that tragedy, she hasn't admitted it to us."

"It was her sister though," Eric said. "He's not likely to bring it up, especially if she holds him responsible in some way for causing Kristy pain back then."

"Then we'll ask her," Tamara said. "We'll be polite but firm. If she's aware of anything Aaron might have discovered regarding Kristy's death, we need that angle. We also know Charlotte had a child with Noah Cook, who also had an argument with Aaron at the reunion. We should confirm Noah's timeline after he left the school the other night too. Tom mentioned that Aaron exchanged words with Noah and Tony Slater before Tom gave him a ride home."

At the mention of Tom's name, the room quieted slightly. Tom was well-liked, but he was still under suspension. Cassie observed Tamara carefully. Tamara cleared her throat.

"For those of you wondering. Tom's involvement here is minimal. He gave Aaron a lift home as a friend, or rather an old classmate. We've already got a statement from him. Let's keep that out of the equation unless something suggests otherwise. He's not a suspect, obviously, but we can't let him get in the middle of an active case either."

Cassie nodded, but her brow wrinkled. "I think we need to run Tom's prints." Tamara looked at her and Cassie shrugged. "He was in the house, so we'll need to know what he touched."

Tamara knew she was right. It was standard. "Okay, they'll be on file. Drop in and let him know though, will you?"

Cassie nodded. It was procedure for all serving officers to have their fingerprints on file in case of officers contaminating a crime scene by their presence. Tamara considered what Cassie had told him Tom said when he brought Aaron's car back to the house in Blakeney. His hinting around suspicious finances lingered in her mind. She chose not to bring it up right now in front of everyone but the bank account analysis might be revealing.

"Right," Tamara continued. "Final points. I want phone records, credit card transactions, and bank statements for Aaron Bell. We need to see if he was meeting someone regularly, socially or through business. That includes any big cash withdrawals, transfers to other accounts, anything that might confirm a secret blackmail scenario or hush money. I know I'm reaching but we're at day two and we don't have a workable motive. Let's find one. Eric, that's up your alley. You're good with the financial analysis. We've got the partial access provided by the widow, Elena Novak, but we'll push for a full production order."

"Yes, ma'am," Eric said. "I'll get on it today. Also, I might talk with the bank directly if we hit a wall with the partial data from Elena. The settlement might keep things locked down, but hopefully we can bypass it with the help of a magistrate."

"Do so," Tamara agreed. "Also speak to Elena more thoroughly. She's not exactly distraught – far from it – and she might be able to shed light on Aaron's finances, even if she's cagey about the specifics. She was in London at the time, with security cameras around her penthouse, so her alibi looks solid. I still want to confirm it though."

There was a moment of quiet as Tamara scanned her scribbled bullet points one last time. Then she turned to the entire team. "Let's summarise our lines of inquiry. First off, the CCTV server. Danny to chase that down today with the security provider. Secondly, phone and the financials. Credit card, bank accounts. Eric, you're to handle the financial data and personal communications. I want a report at the end of play today detailing where we are. Cassie, you are going to speak to the housekeeper, Carol, about their possible relationship. Check if she was there after hours and how often she spent time at the house. Who did she see. That type of thing."

"I'll leave straight after this," Cassie said.

"Charlotte Sears and her sister's suicide. We need to press Charlotte on why Aaron might revisit Kristy's story. Cassie, you can handle that too. Possibly we'll bring her in for a formal statement if she's evasive, but try to keep it low-key for now. We don't want it to look like we're going after her. Danny, you are going to follow up on the burglar and the missing hammer."

"Yep," Danny said, not looking up. "That's me."

"Noah Cook and Tony Slater. We've spoken to Tony but we need to follow up with Noah Cook. How deep was this antagonism between the two of them? Revisited as part of the reunion or did it spill over outside before and, or after the party? Let's confirm their timelines after the reunion thoroughly."

She lowered her pen, exhaling. "I know it's a lot, but this case is a tangle of personal grudges and potential burglary angles. My instinct says it's more personal than a random act, but I won't ignore the possibility. So let's keep an open mind. Understood?"

They all nodded.

"Good," Tamara said. "Questions?"

Cassie put up a hand. "Just to clarify, boss. The forensics are sure it's a ball-peen style hammer? Are we checking local sales or hardware shops for that kind of tool?"

"Already in progress," Tamara said. "I've collared David Marshall for that task. But you know how common those hammers are and plenty of tradespeople have them. We'll keep an eye out for any suspicious purchases if any of our potential suspects have been spotted buying one recently."

Eric ran a hand through his hair. "Any chance we get a forensic match from the footprints in the mud?"

"That'll be difficult, but let's not rule it out," Tamara said. "We'll keep working with the lab. The soil was wet, so with the partial tread pattern, we might get lucky and find a suspect's shoes with mud present. Forensics can do a match in that scenario."

Danny flipped through his notes. "One more thing, ma'am. Are we going to push the press for help? Asking the public if they saw anyone lurking near the property that night?"

Tamara considered. "Yes, we'll do a statement appealing

for witnesses. But not too many details, just enough to see if any neighbours or passers-by saw unusual activity near Aaron's house around midnight. That said, it's quite isolated. Not sure how much we'll get, but it's worth a shot."

She set the pen down. "All right, that's it. Let's get moving."

Chairs scraped the floor as Eric, Danny, and Cassie stood. The air felt charged with purpose. Before they dispersed, Tamara lifted a hand. "One last thing. Don't forget to treat the housekeeper carefully. If she was indeed in a sexual relationship with the victim, she might be vulnerable. She might even be scared. Let's not approach this like she's automatically a suspect. We need her cooperation."

"Yes, boss," Cassie said.

Tamara nodded. "All right. Let's go and get a result and solve this."

Eric and Danny filed out first, each hurrying to their desks in the open-plan office beyond. Cassie lingered a moment, gathering her notes, her features pensive. Tamara locked eyes with her.

"You have something on your mind, Cass?"

Cassie shrugged. "Just… it feels like every new piece of evidence leads to more questions. Aaron's entire life was a spiderweb of secrets. Plus, that Kristy Sears' angle. I can't shake the feeling there's more to it."

Tamara's gaze flicked to the board where "Kristy Sears: Teen Suicide" was pinned in black marker. "I agree. Follow up on that thoroughly. Don't let Charlotte Sears brush you off."

Cassie nodded, gripping her notes. "Understood."

They walked out together, the murmur of phones and the hum of computers filling the corridor. Tamara turned to the main office. Cassie headed towards the exit, already dialling to arrange the next interview.

CHAPTER FIFTEEN

TOM JANSSEN STOOD at the kitchen window of his house, arms resting lightly on the counter, gazing out over the garden. The past twenty-four hours had drawn him back towards old haunts and old friends – or at least old acquaintances – far more than he'd anticipated. And with that had come old memories.

He couldn't quite shake the nagging weight of Elena Novak's words about suspicious funds or the persistent memory of Cassie's face as she told him he should keep away from the case. But how could he ignore it? Aaron had been an old school mate, however distant or complicated their relationship. If Tom had lingered longer, would it have changed anything? He couldn't say with certainty. Maybe the killer would have been spooked and left. Maybe they were there, waiting in the shadows for Tom to leave.

His house felt oddly still this morning. Saffy was at school, Alice had gone to work, and Tom was simply there. The only sound was the low murmur of the television left on in the living room for background noise. Russell, their long-legged Jack Russell terrier was lying on the sofa and Tom could hear his snoring. At least someone wasn't feeling the stress or tension of the situation.

His phone buzzed once. Not a call, just some media notification he had no interest in. Setting it aside, Tom glanced at the television. The regional BBC magazine-style daily programme was on. A panel discussion had just wrapped up. More bulletins about the cost of living, local events in Norwich, a quick weather forecast. It was only half-absorbed noise until he recognised the name of the station's anchor – Amelia Warren – someone he'd occasionally seen at press conferences.

The doorbell rang.

Tom turned, leaving the TV running behind him. Nine times out of ten, if someone came by at this time of day, it was someone pushing junk food flyers or cold calling to sell something or other he wouldn't want or need. But today, something told him it was neither of those.

He stepped to the door and peered through the frosted glass panel. Outside stood DS Cassie Knight, her hands tucked into the pockets of a plain black jacket. She caught sight of his silhouette, and her lips curved in a polite almost-smile.

"Morning, Tom," she said the instant the door opened.

He stepped back to let her in, ignoring a sudden swirl of tension in his gut. "Morning, Cassie. Come in." In his peripheral vision he saw Russell open his eyes and lazily lift his head to see what the commotion was before settling back down again. Cassie came inside, glancing around the narrow hallway as he shut the door behind her. "Alice at work?"

"She is. And Saffy's at school." Tom paused, reading the purposeful stance of the detective sergeant. "Tea? Coffee?"

"Coffee would be good, thanks," she said, though her tone carried the dryness of someone who wasn't here just for casual chat. "As long as it's real coffee and not that instant rubbish."

Tom led her through into the kitchen, smiling as he moved to switch on the coffee machine. He absently pushed aside a small stack of Saffy's colouring books that she'd left on the breakfast bar, gesturing to one of the stools, so Cassie could take a seat if she wanted. The TV was still on. A fresh news segment was rolling now, some snippet about rising tourist numbers in Norfolk coastal towns and the anticipation of a strong year ahead for the hospitality trade.

He left her for a moment, heading into the adjoining living room and gathering up the remote control for the television. He turned the sound down a touch before returning to the kitchen.

"Are you watching a lot of daytime telly these days?"

"Not usually. Just... needed background noise." Tom pressed the button on the kettle. "It's too quiet in here otherwise."

Cassie's expression suggested she understood. She was quiet for a second, considering him. "You, uh... holding up okay?"

He shrugged. "As well as can be. I've had worse days, but... yeah, I suppose I'm restless."

"That's understandable."

He offered a small nod in response, fetching two mugs from the cupboard. He ran the grinder and then transferred the filter head into the machine. "So, is this a social call, or...?"

She gave a slight grin. "I'm afraid it's more official than social, but not an interrogation or anything." A beat passed. "We do need to talk about something. If you're all right with that."

He breathed out. "Sure."

"I'd normally do this at the station," Cassie said, "but we're still sorting out the who, what, and how. It's not your statement about driving Aaron home, Tamara has that. This is more about… something else."

Tom nodded, passing Cassie a mug of coffee, "Milk or sugar?"

"No thanks, Tom. I'm sweet enough," she said with a wink.

"Go on."

In the background, Amelia Warren's voice from the TV said, "With us now is Professor David White, criminologist at the University of East Anglia, to discuss the shocking death of local man, Aaron Bell…"

Both of them glanced at the screen involuntarily. A camera cut to Professor White, a tall, slim man with salt-and-pepper hair, wearing a crisp suit jacket. David White was DCI Tamara Greave's partner. Interesting timing. Cassie's eyebrows shot up in an expression of mild surprise.

Tom reached for the remote and increased the volume. "Let's listen," he said, stifling a grin. "This is going to be interesting."

On screen, Amelia Warren, smartly dressed, a microphone pinned to her lapel, looked earnest. They appeared to be in David's office at the faculty, a number of books on the psychology of crime were strategically placed on shelves behind him. One of which, Tom noted, was written by David. "Professor White, from what little the police have released publicly, it seems robbery is not the motive. What else can you infer about this killing?"

David White nodded gravely. "Well, Amelia, I don't have inside knowledge, so I can only speak generally as a criminologist. But the suggestion is that Aaron Bell died from drowning after a severe blow to the head. The lack of evidence pointing the investigation towards a robbery is indicative of a crime originating from an emotional impulse, or at least a sudden escalation rather than premeditation."

Tom exchanged a sidelong glance with Cassie, both listening. White continued, "Statistics show that in around ninety per cent of homicides, the victim and the perpetrator know each other: friends, family, acquaintances, business partners. It's rarely a true-stranger crime. If the police are ruling out a simple burglary, that heightens the likelihood this was personal. Potentially a confrontation that turned deadly."

Amelia Warren nodded fervently, leaning forward. "Would you consider the perpetrator to be potentially psychologically unhinged? I mean, to knock someone out and then leave them to die in a swimming pool—"

Professor White pursed his lips. "Not necessarily. Many murders of this nature are crimes of passion or reactions with strong emotion. If it were premeditated, we might see more structured planning, removing the victim discreetly, staging a scene more thoroughly, or a different choice of weapon. A blow to the head often suggests a tool of opportunity, especially if something suitable is found on site. Although, the investigation team have not furnished us with the murder weapon as of yet. So, I suspect this is an impulsive scenario. Possibly an argument that escalated out of control."

Amelia pressed him. "And the alleged removal of CCTV or missing footage? Does that not suggest planning?"

White spread his hands in a mild gesture. "It could indicate that once the killer realised what had happened, they decided to cover their tracks. Destruction of evidence can be an opportunistic afterthought. Murderers do not always plan every step. I stress, though, I'm hypothesising based on standard patterns, not specifics relating to this particular case."

The journalist nodded. "Thank you for your insights, Professor. It's a perplexing case indeed."

The interview ended, cutting back to the anchor who teased the next story about local tourism. Tom sighed and picked up the remote, muting the sound. Cassie sipped at her coffee, then let out a slow breath. The corners of her mouth twitched in mild amusement. "Well, the boss isn't going to be thrilled about that one."

Tom set the remote aside. "I can see Tamara's face now."

"Oh yeah," Cassie said with a smirk. "David is going to get it tonight... and not in a good way. He was fairly neutral and passive, but still..."

"He basically said it was personal, likely someone Aaron knew. So, the official line from the police is the same, or close, I guess?"

Cassie wrinkled her nose. "Yes and no. He's not necessarily wrong. We're leaning that way, looking for someone from within Aaron's orbit. I just wonder why he couldn't wait. It's not like him to wade in, and doing it to the Beeb is not going to sit well with the boss... at all."

Tom frowned. "Maybe they cornered him at the university."

"Aye, maybe." She sighed, setting her mug down. "Okay, so..." She looked more serious now. "I came here to talk to you about Kristy Sears."

A little prickle ran along Tom's spine. "You want to know about Kristy's suicide," he asked softly.

"That's it. She died the summer after you graduated high school, right? Tom nodded. "It sent shock waves through the community, I'm guessing."

"It shook us all," Tom admitted. "She was only sixteen, well, nearly seventeen. She jumped off the cliffs above Sheringham. The entire town was rocked." He took on a faraway look, staring straight ahead. "Kristy was bright, a bit shy maybe, but well-liked. She and Charlotte were close. Or at least that's what it looked like to me."

Cassie nodded, taking notes. "Yeah, that matches bits of info we've gleaned. Charlotte was younger than you, though, so Kristy was... your year?"

"Correct. Kristy was in the same year as me and Aaron. Noah, too. Charlotte was a year below, I think. Young in her year though, so there were more like eighteen months between us but my memory of that period is a bit sketchy."

Cassie let out a small hum. "So, Aaron had dated Kristy Sears. For how long?"

Tom's eyes flicked from Cassie to the muted television, his mind replaying old memories. "They were... yeah, they were a couple for a few months. Maybe longer. Hard to say, as teenage relationships can be very on-and-off."

"And some blamed him for her suicide?"

Tom spread his hands. "Yes, but it was never official or anything. People talk. Some said he dumped her in a harsh way. She might have been depressed. She might have had other issues at home. The truth is, no one outside the Sears family really knew what was going on with her. But Charlotte definitely took it hard. She was openly angry with Aaron for a while, but people move on, or they bury it."

Cassie's expression was thoughtful. "We found reprinted articles in Aaron's house. News articles about Kristy's death. It might be almost understandable if he'd felt the need to hold onto her memory at the time but these were freshly minted, so to speak. Strange he'd have them."

"They were printed recently?"

She nodded. "Yes. Possibly within days. It's odd. That's why I'm here asking."

Tom inhaled sharply. "So what's the link to his murder?"

Cassie shrugged. "We can't jump to any conclusion like

that. But it's definitely something we need to look into. It might be something or nothing. Did he discover new info about Kristy's death? Was he feeling remorseful for something? Or was he using it as leverage against someone?"

"Like who?" Tom asked.

"That's the question, isn't it?"

Tom frowned. "I met Charlotte for a coffee and she asked me to come to the vigil they had planned for Kristy. It was the anniversary of her death."

"Odd that Aaron happens to die at the same time, huh?" Cassie said.

"Charlotte was emotional, but it didn't seem like she harboured any animosity towards Aaron. If anything, she'd made some peace with the tragedy, even if it still hurts her. She spoke of him at the vigil too."

"Aaron?"

Tom nodded. "Yes."

"Guilty conscience?" Cassie asked. Tom shook his head.

"That wasn't my impression."

"Shame." Cassie studied him. "That would be nice and neat."

"It's never nice and neat though is it?" Tom said with a wry smile. "Why do you think he was collecting those articles then?"

"No clue," she said.

Tom considered it. "Maybe he was seeking closure. Aaron had that side to his personality. He was cocky, but sometimes privately conflicted." Tom rubbed his temple. "Listen, Cass, it always struck me as harsh to blame him for Kristy's suicide. Relationships break up all the time. People needed a scapegoat for their grief. He... kind of became that."

Cassie took that in quietly, her gaze flicking around the living room. "Maybe so. But if there's anything else you recall

– like rumours that the break-up was especially ugly – it could be relevant."

Tom shook his head. "He was never physically violent with her, as far as I know. They seemed to be the perfect fifth form couple. Neither of them was unattractive. They were the Posh and Becks of their day. At our school anyway. Besides, people would have found out. It was more that he could be callous or manipulative. Or, to put it simply, a typical teenage jerk at times. He had that streak, being popular, good-looking, you know how it is."

"Right," Cassie murmured, tapping her fingernails softly on the rim of her mug. "Thanks, Tom. That helps frame the bigger picture. I have an unofficial interview lined up with Charlotte. I'll have to ask her directly whether there's animosity around Kristy's death."

Tom nodded. After a moment, he glanced at the screen again. The interview with David was still on his mind. "So… is your official line that the killer is someone close to him, like David thinks."

Cassie let out a sigh. "Yes. That's the working theory. We're leaning heavily on the personal angle—"

"Has the name Whale come up at all?" Tom asked. "Shaun Whale?"

She put her mug down. "Who is Shaun Whale?"

"Someone Elena Novak mentioned," Tom said carefully. "She told me Aaron had been making payments from their joint account, or maybe some trust funds, paying significant sums to a man called Shaun Whale. She thought it suspect. She was insistent it might tie in."

Cassie's eyes narrowed in interest. "We haven't come across that name yet. If Elena's worried about it, she didn't share it with us when we spoke to her."

Tom shrugged. "She's protective of her father's business,

the Novak family business. She spoke of Aaron trying to undermine them. Possibly."

Cassie raised an eyebrow. "She told you that? You told me you're not actively investigating."

"No, you told me not to do anything," Tom said, "and I'm not." He spoke a bit too quickly and Cassie cocked her head, marking him with a steely gaze. "She cornered me, basically. She wants… well, she wants answers."

Cassie nodded slowly, measuring his words. "All right. I'll bring that name up. Eric is looking at the finances today, so we'll cross-check bank statements for any reference to him. See if it's legit or if Elena's fishing."

Cassie finished her drink. "Anything else you think we should know?"

He paused, mind flicking through half-formed thoughts relating to Tony Slater and Noah Cook. "What about Noah? Have you interviewed him yet?"

"Not yet. We plan to. Tony Slater was the primary one, seeing as he told us they had an actual fight. Noah was an exchanged word." She gave a wry grimace. "I'm collecting them like stamps. Don't worry. He's on the list. I can already guess how the conversation will go; we parted ways and I never saw him again."

"Yes, that's usually the way." Tom let out a faint laugh, but it died in his throat. "I suppose if it were a spontaneous argument, the killer wouldn't be too quick to admit it."

Cassie pursed her lips. "We'll keep pressing. Thanks for the coffee. And for your insights. We'll see how it lines up once I've spoken to Charlotte. If you remember anything else about Kristy, or anything relevant, let me know."

"I will," Tom promised. "You see Charlotte as a suspect?"

Cassie shook her head. "Not especially. You know me, cynical as hell. I see everyone as a suspect."

"Fair enough."

She glanced again at the muted TV, which was now airing a cooking segment. "I have a suspicion the boss is going to be fuming about David's little cameo. I'll probably find out in the next hour."

"I don't envy you," Tom said, smiling.

Cassie headed for the front door and Tom went with her. "Hey, Tom… maybe you should switch off from the coverage of this case for a bit."

He inhaled, nodding slowly. "Easier said than done."

"Yeah," she admitted, opening the door and feeling the draw of warm air wash over her. "I understand. See you soon. Oh, one more thing," she said. Tom arched his eyebrows quizzically. "I have to run your fingerprints—"

"To finalise the crime scene," he said and she nodded. "No problem."

Cassie smiled, turned and resumed her course, offering him a wave as she headed towards an unmarked car across the street. He watched her go, the sense of being left behind again creeping in. She'd kindly told him to step away, but the more he tried, the more the case seemed to find him.

CHAPTER SIXTEEN

Tom tried to distract himself with chores but none of them fully occupied his thoughts. The interview with David White kept replaying in his mind. An emotional murder, a personal spat. Meanwhile, the name Shaun Whale echoed. If Aaron had poured thousands into someone's account, that spelled blackmail, hush money, or a potential partner turned enemy. Or it could be nothing of the sort, and be something completely legitimate.

By mid-afternoon, it was time to fetch Saffy from school. Tom let Russell know he wouldn't be long – a habit he'd formed of late – locked up, pocketed his keys, and made the short drive to the small primary school. Cloud cover had thickened, but the air was still fairly bright, feeling much like the transition from spring to summer.

He joined the throng of parents at the school's tall iron gate, nodding hello to one or two faces he'd become familiar with since he'd been doing the daily drop-off. Today, no one seemed particularly chatty. As usual, the queue had clusters of mums deep in conversation and some lone dads waiting quietly. Tom made a habit of reading faces. It was a subtle habit he'd learned on the job.

He noticed a couple of parents standing off to one side. The man was absently scrolling through his mobile, or that's what he seemed to want people to think. In fact he was flicking glances at the other parent, a woman, standing nearby. She was in a casual conversation with another mum but was only making a show of listening. Her eyes though, were elsewhere.

Tom recognised the man. James, if he remembered rightly. He was the father of a girl in Saffy's class. The woman was shorter than he was, dressed elegantly, and Tom had seen her around before but didn't know her name. He thought she might have a little boy in the year below Saffy's, but he wasn't sure. They were not obviously interacting, but Tom caught the quick, meaningful looks they exchanged. The subtle flicker of a smile that was almost intimate.

He sighed inwardly. People thought they were hiding their private alliances or yearnings, but even in mundane locations like a school playground it was clear if you knew what to look for. Maybe it was just a silly flirtation, or maybe more. He spotted how they casually stood a few yards apart, never letting their gazes linger too long. But they mirrored each other's posture. Subtle.

It made him think again of hidden secrets. One moment you see a friendly neighbour or colleague and the next, you discover an undercurrent that changes everything. He thought of Charlotte and Noah, of Tony Slater, the tension in the reunion hall. They'd all had old resentments buried for decades. Then there was Elena Novak. Now she had a back story he'd love to get into and he'd only scratched the surface.

The school doors screeched open and pupils began to spill out, eyes searching among the gathered adults for their parents. Tom straightened and waved, and soon enough,

Saffy's bright face appeared. She beamed at him, lifting her book bag into the air in triumph. She was near the front of the queue as they were led out and her teacher touched her shoulder, indicating she could go. Saffy broke into a run.

He crouched slightly, arms out, and she nearly bowled him over with the force of her hug. "Hello, munchkin," he said, ruffling her hair. "Did you have a good day?"

She nodded vigorously, stepping back to give him a big grin. Her face and uniform were neat enough, though there was green chalk residue smudged on one sleeve. "Yes, we had to sketch in class and I pictured a story about pirates!"

"Pirates, huh?" Tom hoisted her little backpack from her shoulders, carrying it for her as they stepped aside so other parents could collect their children. She offered him her book bag as well but he declined the offer, insisting she carried it herself.

"Can we read something about pirates tonight?"

He laughed, taking her hand. "Absolutely. I'm sure I can find something at home and, if not, we can make up our own story."

"That'll be so lame," Saffy said.

"Lame?" Tom repeated with mock indignation. "Let's just see if my creativity can match up to your own pirate knowledge, young lady."

As they moved through the gates into the car park, Tom clocked the same pair of parents – James and the elegant woman – walking out in close proximity. They chanced a quick glance at one another. The barest flicker of a shared smile. Then they looked away again, as if they'd never met.

Tom ushered Saffy along, the hum of conversation drifting behind them from the rest of the parents asking questions of their children as they walked. The pair parted in different directions, no words exchanged. Tom's detective instincts could almost script it. They're either in a secret relationship or flirting on the edge of one. He forced himself to focus on her, to be present.

"So, who did you pretend to be in the pirate story? The captain or the fearless first mate?"

"Me and Isobel took turns! Sometimes I was the captain, but I like being the treasure map maker more." She marched forward, brandishing an imaginary scroll.

"Treasure maps, huh? A new calling."

She giggled, and Tom's heart filled with warmth. For a moment, the heavier reflections from earlier – David White's theories, Kristy Sears' tragedy – receded behind the simpler joy of Saffy's delight. They reached the car but by this time his thoughts had drifted back to Charlotte and her sister's vigil.

The image of people standing in solemn silence, tears in Charlotte's eyes, and the wind whipping her hair as she spoke about her sister's memory. Was it all heartbreak or was there resentment too? Noah was there too, watching on despite the apparently strained relationship between him and his ex regarding their son's future. He considered the would-be couple with the potential for their secret tryst. They were regular people. They had regular lives, and yet they could be leading a double life. A life so secret and hidden that no one would know about it. What secrets did people keep? Hidden lives, passions or desires, that could lead to murder.

In the end though, was it something as straightforward as David White's commentary suggested? Tension building, a confrontation, a single strike, panic. Then, an attempt to erase the evidence. Or perhaps it was more cunning if the CCTV was removed. The gulf between an emotional outburst and a meticulous cover-up troubled Tom.

"Daddy?" Saffy's voice cut through his reverie. "Are you listening?"

He realised he'd drifted. "Sorry, munchkin. My brain got stuck on something. Say that again?"

She gave him a forgiving smile from the passenger seat beside him. "I was saying, can we have pasta tonight? Like the cheesy one you make but without cheese."

Tom laughed. "With bacon? The British carbonara recipe?"

"Definitely with bacon," Saffy said. "But I get the most of the bacon, because it's my favourite bit."

"Sure. Non-cheesy pasta it is."

Saffy beamed again, kicking her feet in the air in delight. Tom tried to quell the thoughts coming to mind. Focus on dinner. On your daughter. He started the car and pulled out of the space. Coming to the main road, he had to wait for oncoming traffic to pass. He caught the eye of a driver coming past him in a white BMW. It was James. He saw Tom looking and offered a polite nod. Tom nodded back, and the car passed. Tom reminded himself that people's secrets were not always sinister. Sometimes they're just private, personal, or even trivial. But sometimes, secrets kill.

He caught Saffy watching him and after he pulled out, he glanced sideways at her.

"Are you tired?" she asked with childlike directness.

"A bit," he admitted.

She gave him a concerned look. "We can read the pirate book tomorrow if you want. If you need to rest."

Tom's chest tightened at her kindness. She was so small, yet so empathetic. "No, munchkin, we'll do it tonight. I promise. I'm fine."

She nodded, seemingly content. They reached their home soon after. Tom unlocked the door and stepped inside, letting her scurry ahead. He forced himself to put aside thoughts of Aaron Bell, Kristy Sears, and everything in between. At least for now, Saffy came first.

An hour later, as Tom stirred a sauce on the hob, he realised the day's events had left him with more questions than answers. Cassie's visit had only heightened them. The conversation about Kristy Sears revived old memories he wasn't sure how to interpret. Why would Aaron have newspaper clippings of Kristy's suicide now? It made no sense.

He lowered the heat under the saucepan. While waiting for the pasta water to boil, he moved to the counter and scrolled quickly through his phone, scanning local news. Indeed, the local stations were replaying David White's interview. Several articles repeated his claims about an emotional scenario amid speculation that the killer was a friend or colleague. He set the phone aside, shutting off those distractions. Cassie said to unplug. That's what he should do. Leave it to Cassie and Tamara. They knew what they were doing.

Minutes later, Saffy tugged at his arm, pulling him to the table where she'd set out cutlery in a slightly haphazard manner. She pointed to a purple plastic cup. "That's for me, daddy. I'm the only one who likes purple!"

Tom winked. "I know. Don't worry." The front door opened and Russell leapt up, excitedly wagging his stump of a tail before running to intercept Alice. "Great timing!" Tom called. I'm just about to serve up.

He drained the pasta, poured the sauce, and within moments they were sitting together, Saffy chattering about her day to her mum. Tom though, engaged with the puzzle of Aaron's death quietly in his mind. He picked up his mobile once everyone had finished eating and did a quick search of the internet with the name of Shaun Whale. There were a surprising number of returns and he realised he'd need to narrow it down. He would do so later on.

Alice gave him a look. One of those looks that said he should be present and not lose himself in his phone. He smiled apologetically and put the phone down, pushing it aside. Alice inclined her head, winked at him and then looked at her daughter who was recanting another pirate moment from her exceptionally busy day. Saffy eventually completed her analysis of her day at school and Alice ushered her upstairs where she had run her a bath.

Once Saffy was settled, playing happily in the water, Alice returned downstairs where Tom had almost finished clearing away.

"So... what's on your mind?" she asked. He looked at her innocently. "I know you, Tom Janssen. Something is eating away at you. Out with it."

He laughed, finishing loading the dishwasher. He closed it and turned his back to the counter, leaning against it and folding his arms.

"It's Aaron."

"I thought it might be."

"There's something going on... but it's like," he collected his thoughts "it's like when you can almost see something but as soon as you turn to look it's gone." He narrowed his eyes. "Do you know what I mean?"

"Sort of," Alice said. "But you know this isn't your—"

"No, no. I know I'm not working. But..."

"You're a policeman," Alice said. "And you can't just switch it off."

"That's it." He sighed. "In a nutshell."

Alice came over to him and slipped her arms around his waist, looking up at him. "So, DI Janssen. What are you going to do about it?"

"Nothing," he said, regretfully. "I can't get involved."

"But you are involved, Tom. Even if you shouldn't be."

Tom's mobile rang and Alice detached from him and he

picked it up. It was Cassie. "Hey, Cass. What can I do for you?"

"Shaun Whale," Cassie said. "I've been doing a little digging."

"Find anything interesting?"

"That depends. Did Aaron say anything to you about what he had going on in his life at the moment?"

Tom was thoughtful. "Marriage in pieces... a lack of direction," he said. "Nothing that isn't common for a man of our age... sadly," he added, spotting Alice giving him another look from across the kitchen. He smiled and she returned it. "Why do you ask?"

"Shaun Whale, or at least the Shaun Whale I've managed to find, is a private investigator."

"Curious," Tom said. "Investigating what?"

"I would love to ask him," Cassie said. I tried to call him earlier but his phone cuts to voicemail every time."

"Maybe he's on a case?"

"Or he's avoiding the police. I wonder why he might choose to do that?"

"It is a mystery," Tom said. "Where is he based?"

"Delightfully vague about that," Cassie said. "He covers London and the east."

"What are you going to do?"

"I'll keep trying him. He'll resurface at some point."

"How did you get on with Charlotte?"

"I'm just on my way to see her now," Cassie said. "She put me back. She said she had something on, but she didn't elaborate and I didn't want to push."

"Sorry I couldn't be more helpful," Tom said.

"Yeah, bloody useless," Cassie said. "But I still like you." She hung up. Tom took a deep breath. Then he typed Shaun Whale into his phone again, only this time added private detective to the search bar. The third return, below the sponsored advertisements for private investigation services, was a website for SWI; *Shaun Whale Investigations*. Tom heard Saffy playfully shout from the bathroom above them.

"I'll go and check on her," Alice said. "I have to wash her hair anyway."

Tom waited for Alice to leave the kitchen and then he dialled the contact number on the website. Just as Cassie had found, the call went to voicemail. Tom listened to the automated voice then when he had the chance, he left a message.

"Hello, Shaun." He angled his head to see into the hallway to make sure Alice wasn't still there. "My name is Tom and I'm a friend of Aaron Bell's. I know what you were doing for him… and it's in your interests for us to talk. Call me back on this number. Any time."

A FAINT BEEP disturbed Tom from his light sleep. At first he thought he'd imagined it, but the screen on his phone lit up the bedroom. He glanced at Alice beside him but she was sleeping soundly. Then he checked the time. It was one o'clock in the morning. He slipped out from beneath the duvet and gathered his phone, hurrying from the bedroom as quickly as he could without running the risk of waking Alice.

He went through into the spare bedroom and pushed the door to as he answered the call. It was from an unknown number.

He was groggy, having been woken abruptly. "Hello."

"We need to talk." It was a male voice. "Tomorrow, if possible."

"I can do tomorrow. Where?"

"Somewhere out of the way."

Tom thought quickly. "Do you know the marina. Over by—"

"Your boat?"

Tom was instantly alert. "How do you know I have a boat?"

"You think I would call you without doing my homework first? You're a detective – or you were – so you know how these things work."

Tom considered that. He'd used his personal mobile phone to call. That leaves a traceable route back to him. It wouldn't be hard for someone to find the owner. Personal data are easy to find on the internet, if you know where to look.

"My boat. Nine-thirty tomorrow morning," Tom said.

"I'll be there at ten."

The call ended. Tom glanced at the screen, then touched the mobile to his lips. He'd just crossed a line. And there was no going back. He made his way back into the bedroom. Alice stirred as he got back into bed but she didn't wake. Tom turned the screen off, placing the mobile face-down so it would hibernate and not disturb them again. He forced a breath, closed his eyes, and tried to slip back to sleep. Outside, the wind gusted through the trees at the end of the garden. Everything was normal.

Tomorrow, he would get some answers.

CHAPTER SEVENTEEN

Tom Janssen knelt below deck on his modest boat, rubbing a smudge of grime off the small gas stove top in the galley. Even though the morning sun had been up for hours, the cabin still felt dim and cool. He hadn't actually taken the old vessel out on the water for months; life had thrown too many detours at him, and his suspension from the force had left him juggling self-doubt, restlessness, and a lingering sense of unfinished business. He should have had more time to do so but, paradoxically, the opposite had occurred.

But the boat was still his refuge, even moored at Blakeney's quay: a cramped-space that smelled of salt and rubber, with pitted wood trim and well-worn seats. It was nothing flashy, just a serviceable little craft that had been something of a hobby for him for many years. He used to come here for peace, and that had been in short supply in recent weeks.

A rhythmic, hollow knock sounded against the hull: two short raps, then a pause, then a third. Tom straightened, brow furrowing. He'd suggested meeting here, a neutral location where he was visible to both his visitor and the general public. He didn't wish to scare Shaun Whale off. Cassie hadn't managed to get hold of him and Tom deduced since Aaron's death, he would have reason to stay low and out of sight.

Was that something to do with Aaron's death or simply the man being unsure and acting cautiously? That was what Tom intended to find out. He carefully set aside the rag he'd been holding and climbed the narrow steps to the deck, stooping low so he didn't clip his head on the overhead beam.

He emerged into the morning sunshine. A crisp breeze rolled in off the marshes between the harbour and the sea, bringing with it the tang of salt in the air and the soft call of gulls whirling overhead. The harbour's water lapped gently at the hull, and the mooring lines creaked whenever the boat gave a slight tilt. On the quayside, a figure stood waiting.

Tom stepped to the boat's starboard side, where a short wooden walkway and the harbour's stone edge met. The man on the quay was in his late thirties or maybe early forties, with a trim, athletic build, wearing a plain blue smock, dark trousers, and practical boots. Nothing about him shouted fashion or flamboyance. Instead, there was a pragmatic efficiency in his stance. Tom found himself scanning the man's posture: straight back, squared shoulders, chin raised just slightly.

"Are you Tom?" the stranger asked, voice low but carrying well over the soft noises of daily life in Blakeney. "Or did I get the wrong boat?"

Tom nodded once, taking in the man's short hair, the watchful set of his eyes. "I'm Tom Janssen," he replied. "Shaun Whale, I assume?"

The man dipped his head. "That's right."

"Go ahead, come aboard. Watch your step though," Tom added, gesturing at the slight gap between the quay and the deck. He'd seen too many people misjudge that small distance and end up stumbling awkwardly.

Shaun hopped over with fluid ease, hardly bothering to glance at where he placed his foot. Tom recognised that sure-footedness. It reminded him of military types who carried themselves in a particular manner.

"So this is your man cave, huh?" Shaun said, casting an appraising look around the deck. The boat rocked lightly beneath them, and Tom gripped a railing post to keep his balance.

Tom smiled. "Yes, something like that." Tom shrugged. "She's not been out in a while, but she's better than a pool table and a dartboard."

Shaun walked a slow circle, stepping carefully around the support strut for the wheelhouse cover. Tom let the silence hang for a moment, both men sizing each other up in the morning sunshine. Finally, Shaun spoke. "You said on the phone that we needed to talk." He spread his hands wide. "So here we are."

"Here we are," Tom repeated.

Shaun slid his hands into his jacket pockets. "You left that message saying, quote, 'I know what you've been doing.' I'm here to find out precisely what you think you know."

Tom gazed back steadily. "I know you were working for Aaron Bell. He's dead, and I'm trying to figure out why." He let the gulls cry overhead for a second or two. "Are you going to deny it?"

Shaun's jaw worked momentarily, then he let out a quiet exhale. "I'm not denying it. But I'm curious why a suspended detective is in the loop, rather than the actual investigating officers. Or, for that matter, why you'd come poking around into my business."

Tom considered the comment. Shaun had been doing his homework on him. He shouldn't be surprised.

"You've been busy then," Tom said.

"I did a little rummaging around after you called me... looking through public records, social media and the like. I know your standing in the police is... complicated at the moment."

Tom managed not to bristle. "You're not the only one who can do his homework, but yes, it's complicated. Aaron was an old friend from school, that's all. This is nothing official."

"You're just helping them out... off the books?"

"Helping myself, more like," Tom answered. "We may not have been close in recent years, but I have reasons to want to see Aaron's killer found."

Shaun's expression wavered. "Well, that's your prerogative. But if the local police want to talk, they can reach out. I'm easy enough to find if they dig a bit."

"Then why not pick up your phone to them? They've been calling."

Shaun's gaze narrowed and they stared at one another. "So... I've been busy," he said, shrugging. "They'll need to be more persistent. As far as I know, I'm not on any official suspect list. Am I?"

Tom ignored the question. "Yet you didn't come forward," Tom said pointedly. "If you're clean, why avoid them?"

Shaun shrugged again, though tension was visible in his expression despite his best efforts to convey the opposite. "Because a man I was working for turned up dead. Murdered no less. That spells trouble for me, no matter what. I prefer to keep my distance until someone figures out who actually killed him and why. Call it self-preservation, if you like."

Tom heard the words echo in his head. The same logic he'd encountered with numerous reluctant witnesses. They never wanted to step into the spotlight of a murder inquiry, no matter how tangential they might be. "You worry about being blamed?"

Shaun's gaze flicked to the water. "You never know. I have a job that often requires a... covert set of skills. It doesn't pay for me to be highly visible to the wider world. It harms business, if you know what I mean?" He sighed. "What I do treads a fine line."

"A line I presume you cross from time to time?"

Shaun tilted his head. "On occasion, if needed. I wouldn't really care for any official scrutiny of my business. I'm sure you can understand that. Besides, everyone wants a convenient scapegoat when things get tough. That's how the world works, especially if Aaron's killer has a better story than I do."

Tom inhaled, nodding. "I understand. But I also know you might hold information that helps lead us to the killer. Or at least figure out what got Aaron into trouble in the first place."

Shaun gave a short, humourless chuckle. "And here I was thinking you might have all the answers already, from the tone of that voicemail, it sounded like you did."

"Maybe I was bluffing a little," Tom admitted, "but that's only because I need to know what you did for him. I'm asking politely, and not as a policeman. Out of courtesy, and off the record."

Shaun looked at Tom for a long moment, as though debating how much to say. Finally, he gave a small nod. "All right. I'll tell you some, but not all. I'm a private investigator and although confidentiality is irrelevant with my client dead, my reputation for discretion still applies—"

"Even though your client is dead?"

"Especially now my client is dead," Shaun said matter-of-factly. "Self-preservation, remember? Typically, my clients want me to run background checks, track suspicious partners or maybe do some discreet surveillance every now and again. More often than not I'm simply serving sensitive documents on individuals." He inclined his head. "My clients don't usually turn up dead, you know."

"Not usually?" Tom asked. "How often has it happened?"

"Never," he replied curtly and took a deep breath. "Aaron Bell hired me about a month ago."

"For what purpose?"

"He told me to focus on two names. Charlotte Sears and Noah Cook. He asked me to build a complete picture of their lives. We're talking finances, relationship history, personal background, that sort of thing. He wanted to know everything about them, plus a full work-up of their family including the child they share, Dean, and how he fits into the wider family dynamic."

"Any particular reason why?" Tom pressed. "Did Aaron say?"

Shaun hesitated, then shrugged. "He never spelled it out. He implied it was personal rather than business. Maybe he had a thing for Charlotte. I couldn't blame him, she is pretty cute, or some vendetta against Noah. Who knows? He didn't share it with me and it's none of my concern at the end of the day. My brief was simply to dig. He wanted me to explore how they ended up, from the time they were at school together until now."

"What about Kristy?" Tom asked. Shaun fixed his gaze on him.

"The sister? Aaron said the starting point for me was the aftermath of her death but, and he was very firm on this point, he didn't want me investigating the actual suicide. He only cared about how people reacted to it, what they said in the media, and how it shaped Charlotte and Noah's future."

Tom felt the gentle sway of the deck beneath his feet. His pulse quickened. It was odd to him that Aaron wasn't curious about the suicide itself. "He specifically only wanted the aftermath?"

"Exactly," Shaun said. "I was surprised. It's not typical. Most clients want me to follow up on everything but Aaron was explicit. Nothing about the actual event. Only the social, emotional, and legal fallout. He said it was a tragedy and best left alone. I guessed, right or wrong, he was looking for leverage—"

"A fancy term for blackmail."

Shaun smiled without humour. "Maybe so, but I didn't ask. Like I said—"

"That's none of your business." Tom ran a hand through his hair, exhaling. "What might he use that leverage for?"

"I have no idea. And I didn't ask."

Tom was thoughtful. "You concluded your investigation recently? Did you give him a report or something?"

Shaun nodded. "I sent him preliminary findings about a week ago. He wanted more details on something specific, but that wasn't easy to establish and I was still working on it. Then, a couple of days later, he… well. He turns up dead. That was a bit of a surprise."

"What was it he was interested in?" Tom asked. "That he wanted more information on?"

"Forgive me," Shaun said, mock-grimacing. "But I think I've gone as far as I'm willing to go."

Both men fell silent for a moment. The gulls overhead circled, and a few voices drifted from the quay, as people strolled past. Tom felt a storm of questions coming to mind, but forced himself to speak calmly. "Can you think of a reason your investigation might have got him killed?"

Shaun let out a slow breath. "No, I can't." Tom watched him closely, gauging his sincerity. He seemed straight enough. "People do drastic things when it comes to secrets but, from what I found, Charlotte and Noah have fairly standard baggage. They married young. They have a grown son, they divorced. There's some financial tension, yes. But I didn't see anything that would incite murder. I'm no expert, though. Maybe something I dug up was dynamite to them, or maybe it threatened someone else in that circle. I can't say. If it did then it passed me by."

"What about Elena Novak, Aaron's estranged wife? There's talk that Aaron was tapping into her funds for unknown reasons. What would you say to that?"

Shaun shook his head, straight faced. "Elena Novak never got a mention with me. If Aaron Bell was up to something dodgy with his estranged wife, then that's news to me. And it's also not my problem."

Tom absorbed that, crossing his arms, and letting the boat's gentle rock steady him. "So as far as you're concerned, that's the full story? Just a routine background check on Charlotte and Noah?"

"That's it. If there's more, then it's above my pay grade. I don't generally handle murder cases, Tom. That's more your field of expertise than mine."

Tom nodded slowly. "Yes, so what is your background?"

Shaun tilted his head. "I'm ex-military police. Drunken fights, petty theft and handing out on-base speeding tickets were much more my scene. Murder? Not so much. If the police want me, they can talk to me, but while there's some nutter wandering about, I'm not volunteering to stick my head up for the attention, if you know what I mean."

"Then I suggest you stay reachable," Tom said firmly. "Because if the lead detective – DS Knight – needs your statement, and you vanish, people will assume you've got something to hide and that might derail the flow of the investigation."

Shaun studied Tom's face. A moment passed, and he spread his hands. "I'm not planning to go walkabout, Tom. I just like to keep out of the spotlight. So let's say I stay... around. If DS Knight wants me, she can phone me. However, between you and me," he said, his nose wrinkling, "I'll say much less than I've told you this morning. I don't want or need the attention."

The tension in the air calmed a touch, and Tom stepped back, leaning an elbow on one of the upright rods near the stairs to below deck. "Let me ask... do you have any theory, any guess, about who you think might have done this?"

A flicker of genuine uncertainty showed in Shaun's eyes. "None. Like I said, murder is not my area. People can kill each other over the smallest thing these days. What can I say, it's an angry world. I didn't see any glaring motive in what I dug up regarding Charlotte and Noah. They have had, and continue to, have plenty of drama in their lives, but it seemed typical, not lethal. It also had nothing to do with Aaron as far as I could tell." He shrugged. "It was easy money for me."

Tom nodded again. "All right. In that case, I appreciate your candour."

Shaun exhaled deeply and glanced back at the quay. "Are we through here?"

"I think so," Tom said. "Where are you staying?"

"Around," Shaun repeated, as vague as ever. "I'm between hotels, caravan parks. Text me if you want me and I'll reply. Fair enough?"

Tom wanted more certainty but sensed he'd get nowhere pushing the man. "Fair enough," he repeated.

With that, Shaun moved to the edge of the boat. He hopped back onto the quay with that same quiet agility. He turned to face Tom once more, voice lower as a couple walking their dog passed by, pitched so only Tom could hear.

"I'm sorry about your friend. For what it's worth, I never pegged him as the type to get himself murdered, but maybe I misjudged the situation."

Tom gave a stiff nod. "Appreciate it."

In another moment, Shaun turned away, the sound of his footsteps drowned out by the general hum of activity in the harbour. The breeze carried the scent of diesel from a skiff passing by his boat, mingling with the salt air. Tom stayed where he was for a while, processing the information Shaun Whale offered him. Eventually, he turned and went back down the short steps into the galley. The confined space felt even narrower than before, as if the conversation with Shaun Whale had added tension below deck.

He flicked on a small light overhead, noticing how the cabin was in half-shadows despite the bright sunshine. Letting out a long breath, Tom braced his hands on the countertop. Aaron had hired a private investigator to compile information on Charlotte Sears and Noah Cook, focussing specifically on the aftermath of Kristy's tragic death and nothing beforehand. The reaction. The blame game, perhaps? Why though?

Tom's mind reeled. He recalled the many whispers surrounding Aaron and whether he was at fault for Kristy's downward spiral. Was it heartbreak that'd pushed her over the edge. That hadn't been Aaron's desire, to investigate the actual cause of her death, and so Tom was puzzled as to what his end goal was. What was he after in all of this? Did he know something that he'd never mentioned before and was seeking to confirm it with Shaun's investigation? But he found nothing. That's what Shaun said, at least, and Tom thought he was genuine in that conclusion.

Could it be that Aaron suspected Charlotte or Noah of something larger, wanting to confirm or disprove a theory about them? The idea that this personal feud – or obsession –

had escalated into murder troubled him. His thoughts flicked to the memory of Charlotte's tearful face during the vigil for Kristy up on Sheringham cliffs. She'd been upset, sure, but was it sadness for her sister or was there something more? Had she known Aaron was snooping into her private life again, stirring up old ghosts? Could that knowledge have driven her or Noah to do something drastic? And, speaking of Noah, Tom had to wonder how and where he might fit into all of this?

He was however reassured that Shaun's investigations had yielded nothing of note. Arguably, it was much more likely that it had nothing to do with Aaron's death. Charlotte was intense, but also warm at times, seemingly genuinely haunted by the tragedy of Kristy's death. And Noah, from Tom's limited vantage, seemed tired, and far from homicidal. But people's external faces weren't always an honest reflection of what lay behind the public mask.

Stepping back up onto the deck, Tom inhaled deeply, letting the damp breeze fill his lungs. The morning was wearing on, and the harbour was getting busier with people making the most of the clement weather and prepping their boats for getting out on the water. Tom decided to head home. He'd garnered what he wanted to know, but it didn't offer him the answers he'd hoped for. He locked up, checked the mooring lines, and stepped off onto the quay.

Aaron Bell's secrets ran deep, and apparently extended to investigating the sister of his teenage girlfriend, Kristy. However, it wasn't in the way Tom might have guessed. If that mystery was indeed the spark that lit the fuse leading to Aaron's death, then the next question was who among that circle of old classmates found Aaron an implicit threat?

Tom moved away, picking his way through what passed for a crowd mid-morning on Blakeney quayside, heading back to his car. As he reached it, he took his mobile from his jacket pocket, considering his next move. Cassie needed to hear this but he thought it was unlikely to be the breakthrough he might have hoped it would be. Driving away from Blakeney's quay, Tom cast one last glance in the rear view mirror. If only one good outcome came from his meeting with Shaun Whale, that he now had a greater sense of Aaron's obsession, then it did give Tom pause for thought. Obsession was a strong term but, in Tom's mind, it was exactly that, an obsession. No one hired a private investigator to look into people unless they had a reason. It didn't necessarily have to be a good reason either. Tom found himself wondering what Aaron was looking for.

CHAPTER EIGHTEEN

Detective Sergeant Cassie Knight eased her unmarked car into the small gravel car park, the crunch of stones beneath the wheels sounding in the cabin. Next to her, DC Eric Collet flipped through his notebook, but he paused to glance at the scene unfolding before them. Two liveried police cars were parked at angles across the entrance, their blue-and-yellow decals reflecting the bright lunchtime sunshine. A gaggle of onlookers had already formed a loose half ring behind the police cordon, necks craning for a glimpse of what was happening. A few smartphones were raised, capturing the drama.

Cassie turned off the engine, exchanged a nod with Eric, and they both got out. Immediately, the chill coastal breeze nipped at them, carrying the scent of brine to them. The building in front of them was a restaurant: a tidy, white-painted single-storey place with a sign mounted on the exterior reading *Tony's Seafood and Grill*. The restaurant that Cassie would expect to be busy with the approach of the lunchtime trade was closed, a uniformed presence standing on the entrance door.

A familiar face stepped away from the taped area, raising a hand in greeting, DC Danny Wilson. He wore a sombre expression, beckoning them over. "Sarge, Eric," he said, lowering his voice as they approached. "Tony Slater," he said, looking between them. "It's a bad one."

Cassie felt a prickling behind her eyes. "Tony Slater. Aaron Bell's old classmate? The same guy who argued with him at the reunion?"

Danny let out a quiet sigh. "Yeah, the same one. He's inside." He gestured with a nod for them to follow him. They ducked under the cordon tape. One of the uniformed constables nodded but stayed put, keeping a watchful eye on the gathering of the curious locals. A handful of them whispered among themselves, pointing at the restaurant. Cassie knew word would spread quickly. Bad news always did.

"Where's the body?" Eric asked, scanning the empty outdoor seating area to either side of the entrance doors, a collection of wooden picnic-style benches with parasols. None of them were open, marking the restaurant as not ready to trade.

"In the kitchen," Danny replied. "Morgan Slater – his wife – found him. She came in just before midday, said she'd been visiting a client in Burnham Market for much of the morning. She says she got a phone call from one of the kitchen hands who'd arrived for work but found it all shut up. When she got home, she found the front door to the restaurant locked and no sign of staff, so she used her key. She came through and that's when she found him in the back."

Cassie could sense Eric growing tense beside her. They all remembered Tony from the earlier interviews. He was the man who'd had the physical altercation with Aaron Bell at the school reunion. The one Tom had broken up. If this was another suspicious death in the same peer group then it was a troubling coincidence, at best, and/or something much more sinister.

"All right," Cassie said. "Show us."

They stepped through the main doors into a modest dining area which had a wall of glass to the rear offering an uninterrupted view over the marshes towards the sea in the distance. Tables were neatly set; tablecloths still pristine, wine glasses arranged in symmetrical pairs. The restaurant evidently prided itself on order and presentation. Now, it felt eerily quiet.

Danny led them deeper inside, weaving through the vacant chairs. "Morgan says—"

"Are you on first name terms with the widow already?" Cassie asked. Danny flushed.

"Mrs Slater… said they don't usually open until five, and only for dinner service these days. They've been struggling with staff retention and so they only have one person come in to give a hand prepping for the evening service. More staff come in closer to four o'clock. Tony was the only one scheduled in the morning for prep work. The one helper who contacted Morg— Mrs Slater when he couldn't get in, and then no other staff until mid-afternoon."

They passed the bar, a compact station with neatly lined bottles, then came to the kitchen's swinging double doors. A uniformed officer stepped aside to let them through. The instant Cassie entered, she caught the metallic smell of fresh blood mingling with the usual kitchen odours of onions, stale cooking oil, and the occasional whiff of cleaning chemicals. There was a strong smell of seafood and Cassie found a crate on the counter with various cuts of fish, scampi and several whole lobsters inside.

"They had a delivery of fresh produce around ten o'clock,"

Danny said, consulting his notes. "After that, we've no idea who came or went."

Tony Slater lay on his side on the tiled floor, dressed in a white chef's jacket and chequered trousers. His jacket was spattered with red and a large crimson stain spread out from the point it'd been pierced. A single, large kitchen knife jutted from his chest, the handle protruding at an oblique angle. The pooling blood spread around him, soaking into the fabric and gradually creeping across the floor's surface. It wasn't a subtle wound. Cassie thought there was a good chance it had pierced his heart. Based on the volume of blood on and around him, he must have bled out quickly.

Cassie and Eric stayed back, letting their eyes sweep the scene rather than stepping too close. They didn't want to disturb any evidence. DC Wilson hovered near a stainless-steel counter, flipping through his notes.

"What was the time of discovery again?" Cassie asked, voice subdued as she studied the crime scene. Danny consulted his notes again. "Morgan Slater called it in at eleven fifty-five."

Eric knelt as close as he dared without compromising the blood spatter. He peered at Tony's hands. "He's got injuries on his forearms, palm and fingers. Looks like defensive wounds to me. He tried to fight off whoever was coming at him wielding that knife."

Cassie followed Eric's eyes around the room before focussing back on the victim. She nodded. The victim's right hand had a deep gash across the knuckles, and on his left forearm there were ugly slashes. They weren't deep but probably caused by wild slashes that he was trying to avoid. It was a sure sign he'd thrown up his arms in an attempt to protect himself. "So he wasn't caught by surprise. He saw it coming," she murmured.

The kitchen itself was in a mild state of disarray. Several pans had clattered to the floor on one side, and a cutting board lay overturned. An onion, half-peeled, rested on a counter near a chef's knife rack, minus one knife, presumably the one now lodged in Tony's chest. The stench of raw onion, fresh seafood left out of refrigeration mingled with the coppery smell of blood.

Eric stood, scanning the counters. "We'll need forensics to do a thorough sweep. The murderer might have left prints somewhere. Or footprints in the blood."

Cassie's expression was grim as she looked at Danny. "Have you figured out any frame of reference regarding the timeframe?"

Danny flicked through the notepad again. "Mrs Slater says she last saw Tony about eight-thirty this morning. He was up early, said he wanted to get ahead with things in the restaurant. He came across here – they live next door – while she had breakfast and got herself ready for work. She's a make-up artist and was off to—"

"That'll explain why you're paying attention, Danny," Cassie said drily.

"And she left for Burnham Market for a hair and make up job," Danny said, ignoring Cassie's jibe. "She returned early, around midday, after receiving that phone call to find this."

Cassie crouched slightly, reading the angle of Tony's body. He'd probably been backing away when he fell. Blood spattered up the side of one of the lower cabinets. "So the killer came in sometime after eight-thirty and left before Morgan arrived." Her mind whirled. "Is there any sign of forced entry?"

"No. The rear access door to the kitchen was ajar when uniform arrived. It doesn't have a proper handle on the exterior and so it must have been opened from the inside. I'm presuming that's the way the killer left anyway, and that's why it's open."

"They'd have to get in through a locked door or be let in by Tony," Eric said.

"Meaning he either knew the killer," Cassie said, "or opened the door to let them in. Or both, I suppose."

"The front door was definitely locked with no sign of tampering," Danny said. "Morgan, Mrs Slater," he said quickly correcting himself with a wince, "said the rear entrance is always locked and only opened during evening service if the kitchen overheats. That's usually in the summer though."

"Did he lock himself in with this person?" Eric asked.

"Maybe," Cassie said. "Or maybe they forced him to lock the door."

From the corner of her eye, Cassie noticed Eric moving towards the small corridor leading to what might be an office or storage area. He glanced back. "I'll see if they have any CCTV here or out in the car park. Then we can coordinate with uniform to do a door-to-door in the area."

Cassie gave a sharp nod. "Good idea. Maybe a neighbour saw someone hanging around or heard an argument." She turned to Danny. "Make sure uniform canvass the immediate area: businesses, houses, any stray dog walkers."

"Already on it," Danny assured. "We'll also check the staff. Morgan said that only one person was scheduled, but he wasn't here when she came back. We'll have to chase them up and see what time he arrived too. It might help narrow the timeframe."

"We should check to see if there were any other suppliers making drops today, too. Let's get his mobile as well, see if a friend called to say they were coming round."

Danny nodded, slipping away. Cassie crossed her arms.

This was a straight-up stabbing, a very personal, brutal act. Often that meant intense emotion or a confrontation. She couldn't ignore that Tony Slater had been in a public fight with Aaron Bell, who was murdered only a few days ago. It was possible, if David White was correct, that he too had been murdered in a similar fashion; an emotional rapid attack that he didn't see coming until it was too late. Two suspicious deaths within the same group of old classmates. It was too big a coincidence to overlook, but they were fighting with one another and she was certain Aaron hadn't returned from the dead to finish the fight they started earlier in the week.

"Right," she said, calmly to herself, her brow set in a deep frown as she surveyed Tony's body. "Let's keep everything methodical, Cassandra." She looked around. "Danny?"

He appeared moments later, his notebook in hand. "Yes, sarge."

"We'll wait for the forensics team to do their part, and then we really need confirmation on that timeline. We'll have to speak to Morgan again… carefully. She might still be in shock. Where is she now?"

"Uniform took her back into her house next door," Danny explained. "There's a paramedic checking her over. She was pretty distraught."

Cassie exhaled, brushing a stray lock of hair behind her ear. "I'll speak to her in a bit, once the paramedic's done." She saw Danny's expression. He seemed uneasy. "What's on your mind?"

Danny pursed his lips, glancing down at Tony's body. "This man argued with Aaron Bell at the reunion. Now they're both dead. I'm worried we're dealing with something bigger."

"What are you thinking?" Cassie asked.

"Whether there's some sort of vendetta at play here that

we're not aware of. That someone is picking them off one at a time."

Cassie forced a wry half-smile. "That's a reach... but it's plausible."

He met her eye. "What's funny?"

"Nothing. It's just good to see you're paying attention for once." She softened her tone, seeing the genuine concern in his eyes. "You're not wrong. Two violent deaths in a short span is alarming. But let's not jump too far ahead just yet."

"Sure," Danny murmured. "What is going on here?"

"Aye," Cassie said. "It's bad. Could be connected, or maybe it's a separate incident entirely, but let's keep an open mind until we know more."

They both returned their attention to the body again. Tony's expression was twisted, frozen in a final moment somewhere between surprise, pain and fear. Cassie tried not to let it unsettle her. She was no stranger to seeing the results of violent crime, but the personal nature of a stabbing always felt more intimate than any of the shootings she'd investigated before. Those incidents were almost always gang related, contacts between rivals and usually around drugs. The defensive wounds on Tony spoke volumes about how desperately he'd fought back.

She cleared her throat, turning towards Eric's footsteps coming from the dining room. "Eric, anything?"

He stopped at the threshold of the kitchen, shaking his head. "I saw a small office with a monitor and an old CCTV system. The screen's blank. I'll see if we can retrieve any footage. If the killer had half a brain, especially if it's the same guy who attacked Aaron then they might have taken the hard drive or wiped it, but we'll try."

Cassie sighed, glancing between the two detectives. "You on that path as well, are you?"

Eric shrugged. "What is it the DI always says?"

"I don't believe in coincidences," Danny and Cassie said in unison.

"Also, I've sent someone along the road to the local businesses to see if they have outside cameras that caught the comings and goings. We might pick up a familiar face. You never know."

Cassie nodded. Her eyes drifting towards Tony one last time. Poor man. She wondered if Eric and Danny were right and the confrontation with Aaron had any part in this. If so, there was the potential for more killings if this – whatever this was – hadn't finished playing out yet. The thought made her mentally shiver.

"All right," she said at last. "We'll let forensics process the scene. Danny, take a formal statement from Morgan Slater and update me if she says anything useful, especially about who Tony might have met with, fallen out with recently or…" She looked skyward, letting out an exasperated breath. "Anything! Just anything that might help us get a motive for what is going on here."

He nodded. "Of course. I'll be outside if you need me."

Cassie motioned for Eric to follow her out of the kitchen, careful not to step in any blood droplets. The hush of the dining area felt jarringly peaceful after the grim scene they'd just left. Distantly, they heard the murmur of voices, the chatter of onlookers, and the rustle of a paramedic's kit bag.

Reaching the front door, Cassie paused, looking back through the quiet rows of tables to the kitchen doors, where Tony Slater's life had ended mere hours ago. Another violent death tied to that same reunion group. Aaron Bell… now Tony Slater. What, or who, was going to be next? She sensed more trouble brewing on the horizon, as if these murders were just part of a larger storm. And she couldn't shake the image of the circle of old classmates, each with histories, grudges, and secrets that no one was sharing. This was personal, and personal murders had a way of quickly escalating.

Stepping out into the bright sunshine, Cassie shielded her eyes from the glare off a nearby police car. The small crowd gathering outside appeared to have grown a little. Word was spreading, and that would only get faster.

CHAPTER NINETEEN

DETECTIVE SERGEANT CASSIE KNIGHT stepped into the dining room of Tony's Seafood and Grill, her shoes scraping lightly on the wooden floorboards scuffed by countless customers over the years. The late-afternoon sun slanted through the tall windows, casting elongated shapes across the tables that were still set for an evening service that would no longer happen. A hush settled over the assembled staff. Seven of them in total, all in their twenties, plus two uniformed officers standing off to one side with statement forms at the ready to record the staff's comments. Eric stood behind Cassie, watching.

An undercurrent of tension was palpable. Tony Slater, their boss, had been found dead just hours before. Murdered in his own kitchen. Now these staff members had been summoned here, not to work their shifts, but to answer questions that most could never have imagined they'd be asked. She paused a moment, scanning their faces.

In her line of sight, near the bar area, Cassie noticed a young woman hugging her elbows, as if warding off a chill. Pale and shaken, she fixed her gaze on the floor. Beside her stood another waitress, eyes rimmed red, occasionally sniffling with a balled-up tissue clutched tightly in her fist. A couple of the kitchen staff, one boyish-looking with spiky hair and another with a small moustache, shifted restlessly, not making eye contact with anyone. One older figure wore a crisp black shirt and black trousers. Cassie had already been introduced to him as the restaurant's assistant manager. Two more front-of-house staff, wearing casual black clothes rather than uniforms, stood in subdued conversation, arms folded in protective stances.

Cassie knew the scene was always the same: confusion, fear, the shock of confronting mortality within the place they earned their living. Usually, her job was to gather facts with gentle but firm guidance, to glean clarity from the chaos. But she was also mindful of the rumour mill that inevitably erupts in the aftermath of a murder in such a small community, let alone one a mere three days since the last.

Clearing her throat, Cassie drew herself up. They'd turned the heating down in the restaurant at the request of the forensic team, to avoid any possible deterioration of any organic evidence. The sunshine that would have warmed the building was now casting long shadows and the wall of north-facing glass did little to heat the space. Cassie noticed a few staff members appeared to be feeling the cold.

"Thank you all for coming in," she began, her voice carrying across the room. "I'm DS Cassie Knight. I know you've had a tremendous shock. We understand how difficult this is." She glanced around, meeting a few pairs of eyes. "I want to start by saying we appreciate your cooperation. We'll take things one step at a time and get through this as swiftly as possible. My team and I," she gestured at the uniformed officers, "are here to speak to each of you privately, get your statements, and to ask a few questions. The sooner we can understand your normal day-to-day routines, the better we can figure out what's happened to Tony. Our deepest condolences to you, and of course to his family."

A ripple of uneasy movement passed through the group. Some stared blankly at Cassie; others nodded stiffly. The young man with spiky hair blinked rapidly, stepping aside slightly as though he needed more breathing room.

"First of all," Cassie continued, "I know this is emotional. Tony Slater was your employer, possibly a friend to some of you. It's natural to feel upset, angry, or even frightened in these circumstances. We'll keep this as brief and straightforward as possible, but we also need to be thorough." She swept her gaze across them again, noticing the flickers of grief in their eyes. "I understand that Morgan Slater – his wife – called each of you to ask you to come in. She isn't here right now. She's obviously had a severe shock and will be staying at home. For the moment, we'll focus on your knowledge of Tony, what you've seen recently, and anything that you can think of that might be of help in catching whoever did this."

The staff parted a little, forming a loose half circle. The oldest of them – a woman in her late twenties, wearing a light sweater with the restaurant's logo stitched on the chest – cleared her throat softly. Cassie nodded at her in encouragement.

"Go on," Cassie said.

The woman didn't speak at first, but gave a shrug. Her expression said it all, *I don't know where to start.* Cassie recognised that look. She smiled warmly.

"Let's keep it simple at first," Cassie said. "Did any of you see Tony this morning? Yesterday? Did he mention meeting anyone here or at home outside of normal deliveries?"

One of the younger women – maybe twenty-two or twenty-three – bit her lip. "I—I didn't. I had the day off yesterday, so I wasn't in." She darted her gaze around as if afraid she might be singled out for not working. "He sometimes comes in early, right? Preps the kitchen or checks the ingredients. We prioritise fresh and seasonal, so it matters to stay on top of it."

There were nods from a few of the kitchen staff. A tall, broad-shouldered man with a faint moustache, wearing a black hoodie, cleared his throat. "I work in the kitchen. Vegetable and salad prep is my thing. Usually Tony would want me in around lunchtime if we're doing a dinner service. He'd come in first in the morning to receive the seafood drop." He thought hard. "That's every other day, almost every day in high season. That's normal. He never specifically said he was meeting anyone today. Not to me anyway." He shrugged, shifting his weight between his feet, glancing at the glass façade that let in so much natural light. He seemed anxious.

"All right," Cassie said softly. "And none of you can recall him mentioning an appointment or something unusual for today? A new staff hire or a meeting with a supplier that wasn't on the schedule?"

Silence.

Eric moved forward, and gently said, "If any of you remember anything, anything at all that stands out, you'll have a chance to detail it in your statements." He gestured at the two small folding tables that had been set up near the bar. "We'll speak to you individually. We just ask for your full name, contact details, and a little bit about your role here."

Cassie picked up from him. "Yes, exactly. We want you to describe your usual interactions with Tony. If there were disagreements, tensions or changes in routines. That sort of thing. If anything stands out from the last few weeks, let us know. No matter how small it is. We will decide if it's relevant."

The staff seemed to collectively exhale. Some of them were hugging themselves, others looked around the room, keen to find a distraction. All of them gave the impression of being unsettled. Tony Slater was not just a name in the news to them. He was their day-to-day boss, the man who might have greeted them in the morning or challenged them for being late. Now he was gone in the blink of an eye, killed in his own kitchen.

"I'm going to break you up into smaller interviews," Cassie continued. "One by one, the officers here will call you over. Please bear with us. We have a few questions for each of you. In the meantime, if you need water or a chair, please do let one of us know. And if you feel overwhelmed, let us know that too."

She scanned their faces, mentally noting their names from the short staff list she'd been given, but she withheld rattling them off for the moment. They needed a sense of calm, not intimidation. Better to let them see the police as helpful and not as a threat. They'd talk more freely. The assistant manager raised a hand. "Excuse me, DS Knight?"

"Yes?" Cassie said, turning towards him.

He swallowed. "Do you know if—" his eyes darting around, "I guess I just want to know... if Morgan's okay?"

Cassie pressed her lips together. She could sense they all wanted some reassurance or detail, but official procedure was not to reveal too much. "She's had a shock. One of our family liaison officers is with her and she is being supported. That's about all I can say." He nodded, no further questions, a certain disappointment in his eyes. She gave him a sympathetic look. "It's all right to be worried. We're worried too."

With that, the group fell silent, waiting for instruction.

Cassie stepped back, giving a slight nod to the uniformed officers. They began calling out names from the staff list. The assembled group broke apart, forming small clusters or standing alone with arms folded in uneasy poses. In the next few moments, the dining room filled with the low hum of voices, as the officers gathered each person's details and preliminary statements.

Cassie lingered near the bar, keeping an eye on the collective mood. A few staff members were tearful, hugging one another or lost in thought. All quite understandable. She noted the young woman with pale cheeks was trembling as she tried to speak to a female constable. The vegetable chef, or whatever his proper title would be, was pacing, hands in pockets. Another man wearing a red hoodie spoke quietly but intently to PC Marshall, occasionally glancing around as if worried about who might overhear him.

Through it all, Cassie moved calmly around paying attention. She'd done enough of these to know that the best approach was to watch for someone who might be holding back, or who might appear more anxious than the situation alone would justify. Guilt, fear, knowledge… there were many reasons someone might be reticent to speak up. Yet, from the quick read of the room, most were simply upset and were trying to process the shock.

She caught sight of a young man near the far window, staring out over the marshland. He was maybe mid-twenties, slim build, with hair cut short on the sides in this modern mullet style that had somehow become popular again. His arms were folded tightly across his chest, his body angled away from the others, as though he wanted to be absorbed into the shadows. She noticed him glancing her way a few times but darting his gaze away every time she threatened to catch his eye. He had a furtive tension about him, as if he was grappling with something he wasn't sure whether to share.

Cassie recognised that look. He knows something or believes something, but he's not sure if it's relevant or how to bring it up. She hovered nearby, waiting to see if an officer would pick him to interview, but he avoided the lines forming at the improvised interview desks. The knot in her gut tightened. In her experience, the people who were truly stunned tended to line up first for an interview, keen to either vent or try to do anything they can to help. The reluctant ones were often those who had something pertinent to share.

A flicker of eye contact at the third attempt. Cassie seized the moment, giving him a small, reassuring tilt of her head. The unspoken message, *come and talk to me*. But he immediately dropped his gaze. All right, she thought, I'll approach him more directly. She cleared her throat.

"DC Collet," she said quietly and he came alongside her. Just then, she raised her voice to be audible to the group. "Excuse me a moment." She stepped towards the young man. He straightened, stiffening as she approached. "Hello," she said gently. "Are you all right?"

"Uh… yeah," he mumbled. "Just… it's messed up. Tony… it's messed up."

"I know," she said, her voice calm. "You look a bit nauseous. Why don't we step outside for a breather? Get some air. The dining room's a bit stuffy, isn't it?"

He looked caught off-guard but nodded, clearing his throat. "Yeah, sure. Fresh air would be good."

Cassie motioned towards the door that led outside to the rear seating area. She noticed some of the staff glancing their way. She gave them a warm smile. Although the restaurant primarily faced the road and car park, the back offered a spectacular view across the marshland. Late-afternoon sunlight bathed the reeds in gold, the wind carrying the faint cry of seabirds and the muffled roar of distant waves. Cassie brushed the hair whipping across her face away from her eyes. A few scattered outdoor tables and chairs, for use when the weather really picked up, were stacked up or partially covered to protect them from the elements.

The chill breeze saw Cassie zip her jacket higher. The young man shivered, folding his arms again. She took in the scene; the salty air, the long shadows stretching across the ground and the setting sun just about visible to their left as it sank below the horizon. The stillness of the scene was punctured only by the sound of the breeze rustling the reeds and the odd passing car on the road.

"Do you mind telling me your name?" Cassie asked. "And what you do?"

"Cole," he said softly, "Cole Davies. I…uh… I work as a server here. Waiting on the tables, clearing away. Sometimes I help in the kitchen if it gets busy. Tony said he was going to train me up over the summer, get me onto an approved apprenticeship or something."

"Right. Tony must think highly of you." Cassie studied him. He was tense. "Cole, you seemed uneasy inside just now. It's like you were holding something back. Is that fair to say?"

He swallowed, his gaze flicking towards the broad, open sweep of the marshland. "I don't know if it's anything, but moving around… doing a bit of everything I get to hear things. What people say and that," he said quickly. "It's just rumours, stuff the staff talk about. And people gossip, you know?"

Cassie nodded slowly. "It might be important. Or it might be nothing. Why don't you let me decide, once I've heard it?"

His brow creased. "I don't want to get anyone in trouble."

"You won't," Cassie reassured him. "But Tony's been

murdered. That's... serious. If there's anything you know that could lead us to find out who did this, then we need it. Even if it's just hearsay or speculation."

Cole exhaled, shoulders sagging. "We're all in shock, yeah? But... there's been talk, especially among the kitchen staff. I don't know if it's true... people chat shite all the time... but they're saying Tony was seeing someone else. You know, he was cheating on Morgan."

Cassie cocked her head. "Having an affair?"

"Dunno if it's an affair, exactly," Cole hedged, his voice quieter now as the breeze strengthened and caught his words, "but that's the rumour. He'd make flirty phone calls sometimes. I heard that myself."

"Maybe he was talking to his wife?"

Cole shook his head. "When I heard him, she was there, at the restaurant. I could see her and she wasn't holding a phone. Tony... was a good bloke, but he liked to flirt with women. Customers, staff... anyone who caught his eye. Not in a nasty way, but still... sometimes it was borderline."

Cassie took a moment to consider. "So Tony Slater was quite a ladies' man, you'd say?"

Cole let out a shaky laugh that had no humour in it. "He had a... big personality. He loved women. He'd flirt with the waitresses, the new hires. He'd chat up the younger ones or the older ones. Age didn't matter to him. Most people sort of rolled their eyes about it. I mean, he was never, like, creepy with it."

Cassie folded her arms against the chill. "And what's the gossip specifically? That Tony was seeing someone behind Morgan's back? One person, like in a relationship, or was he putting it about all over the place?"

Cole nodded hesitantly. "Right. I don't know. I'm not sure anyone does, not really. He'd disappear some afternoons for a while, saying he was going for a round of golf or something but…" Cole smiled. "He wasn't off playing golf, not the way he looked when he took off. And it was always when Morgan was away working or had left for the day."

Cassie eyed him closely. "You're sure it's not just him being flirtatious though? You actually suspect there's something going on?"

His gaze broke from hers. He stared at the marsh for a moment, as if seeking courage from somewhere in the landscape. "Yeah," he said finally, "some people reckon it's more than a fling. Recently, there's talk that the woman might be pregnant."

Cassie's eyebrows flicked up in surprise. "Pregnant. That's… quite a rumour. You have any idea who she is?"

He rubbed his neck. "No," he said. "No idea, I swear. If I did, I'd tell you. Morgan definitely doesn't know, though. Or at least, that's what everyone's been saying. She's been acting so normal. To think… Tony would cheat on a class act like Morgan." Cassie cocked her head inquisitively. "Well… she's a damn sight closer to my age than his… and she's…" He shrugged. "She's well fit. I mean, he's always been punching way above his weight, you know?"

Cassie let that sink in. A possible pregnancy. If it was real, it might be a motive for murder. It didn't tie in with Aaron Bell's murder though. Then there was Morgan. Could she have heard the same whispers. Would that cause a confrontation that might see her lash out? Or perhaps the unknown woman might have pressed Tony to formalise their relationship, especially with a child on the way. Had he rejected her? Did that rejection escalate into violence? Cassie forced herself not to jump ahead. She needed more evidence than hearsay from the mouth of one man.

"All right," Cassie said gently. "And you're confirming you

did personally overhear those phone calls? It's not just hearsay or second-hand info?"

He shook his head. "I heard Tony talking on the phone a couple of times, but I never caught the specifics. He'd get this low tone, you know? He'd laugh in that smooth sort of way, but I was always close enough. Not that I was eavesdropping. Not at all." He paused. "Close enough to hear the gist of it every now and again."

Cassie mulled over the scenario. "And you say Morgan was sometimes around, but obviously not the one on the other end of the line?"

"Yeah. She'd be in the office or out front, and Tony would slip away. Thinking about it, he was quite brazen sometimes. He'd get all edgy afterwards, sometimes weirdly moody, like the phone calls brought him stress or excitement. It's hard to describe. A few nights ago, one of the others said they heard he might have gotten some woman pregnant." Cole shrugged, a pained expression crossing his face. "One of the girls even congratulated Morgan on being pregnant... and then had to back pedal like nobody's business when she said she wasn't."

Cassie folded her arms, letting a moment pass. The breeze played with her hair, tugging it across her face again, and she tucked it behind her ear. "All right, Cole. Thank you. That does help."

He lifted his eyes to hers with hesitation. "You're not going to... pin this on me, right? I mean... it's only gossip."

She gave a small smile, attempting to reassure him. "No, of course not. I appreciate your honesty. We're looking into all aspects of Tony's life. If he was involved in a tryst – especially one that might have led to a pregnancy – then it's something we need to look at, but if it's not relevant to his death then there's no need to include it."

Cole relaxed slightly, though his arms remained folded.

"It's just so screwed up. Tony… sure, he wasn't perfect, but he was always a pretty decent bloke to have as a boss. I never thought… you know, that something like this would happen. Not in a million years."

"I understand." Cassie smiled. "Look, after we finish talking, one of my colleagues will want your official statement. Mention that you spoke to me, and go over what you told me about the rumours." Cole looked anxious.

"But what if Morgan—"

"It's important we record it properly," Cassie said, "but we will be discreet."

He nodded, swallowing hard. "Okay."

"You're doing the right thing," Cassie said.

Cole went back into the dining room while Cassie stayed where she was. Moments later, Eric appeared at her side.

"What was all that about?" he asked.

Cassie took a deep breath, checked that no one else was within earshot and then looked at Eric. "The word is that Tony Slater was having a bit of something extra. A side dish to the main meal that is his marriage."

"Ooo," Eric said, wincing. "Do we know who with?"

Cassie shook her head. "We need mobile phone records as soon as possible." She glanced back, first at the restaurant and then towards the house. "See if Morgan will allow us to search the house too. If not, we'll have to see a magistrate and obtain a warrant."

"In search of what?"

"A second mobile phone, hidden from the wife… secret letters… I don't know. Whatever a man who's playing away keeps hidden from his wife. That sort of thing. Do you have any experience of that, Eric?"

"Me?" Eric said, exhaling sharply. "I have enough trouble keeping one woman happy, let alone a second."

"The rumour is Tony got this woman pregnant as well."

"That brings jealous wife or husband into play," Eric said. Cassie nodded.

"It doesn't tie his murder to Aaron's though."

Eric frowned. "Maybe they're not connected at all."

"Maybe," Cassie said, then arched her eyebrows. "And maybe not."

CHAPTER TWENTY

Tom Janssen pulled his car up along the short driveway leading to Tamara Greave's home. The beams of his headlights illuminated the expansive front lawn to either side of the drive, casting stark shadows against the mature hedgerow running along the perimeter. Night had fallen properly, and despite a relatively clear sky, Tamara's property sat in the darkness, overshadowed by established trees.

He noticed the garage door was open. Inside, her old Austin Healey lay half-exposed under the strip light, its bonnet propped up on a metal rod. Various tools, oily rags, and scattered parts covered the work surface near the front bumper. Tom got out of his car and approached the garage. There was no sign of Tamara though, but he did note the engine bay was open, wiring harnesses partly visible. Tinkering with cars was a passion of hers, and he knew she often lost herself in projects when she was stressed.

"Tamara?" he called. The faint echo of his voice returned to him. No response.

He crossed the drive to the house and tried the front door, pressing the bell. Again, there was no answer. Tom frowned.

She must be home. She wouldn't leave the garage open like that. Pulling his jacket collar up against the chill, he made his way along the side of the house towards the back garden, shoes crunching gently on gravel. The wind whistled through the branches overhead. Reaching the rear, he saw a soft light in the kitchen window. The blinds were half down but he caught a glimpse of Tamara inside. She was alone at the dining table, her back to the glass, shoulders slightly hunched. A half-empty bottle of red wine stood on the table, and a single glass in her hand as she stared into space.

Tom tapped lightly on the door frame. "Tamara?"

She turned, startled at first. But upon seeing him, her features softened. She rose, crossing to unlock the back door. "Tom," she said, her voice subdued. "I didn't hear you come. Sorry."

He stepped inside, finding the kitchen noticeably warmer than outside, and he picked up a sense of tension in the air. The television, on in the adjoining dining area – visible through an open archway – chattered quietly, the evening news running a segment that Tom recognised. The reporter's voice carried enough that he could make out references to Tony Slater's murder.

"You left your garage open," Tom said gently, nodding in the direction of the side window. "Looked like you were mid-project."

She shrugged, but the gesture lacked energy. Her hair was loosely pinned up, a few strands slipping free. She wore a plain sweater, rolled to the elbows, and jeans. "I needed something to do with my hands earlier, so I was poking around the old bird."

"Problem?" Tom asked.

"More of a list," she said, returning to her seat. "But that's the fun of these things. I'm trying to see if I can fix a misfire and then there's an electrical fault that I can't seem to pinpoint too. I might've lost track of time. Then..." She waved vaguely at the wine bottle on the table. "I got sidetracked."

Tom understood. Tension, stress, frustration. Everyone had ways of coping, and tinkering with an old car was Tamara's. "I can close the garage if you like," he offered.

She shook her head. "It's fine. I'll handle it later." She set her glass down, rubbed the back of her neck. "Can I get you a glass?"

He shook his head.

"No, that's right," she said, looking sleepy for a moment. "You're still not drinking?"

"No."

"I thought recent events might have changed that."

"Recent events are exactly why I shouldn't change that," he said, smiling.

"Your loss," Tamara said. She sat back down, gesturing for him to take a seat if he wanted to. "Are you here about Tony Slater?"

Tom nodded, exhaling. Another murder. "I am. News travels quickly, especially about something this big." He let his gaze pass over her. "Are you all right?"

She gave a short, joyless laugh. "Does it look like I'm all right?" She gestured at the half-empty bottle.

"No... not really."

Tamara nodded and leaned back in her seat. The television's volume rose slightly as the segment changed, replaying an excerpt from David White's recent interview. The banner at the foot of the screen, bold white letters on a red background, read, *Two murders of Sheringham residents*. Tom shook his head. Aaron Bell lived in Blakeney, not Sheringham. But that was news coverage, never let the truth get in the way of sensationalising a story.

The footage cut to David, wearing a neat tweed blazer, speaking calmly about *crimes of a personal nature*. While the on-screen caption asked if the same killer might have struck again. Tom watched Tamara's jaw tighten, her eyes blazing with frustration. The reporter's voice came over the footage.

"Expert, local criminologist, David White spoke earlier this week about the murder of Aaron Bell, citing an emotional, impulsive act. Now, with the murder of Tony Slater, a local man familiar to Aaron Bell, speculation is mounting. Is there a killer on the loose, targeting men from the same group? Are the police doing enough to keep us safe in small rural communities and coastal seaside towns? With the tourist season ready to get underway, will this affect business?"

"A killer on the loose, stalking middle-aged men in and around Sheringham?" Tamara repeated bitterly, snapping off the television using the remote on the table in front of her. "Great. Just wonderful."

Tom pulled out a chair, sitting down opposite her. "The media's making leaps. They always do."

She nodded, lifting her glass of wine but not sipping yet. "True. And my other half has fed them some wonderful content that comes back to bite me again and again. Remind me to thank him, won't you."

Tom winced. "Statistically, it's rare for a so-called serial killer to target middle-aged men – especially heterosexual men – unless there's some deeper angle, like a hate ideology aimed at gay men for example."

Tamara tipped her glass towards Tom in a silent salute. "Please pass that on to David, would you? He might keep his mouth shut, " she said, bitterly, "but I doubt it."

"What's the connection, Tom?" She shook her head, staring blankly forward. "They were at school together, and they didn't like one another very much." She spread her hands wide. "I'm out."

"They weren't even friends," Tom said. "Tony told me they used to rub each other up the wrong way. So yes, they were school acquaintances, and there was friction."

"And friction can lead to murder now?" Tamara said sarcastically. "A dead man didn't resurrect himself to settle a score. I'm sure of that."

Tom spread his hands on the table. "Obviously not. So, why would a third party target them both? Are you linking the two murders yet?"

Tamara let out a heavy breath. "I can't say definitively. I mean, the official line is that both investigations remain separate but are running in parallel. We can't ignore the coincidence. If this was London or Manchester, you might guess it's just an unfortunate occurrence. But here? In rural Norfolk? The population's small, the chance of two brutal murders of men from the same year group at school within days of each other is... minuscule."

Tom nodded, glancing at the television, now a black mirror, reflecting the light from the kitchen back at them. "And you suspect something's behind it, some old secret or new disagreement? Tony and Aaron had that fight at the reunion and that altercation set something in motion?"

Tamara sipped her wine, setting the glass down carefully. "That's exactly the question. Why did Tony and Aaron fight a few days ago? Was it something carried over from school or something from adulthood? We're trying to figure out if that argument was just old teenage rivalry rearing its head or if it was part of a bigger feud. And if so, how it ties to both murders. Possibly, someone else had a grudge involving them. But it's all speculation right now."

Tom's brow furrowed. He rested his elbows on the table,

chin on his hands. He recalled Aaron's brash manner at the reunion, Tony's exasperation. "I don't know what they were fighting over. They parted ways afterwards, and each was seemingly dismissive of the other. Tony told me it was a drunken, childish tussle. Aaron basically told me he found Tony arrogant. It was a nonsense."

She nodded. "That's all we're hearing so far. But there must be more." She paused. "You spent time with both men right before they died. Did you see anything that might hint at a bigger conflict?"

Tom exhaled, leaning back. "No, not that I recognised. Aaron had personal troubles, his marriage was failing, and he was struggling to reach a settlement. Tony... I only learned from the reunion that he was nursing old grudges. But I didn't sense anything connecting the two that would tie to a common enemy. This is all so bizarre."

Tamara stared at her wine. "I'm beginning to think everything that's happened here is bizarre. Two homicides in under a week; both local men, ex-schoolmates." She rubbed her temples. "We think Tony was having an affair with someone."

"Really?" Tom asked.

"Yes. Possibly got someone pregnant too. That doesn't bring a link to Aaron's murder though." She topped up her wine glass. Tom wanted to suggest she took it easy but she was a grown woman and it wasn't his place. "David's interview is only adding fuel to the media fire." She sniffed, swirling the contents of her glass in a circular motion. "They keep quoting him talking about an *emotional crime*. Do you realise how that looks for me? My partner going on television, speculating about possible motives and bordering on suggesting it might be..." she sighed. "Whatever he said it might be."

"I should imagine you're not exactly thrilled."

"Understatement," she said flatly.

Tom laced his fingers on the tabletop, watching Tamara carefully. "So you and David... not seeing eye to eye at the moment?"

She barked a short laugh, and raised her glass. "You are the master of the understatement tonight, Tom. That's putting it mildly. He went behind my back, or rather, he didn't consult me, to say the least. Now I'm being hauled over the coals by the senior ranks for failing to keep my house in order or some other bollocks. Why's he spouting theories that we haven't confirmed?" she scowled.

"He might be right—"

"Which would be very annoying," Tamara said, "but that's not the point. I'd rather he'd told me privately, not told the entire East Anglia region on the six o'clock news."

Tom gave a small nod, empathising with the tension. "He might have been cornered, or maybe the press seized on him for a statement."

"He's no innocent in that," Tamara said sharply. "He likes the spotlight sometimes. He fancies himself as the local crime psychology guru." She locked eyes with Tom. "It doesn't help that he has a new book coming out soon." She snorted. "Let him see how it feels when the official investigators have to do damage control and the calls from the chief superintendent start coming to his office. He was furious!"

"I can imagine." Tom fiddled with a stray crumb on the table. "Is David still at the university now?"

Tamara's mouth tightened. "He texted me earlier, said he'll be at the campus late, finishing some departmental meeting. He's conveniently absent, which is probably wise for him right now." She sipped from her glass. "He's not daft. He knows I'm in the mood to kick him in the arse."

Tom studied her, noticing how frustration warred with underlying hurt in her eyes. "I'm sorry."

She set the wine glass aside, pressing her lips thin. "Don't be. It's not your fault. It's just... it's all landed in my lap. Two murders, the press nipping at my heels, David spouting theories all over the place—"

"One interview," Tom corrected.

"On *television*," she said. "The BBC no less. And here's me, stuck in the middle. I want to solve this case, not spend my time juggling politics."

Tom softly laid a hand on the table near hers. "I wish I could help more. You know I do. If I were still on the team—"

She looked at him sharply. "Tom, I know you mean well, but you need to stay out of it. The last thing I need is them thinking I'm passing you details or letting you run an off-the-books parallel investigation."

He nodded slowly. "I understand." Then a faint sigh. "Still, if there's anything you do want me to help with—"

Her expression softened. "I know. You have good instincts. But I have to be careful, and protect you as much as I protect myself. One of us has to be here to run CID."

"Cassie?"

"Can run a bath, maybe," Tamara said. Tom knew she held Cassie in very high regard. Her gaze flicked towards the silent television. "David said these murders are personal. He might be right. We both suspect that. He just shouldn't have said it publicly."

Tom shifted in his seat. "Well, personal can mean a lot of things. They might share a blackmailer, a deep-held secret. Or someone they both crossed, perhaps decades ago. But a random maniac targeting them for no reason is less likely, especially here. So David's logic isn't flawed, just inconvenient."

She rubbed her forehead. "Precisely. Inconvenient." Then she inhaled, forcibly changing the subject. "So, Tony… have you heard details? He was found with a knife in his chest, defensive wounds, a messy scene. Everyone's reeling."

Tom grimaced. "He wasn't a close friend, but still…"

"That's the talk all over Sheringham," Tamara murmured, eyes wandering to the window where lights from a neighbour's house glimmered through the trees. "People are frightened. And the news is stoking that fear with speculation of a killer on the loose. That's the phrase they keep repeating. We want them to remain cautious, obviously, but not to panic. It's just so damned irresponsible."

Tom rubbed his jaw, remembering how unusual it was for Norfolk to have two murders so close together. "That's the news for you. They want clicks and interaction. Negativity sells."

"Even the BBC?"

"Everyone wants to stay relevant," Tom said. "When did Tony die? Do you know?"

"Early. Before lunchtime. The forensics team haven't pinpointed it exactly, but it's likely mid to late morning. The post-mortem will confirm it."

Tom shook his head. "Brazen to do it in broad daylight when staff would be expected to come in for work."

"Or personal," Tamara said. "Maybe it was someone he allowed in, someone he wasn't afraid of. So yes, David's personal crime hypothesis might ring true. All the same, I wish he'd keep it to himself." She drummed her fingers on the table. "At least until we had made some headway. Now I'm spending half my time fighting fires in the media and upstairs with the top brass. Are you sure you don't want a drink. I might just open another bottle soon."

"Hey," Tom said softly, "I think you've had enough liquid

therapy, at least if you want to stay clear-headed." He offered a gentle smile. "Anyway, you never told me how you're getting on with the misfiring Healey."

She let out a small, genuine laugh for the first time. "Probably needs half its wiring replaced. I can't focus on it properly tonight, not with everything going on. Right now, I'm just too wound up."

He nodded. "I'll close the garage door for you if you like, then get out of your hair. Let you calm down a bit."

She stared into her wine glass, nodded, and set it down. "All right. Thank you."

He reached out, a soft gesture, and she squeezed his hand in gratitude. For a moment, they sat there, two old colleagues caught in a tangle of professional ethics and personal friendship. He broke the contact first, drawing his hand away. He checked his watch. "I should go. I want to spend some time with Saffy and Alice this evening."

Tamara nodded, arms still protectively around herself. "Thanks for stopping by."

He paused at the door, glancing back at her once more. "You'll be okay?"

She forced a reassuring nod. "Yes. I'll be fine." Then a faint flicker of warmth. "Go home, Tom. Don't worry about me. We'll talk soon."

With that, he left via the back door and made his way around to the front of the property where his car was parked. He crossed the short distance, looked into the garage and found the light switch. Then he dropped the door and walked the short distance to his car, his thoughts dominated by the loss of two childhood friends.

CHAPTER TWENTY-ONE

DAVID WHITE SAT HUNCHED over his desk in his faculty office, listening to the quiet hum of the overhead strip lighting. His monitor cast a pale glow across his desk, illuminating several books on his specialist subjects of criminology and psychology along with a stack of half-graded essay papers. Outside his window, lamp posts punctured the darkness of the car park and adjoining paths where only a handful of vehicles remained. At this hour, the campus resembled a deserted island, albeit one covered in asphalt. The odd light from offices in the building opposite split the brick façade of the university faculty buildings where some colleague, equally overcommitted, must also be working late.

It was almost pushing ten o'clock. Officially, the building closed half an hour ago, but David's staff pass gave him after-hours access, and the security guards knew to expect him to stay on. He'd been doing so most nights for several weeks what with the impending deadline of his latest book hanging over him. He was behind on marking and the requests for comment and interview were piling up ever since he went public with his opinion on the recent murder in Blakeney.

He'd had to turn his mobile phone off for a while when the news broke of a second murder.

He couldn't deny that a tiny part of him – perhaps the professor who loved being consulted – felt a thrill at being able to apply his expertise in real time. He was the senior lecturer at the university in all things criminological. His expertise in psychology furthered his position as an expert. Journalists loved experts. It gave them an easy headline. That had led him onto that television interview earlier in the week. Agreeing to it was probably, in hindsight, an error in judgement. Bearing in mind his relationship with Tamara, Senior Investigating Officer in this particular case, more discretion would have been advisable.

However, here he was, in a bed of his own making. There was little he could do now. His vision briefly went double and he removed his glasses, pressing thumb and forefinger into his eyes. Tamara was furious. Furious was actually an understatement, if he thought about it. Part of the reason he was still here was because he was avoiding her wrath.

His mobile phone broke the silence, the shrill sound startling him. David jolted, nearly knocking over his glass of water. With an exasperated sigh, he fumbled for the phone on top of a paperback titled *Dark Obsessions: A Study of Passionate Crime*. The call was from an unknown number.

"Hello?" he answered, setting his reading glasses aside on the desk.

"Professor White?" An upbeat female voice. Professional yet eager. "This is Jade Murray calling. I'm a production assistant working for the BBC Breakfast, Look East team. I do hope I haven't caught you at a bad time."

He blinked. "No, it's fine. Good evening, Ms Murray. How can I help?"

"Well, Professor, I'm sure you're aware that Tony Slater's

murder, following so soon after Aaron Bell's, is causing quite a stir. We'd like to invite you into the studio in the morning for tomorrow's programme to do a follow up interview after the one you kindly did for us earlier in the week. We're keen to discuss any possible patterns you see, whether there's a serial killer in the area, and so forth. Would you be available?"

David's stomach did a little flip. Another interview. Tamara's voice thundered in his mind, warning him about speaking to the media unilaterally. The chance to shape the narrative, to clarify the complexities of violent crime, appealed to him though. Also, his students had seemed so fascinated by his appearance on television. Seemingly, once you made it onto the small screen you became more credible. He also couldn't help but find the attention somewhat flattering.

He hesitated. "That's… rather soon. Tomorrow morning, you say?"

"Yes. We can send a car for you, if necessary," Jade replied, sounding hopeful. "Or you can come into our Norwich studio for a segment at around seven forty a.m. You'd be on the sofa with our regular presenters, they are very excited about the prospect, just to give your professional perspective. It wouldn't be anything too heavy. Seven or eight minutes of your time."

Professional perspective. David felt an old excitement stir. He glanced at the pile of unmarked essays, telling himself another interview wouldn't kill him. Tamara might though. On the other hand, if he was more careful and took the time to measure his words more cautiously then it could actually be beneficial for all parties.

"Yes," he said at last, couched in caution. "I think I can manage that. Let's say I drive down, so no need to send a car for me. I'll be there by… what time do you think I should be there?"

"By seven, to give us time to prepare you, would be ideal."

"Yes, I think I could manage that."

"Wonderful, Professor White. Thank you ever so much. I'll email you the address along with a quick run through of the segment we have planned, just so you can be ready. We'll be focussing on the emotional dimension of these crimes, as well as who might be behind them—"

"Oh, I couldn't possibly name any names, you understand—"

"Of course not, no," Jade said. "But with your background in criminology, you will have a keen insight into what lies behind all of this, I'm sure."

They exchanged farewells. David hung up, letting the phone settle on his desk. The enormity of what he'd just agreed to sent a wave of doubt through him. Immediately, the thought occurred that he should call back and cancel. This wasn't a clever idea. He hadn't taken her number though. She was Jude someone. No, not Jude. It was... he couldn't even recall her first name let alone her surname. He'd wait for the email. Then he could decline. That made sense.

With a sigh, he picked up his glasses and put them on, turning back to his computer. The screen displayed half of an overdue analysis of local violent crime patterns. He forced himself to resume typing. Focus. Just get another hour in, then go home. He tapped out a few lines of commentary about how a murder in a small community often triggered disproportionate panic in rural communities. These were called A+ category murders, ones likely to generate anxiety in a population.

A gentle rap on the door interrupted him again. "Yes?" he called, setting aside his frustration at being disturbed again so soon.

The door eased open. A young woman poked her head inside. She had large, inquisitive eyes and a cascade of dark hair pulled back in a simple ponytail. "Professor White?" she asked. "I hope I'm not bothering you."

He recognised her at once. Kateryna, one of his second-year criminology students from Ukraine. She had a sharp mind, always engaged in discussion, though sometimes she came across a little shy in seminars. "Kateryna," he rose to wave her in. "It's late. Is everything okay?"

She slipped into the office, holding a slim laptop to her chest. "I'm sorry, Professor. I saw your office light on and thought I'd take a chance. I wanted to ask about the essay you set us. The subject matter, you know, men using violence, coercive control and manipulation to commit their crimes?"

David nodded, remembering the prompt. "Yes, of course. The final deadline's next Monday, right?"

"Yes." She clutched the laptop tighter still. "I've made a start, but I have questions. The assignment notes reference historical case studies of men using their emotion and passion to justify committing acts of extreme violence." Her English carried a slight accent, though her words were crisp and clear. "I am wondering how relevant this could be, you see, with these two murders recently. Don't you think these two murders could fit into this scenario?"

"It might be relevant in a broad sense, yes. But we don't have any direct evidence that either of these murders is resulting from such matters."

"But you said, earlier, about the Aaron Bell case being very personal, with the hallmarks of an emotional murder."

"Yes... but we're still in the realm of speculation. The authorities haven't suggested they agree with me, but... broadly, yes."

She gave a half-shrug. "Still, the pattern of men in conflict, sometimes they leverage their positions, or relationships, to manipulate or harm others. Could these murders be, in some twisted way, connected by that theme? Like a vigilante scenario?" She sounded eager, curious.

David carefully weighed his words. "Possibly, but vigilante scenario is quite a leap without supporting facts to add weight to the argument. We only know they were ex-schoolmates who died violently. I wouldn't advise you to structure your essay around conjecture."

Kateryna offered a slight smile. "I'm not intending to. I just find it interesting. And... forgive me, but I also overheard you in your conversation a moment ago. You're going back on television."

Surprise flickered across David's face. "Yes, I was just asked." He paused, thinking it might be wise not to broadcast it, especially if he was going to withdraw. "They want me to discuss whether these murders share a pattern."

She beamed. "You should do it, sir. I saw your last interview. Many of us thought it was brilliant; you were brilliant. You are on real television, analysing a live case. You should have seen yourself... it was quite something to hear you speak of it."

David felt warmth at the praise. So it was well-received among students. "That's... flattering. Thank you. Though I must be careful. My partner," he nearly said the police detective but managed to keep Tamara's identity vague, "thinks I should be more discreet on these matters."

"It's good for the reputation of the faculty," Kateryna said. "It shows we have real experts teaching us. The media rarely highlight academic perspectives this way. It's a big deal." Her eyes shone with admiration. "You really think these murders are crimes of passion or personal vendetta, right?"

He hesitated. "On the surface, they seem personal. Both victims died under violent circumstances, with no obvious sign of robbery or a profit motive, as far as I understand.

Certainly nothing of that was reported in the first case and the details of the second aren't commonly known… yet. As for a vendetta? I'm not so sure about that. We shall have to wait and see. The killer might be punishing them for wrongdoing, perceived or real."

She nodded intently, leaning closer, almost perched on the edge of his desk. "Yes, yes. That aligns with what we're reading about 'passionate sprees.' We saw your commentary on how emotional factors can lead to impulsive violence. But is there a chance it's a spree killer or serial killer scenario, continuing the same pattern? People are talking about that."

David briefly recalled Tamara's caution. He cleared his throat, keeping his tone carefully neutral. "A spree or serial scenario is possible, but it's not the most common pattern for two murders within days. Usually, spree killers either target random strangers or focus on a single event with multiple victims. This is more spaced apart, with the same broad social circle of peers – ex-schoolmates – and I suspect a personal link rather than a random spree." He frowned. "Serial killers are not particularly common. And certainly not in small communities such as rural north Norfolk."

Kateryna's face lit up in fascination. "Exactly what I was thinking. Two men with some old tension, perhaps. Or someone they both triggered at one time? If the killer enjoyed the sensation of the aftermath, perhaps they thought about settling another score?"

David nodded slowly. "Yes, though again, speculation. The official inquiry has more data than we do. Academically speaking though, you can analyse parallels. The similarity in type of homicide, both within a short time, and some bridging factor, like mutual acquaintances. The question is why. That's what your essay can't answer definitively but can certainly explore with historical examples."

She offered a mischievous grin, placing her laptop down on the desk. He could detect a hint of perfume on her, nothing too strong with a pleasant bouquet. "I actually wrote a short section on famous cases where a killer targeted members of a group who once wronged them. For instance, certain spree killings in the U.S. where the perpetrator returned to a workplace or a school. If it's relevant, maybe it's a lead."

David found himself nodding at her reasoning. She was bright, no question. A kernel of discomfort lodged itself in him though. The conversation felt too conspiratorial for a standard student essay chat. He pushed back gently. "We must remember not to seek to cross boundaries and to follow the facts."

"Of course," she said, eyes shining. "Thank you, Professor. This is so interesting. My home country has had enough conflict without me taking an interest in crime, I know, but I can't help it. Studying – this is my passion."

He offered a kind smile. "You've got a sharp intellect, Kateryna. Just keep your focus on academic sources. Real police work is often more mundane than you'd think." He glanced at the clock on his monitor screen. "But it's late. I should finish up. And you… you need to get home, too."

She blinked, glancing around as though noticing the darkness for the first time. "Yes, I suppose so. Thank you for your time, Professor White."

David stood, stepping aside to open the office door for her. As she passed, she paused just a fraction of a moment, her shoulder nearly brushing his. Her eyes flicked up at him. For a split second, he sensed a certain closeness, an intensity. Then she stepped into the corridor.

He cleared his throat, feeling self-conscious. She's just an admiring student, he told himself. Don't read too much into it. Still, he was acutely aware of how precarious any hint of impropriety would be in this environment. "All right, then. Take care, Kateryna."

She must have picked up on his sudden caution because her cheeks reddened faintly. "Yes... sorry. I'll see you in tomorrow's lecture." She turned and walked away, footsteps echoing on the linoleum floor.

David exhaled, leaning into the door frame as she disappeared around the corner. Young, bright, enthusiastic, he mused. A pang of worry about the line between professor and student hovered in his mind. But, academically, she seemed sincere.

He was about to close his door when a soft thud echoed down the hallway, as though someone bumped into a wall or door. Frowning, David poked his head out, scanning the corridor. "Kateryna?" he called quietly. There was no response. The overhead lights had been switched off in sections, leaving alternating pools of shadow. Usually a cleaner or a security guard might pass by on their nightly routine.

He listened. Nothing but the faint whir from the air conditioning unit mounted overhead in the ceiling. The corridor was empty. Perhaps one of the facilities management team was moving equipment in a nearby room. He waited a moment, the hair on his arms prickling with an unexpected sense of being watched. But no one appeared and after a moment, he brushed the feeling aside.

David shivered. *This building can feel eerie at night.* Enough dramatics, he told himself, stepping back into his office. He quickly gathered his papers, slipped them into a battered satchel that he'd used for well over a decade now, and shut down the laptop. A wave of guilt washed through him. *Tamara won't be happy about this second television appearance.* Backing out came to mind again, but he hated letting people down and he'd said he would do it.

He shoved the last essay pile into a drawer for tomorrow, then, with one final look at his desk from the door, he switched off the lights. He locked his office door, rattling it to ensure it was secure. He heard the echo of footsteps on the polished floor but they were some way off, maybe in the adjoining corridor. He was on edge but couldn't understand why. Don't be daft, he chided himself. You're not the only one here.

Clutching his satchel, he headed towards the stairwell under the night lighting, every third light above was on, casting shadows about him. He didn't see or hear anyone else as he descended the stairwell. Floor by floor, the building was deserted: empty staff rooms, silent offices, locked labs. He half-expected to see Kateryna waiting somewhere, but she'd presumably gone home as instructed. Every so often, he heard tiny clicks or distant humming; typical night-time sounds in an old building. It was probably nothing, anxiety brought on by studying recent murders, but he felt vulnerable.

Finally, he reached the lobby, and swiped his card to unlock the doors and allow him to step out into the crisp air. A single security guard booth stood by the main entrance, but it was empty. The campus green lay beyond, shadowy except for lamp posts scattered along the paths. David's car was in the near-empty faculty car park on the far side of the green. He took a breath, heading towards it. You're being paranoid, he told himself. You've walked these routes a thousand times. A few students strolled across the distant pathways, laughing amongst themselves.

He cut behind the library, a route that usually saved a few minutes. The library windows loomed over him, mostly dark except for the ground floor's twenty-four-hour study area. No one was visible behind the glass. The wind picked up as he walked. He kept thinking he heard footsteps behind him, or saw the flicker of a silhouette at the edge of his vision, only to turn and see nothing.

Finally, the staff car park came into view, a rectangle of tarmac with bays marked by faded white lines. Perhaps two or three vehicles remained, including his own hatchback at the far end. The sense that he was being watched pressed upon him again, making his shoulders tense. Focus, he thought, fishing for his keys in his jacket pocket.

"Professor White!" a voice barked suddenly from behind.

David jolted, heart pounding. He spun around, nearly dropping his keys. A campus security guard, a stocky middle-aged man in a high-visibility jacket, stood a couple of strides away. "Apologies, sir," the guard said, raising his palms. "I didn't mean to startle you. I was just doing my rounds."

Blinking, David caught his breath. "Ah... no, it's fine. My fault for not hearing you." He forced a smile. "Late night for both of us, I guess."

"Indeed, sir. Are you heading home now?"

"Yes. I just... got carried away with a few bits and pieces. I'll be out of here in a moment."

The guard nodded. "Very good. Have a safe journey home, Professor."

"You too," David managed, stepping quickly to his car. He unlocked it with a click of the fob, glancing over his shoulder once more as the indicator lights flashed momentarily. The guard had already moved on whistling a nameless tune. David sighed. I'm being ridiculous, he told himself. He slid into the driver's seat, started the car, and locked the doors before they locked themselves. Now he felt secure.

As he pulled out of the space, headlights illuminating the deserted car park, a fleeting image of Tamara rose in his mind. She *really* won't be thrilled about tomorrow morning. He would have to address it tonight, so that she was aware. He'd have to manage that conversation gently. Perhaps he could explain how controlling the narrative might help contain the threat of anxiety among the locals. Yes. That's how he'd spin it.

Driving away from the campus, that nagging sense of being watched followed him until he was some distance away from the entrance. He took a steadying breath, glancing in the rear-view mirror, his eye caught by another vehicle coming along behind him. It was some distance away though, and he settled in for the hour-long drive back to the house he shared with Tamara.

CHAPTER TWENTY-TWO

David White pulled into the driveway just after eleven o'clock. As he switched off the engine, he allowed himself a weary sigh. The day had been an exhausting one, albeit one of his own making. The edits to this manuscript he was writing, going through the detailed changes the editor wanted, were proving more frustrating than he'd experienced with his previous books. They were also coming into the period running up to the exams. Then there was this phone call from the BBC. He'd spent the entire drive home dreading how Tamara would react. He'd reassured himself that he'd deal with it when he got here.

Now he was here, and the knot in his chest was evident.

He parked the car in front of the garage and got out. The chill of the night air made him shiver. Light spilled from the downstairs windows of the house he'd shared with Tamara for almost a year now. Through a gap in the curtains, he could see the living room lamp lit. She was still awake, waiting for him.

Entering through the front door, David paused in the hallway. The tightness in his chest grew. Tamara was seated on the sofa, arms folded, posture rigid. The television was muted, some rolling news channel playing silent headlines at the bottom of the screen. At the sight of him, Tamara picked up the remote and switched the television off with deliberate care.

"Hello," David said softly.

She nodded but didn't move from her seat. "You're late tonight."

He hung his coat on the rack beside the door, speaking to her over his shoulder. "Yes, sorry. I—"

"I know why," she cut in, her tone sharp. His brow furrowed.

"I had to focus. I have a lot of papers to mark," he said, sighing and rubbing at his face with the palms of his hands, "as well as finalising a lecture plan for the remainder of the week. I did tell you I'd be late."

He heard the tension under her calm tone. "I'm not talking about your day at the university," she said. "I mean your next brilliant television appearance." She pointed at the blank screen. "The BBC just announced they'd have you on the programme tomorrow morning." He saw her work her jaw. "That'll be nice. A seat on the sofa chatting about my case."

David's stomach lurched. He'd been bracing for this ever since the phone call inviting him back on air. "They promoted it already?" he asked quietly, pinching the bridge of his nose. "I... thought I might... break it to you more gently. I got the call last minute. I was going to tell you, I promise."

Tamara rose from her seat on the sofa, the overhead light casting hard shadows across her face. "Break it to me gently," she repeated, with evident sarcasm. "Perfect. As though me finding out from the BBC isn't humiliating enough. This is exactly the kind of stunt that makes me look utterly incompetent to my superiors."

"Now, that's unfair—"

"They already think I must be feeding you inside information, or worse, that you're capitalising on what I say at home for your own gain."

He bridled at the implication. "I'm doing no such thing," he said firmly. "They want me to help calm local fears, to speak about this matter from an expert, criminologist's perspective. That's beneficial, Tamara. People are scared; there's talk of a serial killer. We both know how these things can be blown out of proportion. My appearance on the television should be welcome, not viewed negatively."

She was in front of him now, arms still crossed tight. "Welcome?"

"Beneficial, then," David said defensively.

"For whom, exactly?" Her voice rose a notch. "Because it's sure as hell not beneficial for me. I've got two unsolved murders in the same group of acquaintances. I've got the senior brass so far up my backside they can tell where I shop for my knickers, and the least they expect from me is to control the flow of information on the murder investigation I'm in charge of."

"That's exactly my point, controlling the narrative," David said. "If I present it calmly and avoid any speculation about some spree killers, then emphasise it's a personal murder—"

"Oh... it's a personal murder is it? Thanks for letting me know," Tamara said, inclining her head. "I don't know why I didn't just ask you first, rather than... I don't know... investigating."

"Oh Tamara—"

"Don't you speak to me like that, David."

"Like what?" he asked, spreading his hands wide.

"Don't be condescending."

"I'm not. Maybe I can help. I can say the police are

working diligently, that it's not random and you are making progress."

"Which... wouldn't sound like I'm feeding you insider knowledge at all."

"That you are *sure* to be making progress, then."

"And in doing so, you undermine official channels." She turned away, pacing to the far side of the living room. "We have spokespeople for that. Trained officers who coordinate with the press office. You're not part of this."

David's jaw tensed. "I'm not giving away confidential details. It's broad strokes criminology, Tamara." His forehead creased. "Come on, you know this."

She swung back to face him, frustration flaring. "You do realise how it looks? Another prime-time cameo."

"What do you think it looks like?" he asked, failing to mask his irritation now.

"It looks like you're making a name off my case. My bosses... you know how much scrutiny I'm under with Tom on suspension? Now, they're expecting me to rein you in. If I can't manage you, my own boyfriend, then how can they expect me to manage a CID department, let alone a double homicide inquiry? I look like I've lost control of the situation."

He lifted a hand, half in surrender. "I'm sorry. Truly, but I don't see it that way."

"You shouldn't do the interview tomorrow," she said.

"I can't simply back out now without making things worse. The BBC will fill that slot with someone else. Maybe it will be some random talking head who stokes the situation rather than calms things. At least I have a measured approach, and you know that I know what I'm talking about."

Tamara looked at him hard. "Okay," she said, putting her palms together as if in prayer, her eyes gleaming. "I'll say this plainly. *Cancel your appearance* for tomorrow."

"That's not reasonable—"

"I can't have you out there, someone in a relationship with the SIO, fuelling speculation on this case. You do this, and it becomes even harder for me than it already is. People will suspect the police, and that's me by the way, just for reference, is feeding you inside info."

He exhaled, dropping his gaze. "I wish you could see it from my side. All of this is coming off the back of me being approached to be the lead consultant for a major new true-crime documentary series."

"Since when?"

He sighed. "I've been meaning to mention it, but—"

"When? Five minutes before it goes to air?"

David winced. "It's not like that. This is… it's… a huge opportunity for me. These interviews, the extra exposure… it all plays into that."

Her eyebrows shot up. "A documentary series? Well that's just fantastic news!"

It was clear to him that the news was quite the opposite. "It came about a fortnight ago," he said. "They approached me about it. I've been mulling it over. I had a call this afternoon from the producers and they confirmed they'd like me to front it. There have been discussions about it going to a more familiar face, but my visibility this week adds to my credibility."

Tamara's face darkened. "So that's what this is about, David? Your career, your big break in prime-time crime commentary?" She let out a scathing laugh. "Meanwhile, you're destroying my career at the same time—"

"That's not fair!" he snapped, stepping closer. "I'm not out to destroy your career. I've never betrayed you." He shook his head firmly. "I'd never do that, ever!"

She shook her head in anger, stepping back from him. "You

don't get it, do you? The more you talk about local murders, the more the media think you have some inside track. It undermines the official updates. My superiors see it as a conflict of interest, and you're dragging me straight into it."

David's pulse hammered. "I understand it puts you in a difficult position. But we're partners, Tamara. We're supposed to support each other's goals, not make demands of one another."

"This isn't support," she hit back. "You made a decision that directly impacts me. You didn't even consult me about it first. Two times, David." She held up two fingers in the air before him. "Two times! That's not how a partnership works in my book."

His hands balled to fists at his sides. "I have sound, professional reasons for doing what I—"

"I have. I have. It's all about you, isn't it?"

He swallowed, trying to keep his voice steady. "That's not my intention. None of this is."

"Well, your intentions don't matter if your actions wreck everything." She stood there, breathing hard. She let out an exasperated hiss. "I'm going out. I need air."

"Tamara... wait. It's too late to—"

But she was already marching past him, snatching her jacket violently from the rack. She glared at him as she put it on. The door opened and slammed shut in an instant. David stood in the silence, heart pounding. He ran a shaky hand through his hair.

"Well... that went better than expected," he whispered quietly. Closing his eyes, he let out a long breath. The knot in his stomach had dissipated. He could understand her viewpoint, he really could. At the same time though, he had a professional opportunity of his own. Pulling away from the argument now felt impossible.

Slowly, David moved through into the kitchen. Seeing the open bottle of red wine on the table, he opened a cupboard and got himself a glass. As he poured, he heard the ring of the liquid, and picked up the faint scent of fruit and spice. He took a careful sip, inhaling deeply. The wine was full-bodied, a harsh but welcome relief against the dryness in his mouth.

He set the glass down on the counter, leaned against it, and rubbed the bridge of his nose. "Damn," he muttered. He didn't want to sabotage Tamara's career. He just wanted to share his expertise, maybe do some good and, yes, it would almost certainly further his own academic reputation within a new circle of people. Namely in media and television. There had to be a middle ground. Maybe, after Tamara calmed down, they could talk it through again only with a more positive outcome.

A sudden knock at the front door jarred his thoughts. He glanced at the clock. Tamara had left only a few minutes ago but she hadn't gathered her keys or anything. She'd locked herself out when she slammed the door. David took another sip of wine, then set the glass aside and walked out of the kitchen and down the hall to the front door. His mind was working overtime, forming apology options he intended to make. The knock came again, only this time it was more urgent.

"I'm coming," he called, picking up the pace. David grasped the handle without the slightest hesitation and pulled it open. "Tamara, I—"

He never finished.

A figure, half-hidden in the darkness, lunged forward. David caught only the glint of something in a raised hand. Then a heavy blow smashed against his temple. Pain flared in his head, his vision swimming with pulsing lights. He staggered back, reeling. Keys? Not keys. His vision blurred under the impact as he stumbled against the doorframe. The door was still open, and he felt the sensation of cold air brush over him.

His attacker stepped forward, a dark silhouette and he thought he saw something within the darkness reflect the hallway lighting for a brief moment. David tried to shout, but the words got stuck and he heard a pitiful moan in place of a scream. The metallic object flashed through the air. Once, twice... he lost count as it struck him repeatedly. A burning sensation in his side, then a dull numbing feeling in his chest. Desperate, he clutched at the intruder's arms, but they twisted free with a terrifying strength. He lost his footing; the wooden surface became slippery underfoot. Movement in front of him was a blur and he felt out of control, his hands flailing in the air.

He stumbled, his knees buckling. The hallway walls seemed to tilt. Breathing was painful, laboured and increasingly difficult. David collapsed, his shoulder striking the floor at an awkward angle. He tried to right himself but couldn't. A cry came from his mouth now, partly from pain and partly from disbelief. Everything felt surreal, like a waking nightmare. His face was flat against the floor now, but he managed to shift his eyes, looking upward as a figure came to stand over him. His vision blurred again, firm edges taking on vague outlines.

The darkness swallowed him whole.

Tamara walked briskly along the lane, the crisp air cutting at her cheeks. She'd left without thinking but at least she'd picked up her coat. It was deceptively cold tonight. She paused, grimacing. They should never have fought like that.

"Never start an argument when you've had a drink, Tamara," she told herself. Turning on her heel, she started back towards the house, hoping to gather her thoughts and maybe salvage something from their disagreement. After all, they had an agreement. They were never to go to bed without settling the discourse. Naturally, that meant they had spent many nights without sleep, but she would try.

She'd only walked about a quarter of a mile before she'd calmed down. Was that the night air sobering her up, or just that she'd simply blown off steam and was ready to be… a bit more adult about the matter? She'd overreacted. She knew that. David was proud, perhaps too eager for the spotlight, getting carried away with the prospect of a little stardom. There was no harm in that. And he wasn't trying to ruin her, he just didn't fully grasp the consequences of his media appearances. As a high-ranking detective, she was under enough scrutiny without him complicating things.

The night felt eerily still. The raised wind from earlier had calmed. The breeze rustled leaves overhead, but there were no passing cars, and only a solitary muntjac crossing the road in front of her broke the stillness. She approached the driveway, standing beside the pillars and noticing with a puzzled frown that the door to their house was ajar, a shaft of light spilling out across the porch. Had she left it open when she stormed out?

A car started up down the street and she looked over to see it making a turn in the road. It was a small van, not a car, and looked beaten up, but in the available light she paid it little attention. The vehicle accelerated gently away in the darkness, the driver switching on the headlights before reaching the bend in the road and disappearing from view. Tamara resumed her walk back up to the house. There was something about the scene that made her heart lurch. David would never leave the door open like that.

"David?" she called quietly, approaching the house and increasing her pace. On the porch, she hesitated, her eyes snapping down. Splashes of red. A lot of them, trailing across the floor, forming a dark pool to one side. A gradually increasing pool of dark crimson, spreading out from beneath him. "David!" Tamara's voice broke.

CHAPTER TWENTY-THREE

Tom Janssen ran through the darkness before dawn, his breath fogging in the cold air. The coastal wind was ever-present, numbing his cheeks. He could taste the salt and feel the dust off the sand in the air as it whipped over the dunes and was swept inland. The habit of running in the early hours became akin to a meditative state for Tom. He was alone with his thoughts with nothing but pounding the earth beneath his feet to distract him. He liked the solitude, the sense of resetting himself for the trials ahead. Step by step, mind and body aligned.

His counsel, provided by the Police Federation, had left him a message the day before. The coroner was preparing his findings. The decision reached would have a massive impact on Tom and his life, his career, whichever conclusion was reached. He didn't know when exactly, and it could be a matter of days. This sword of Damocles, hanging over him these past few months, was about to strike down and he was powerless to affect its path.

He was halfway through his usual route – a looping track

that skirted farmland and an old church before bringing him along the inland edge of the nature reserve – when headlights appeared behind him. Tom slowed, glancing over his shoulder. The car pulled alongside, dipping forward as it braked. The passenger window slid down, revealing DC Eric Collet at the wheel. One look at Eric's face told Tom that something was badly wrong.

"Sir," Eric said, his voice low as he craned his neck to see Tom. "I've been looking all over for you."

Tom's pulse, already thumping from the run, kicked higher. Eric's expression bordered on frightened. Tom glanced around, then jogged over to the passenger door, leaning down. "What is it?" he asked, eyes flicking between Eric's taut features and the faint glow of the dash lights.

"There's been another attack," Eric said. Tom baulked. "Only… it happened at the DCI's house."

Tom's heart lurched. "Tamara?" His voice snagged on the name.

"No, she's… she's okay. Physically anyway," Eric said, though he still looked grim. "It's David."

"David?"

Eric nodded. "He was attacked in the hallway, late last night. He's in hospital."

"Is it bad?"

Eric frowned. "I don't have an update… but he's critical."

Tom pulled open the door and slid into the passenger seat. "Tell me everything," he said, still catching his breath. Eric shifted into gear and pulled off the verge, turning the car back towards the main road. "It happened last night. We got the call after eleven. The paramedics and uniform were first on scene, and they were there fast too."

"And David?"

"Multiple stab wounds," Eric said, eyes on the road but occasionally flitting across to Tom. "They managed to get him to hospital alive but…" Eric grimaced. "The last I heard it was touch and go."

The words landed heavily. Tom pulled a hand through his mass of sweaty hair, leaning back against the seat. "Tamara found him?"

Eric nodded. "She wasn't at the house when it happened and I think she'd returned just after it happened." Eric slowed, indicated and took a right turn. He was heading towards Tamara's house. Tom knew the route. "When she got home, the front door was open and David was on the floor… in a bad way. Honestly, you should see the place." Eric shook his head. "It's a mess. How anyone could survive it… I don't know."

Tom closed his eyes, taking a deep breath. The image struck him with grim clarity. Tamara, coming home to find David lying there. "She must be beside herself," he said quietly.

"She is. Francesca, her mother, is with her at the hospital right now." Eric glanced at him. "Cassie's on the scene with Danny Wilson. They're overseeing forensics. Cassie really wants you to take a look."

Tom simply nodded. Another violent attack. This was too soon to the previous ones. And it was far too close to home.

THEY TURNED off onto Tamara's road, greeted immediately by the bright glare of rotating blue lights. Even at this early hour, the place looked on edge: a uniformed constable guarded the driveway, while a second officer directed the occasional curious onlooker away. Despite the hour, people were getting in the early morning dog walk before going about their day. In such a small community there was bound to be interest. The sky had a pastel, pre-dawn, quality to it as if the sun was considering making an appearance but had yet to show itself.

Eric pulled up at the edge of the cordon and the constable peered inside, nodded to them both and gestured for them to pass through. They drove up to the front of the house, Eric pulling in some distance away from the front door alongside another liveried patrol car and the scenes of crime forensic van. Tom got out, shivering against the chill of the breeze. Whilst running he'd been sweating, but having sat still for the brief car journey, he was now feeling that moisture cool his skin.

The raised porch was cordoned off with police tape. Technicians in white suits could be seen milling around the entrance hallway with the occasional flash of a photographer's lens. Even standing at the edge of the cordon, Tom could see smears of blood on the threshold. His stomach twisted. Cassie saw their approach and she side-stepped the pool of blood on the wooden floor, coming out to meet them. Once clear of the scene, she removed the boot covers on her shoes and motioned for Tom and Eric to join her. There was no humorous banter, no attempt at lightening the mood which they often did even in the darkest of crime scenes.

On this occasion, it was pure professionalism.

"Thanks for coming," Cassie said, her tone flat. She glanced over her shoulder back at the front door. "That's where it happened. It's where David was attacked."

"Do you have any news on him?"

"No, but Sheriff is there with Tamara. He's there to keep us informed but also to make sure no one comes to finish the job."

Tom cocked his head. "You're confident he was the target?"

"If it wasn't him, then it was Tamara," Cassie said. She shrugged. "Either way, Sheriff is with them."

"Eric says it's not looking good for him."

"He passed away at the scene but the paramedics were able to get him breathing, but the injuries… they're severe." Cassie exhaled shakily, then nodded to the side. "Come through."

Cassie handed Tom and Eric a set of covers for their feet from a box, and she drew a fresh set for herself too. Then she lifted the cordon tape and Tom ducked beneath it. They walked up to the house, pausing on the porch, before circumventing the immediate area. Cassie pointed to the mat and the quarry tiles beneath it.

"There are some muddy footprints here. Whether it's from our killer or someone else, we can't say."

Tom noted the sticky sheen of dried blood on the porch. Someone had placed evidence markers, in the form of numbered arrows, near the spatter.

"We think he opened the door to his assailant," Cassie said, pointing to the spatter on the floor beneath the canopy off the porch. "Then he backed away, possibly trying to retreat from the ferocity of the assault. The attacker followed, driving him back."

Tom looked inside. A wide patch of dark blood stained the floor, indicating where David had collapsed. The volume of blood, as well as the colour of it, told him David lost a great deal of blood and it pumped from vital organs. The darker the colour, the more vital the location of the wound. He wasn't surprised to learn that he'd died at the scene. If the paramedics hadn't arrived quickly then he would have bled out within minutes.

"Tamara found him?" Tom asked.

Cassie inclined her head. "Yes, she'd just stepped out for a minute and gone for a walk. She came back, found the front door open, and David—" she sighed, letting the rest speak for itself.

Tom grimaced. "What time was this?"

"After eleven," Cassie said. "I'm not sure exactly. I haven't had a proper chance to speak to Tamara."

Tom nodded. He glanced at the forensics team working methodically. A camera flashed, capturing the disarray in the hallway. Another technician was busy dusting the door and its frame for fingerprints. The house, which Tom had visited countless times stood silent except for the hum of electronics and the quiet chatter of investigators.

Cassie pursed her lips. "Third victim in under a week. One dead in Blakeney, one in Sheringham, and now this."

Tom steadied himself. "You think it's the same attacker?"

Cassie steadied herself. "It fits the pattern, or at least it looks that way. David is a white, middle-aged male, attacked in his own home. A place he considered safe. Aaron Bell was attacked in his home in Blakeney. Tony Slater in his restaurant which adjoins his home, so it's near as the same thing…"

Tom took a breath, studying the crime scene. "The difference is, David's not in their circle. The other two were classmates."

"Aye," Cassie said. "But maybe we've been too fixated on the fact the first two knew one another. We haven't found any other common thread between them other than they went to the same school, attended the reunion and fell out with one another."

"Maybe," Tom said.

"This is north Norfolk," Eric said. "If you had someone attacking people then there's a decent possibility that the victims might know each other."

Tom frowned. "Right. No sign of forced entry?"

Cassie shook her head. "We think he came right up to the front door. David never knew what was coming when he opened it."

"So the question is, why David?" Tom asked.

"We haven't found a reason why for any of them," Cassie said, visibly frustrated. "Other than their age range and demographic—" She was interrupted by her mobile phone ringing. She stepped aside to answer it. Tom moved closer to the front porch, careful not to disturb the crime scene and contaminate any potential trace evidence. DC Danny Wilson, came into view from the kitchen. He offered Tom a subdued nod. Tom nodded back in acknowledgment, noticing the younger man's glum expression.

"With respect," Cassie said, raising her voice, "the man's an idiot!"

Tom glanced over at her but Cassie didn't notice his attention, and shook her head, building up to saying something else and then visibly deflated.

"Yes, sir," Cassie said. "I understand. I'll be ready to brief him when he arrives."

Cassie ended her call and returned to join Tom, with a face like thunder.

"Problem?" Tom asked.

"That was the Chief Superintendent," she said, her tone betraying her frustration. "With Tamara having to be recused from the case, obviously, and the apparent escalation in attacks – now we seem to be looking at three – he thinks it's escalating beyond our control." She glanced at Tom. "And he wants to bring in another DCI from King's Lynn to take the lead in the investigation."

Tom's eyebrows rose. "Who?"

"DCI Talbot," Cassie said. Tom exhaled, wincing.

"I suppose he's been around," Tom said.

"He's a buffoon. And you and I both know it. A stable pair of hands, the chief called him. Stable my arse. He's on the countdown to sealing his thirty years. We'll be lucky to get a result before he retires."

"He might not be that bad," Tom said, but inside, he agreed.

"They want a fresh lead with more experience. It's ridiculous—" she broke off, inhaling, then forced a more measured tone. "I told the Chief Supt we could handle it, but he'd already made up his mind. DCI Talbot will be here mid-morning. I'm to brief him back at Hunstanton on progress."

"DCI Talbot." He inclined his head. "A new SIO. That's going to slow you down."

"He's proper old school," Cassie said. "Thinks he knows everything. By the time he's fumbled around for a day or two we'll have another body in the morgue at this rate."

Tom stepped closer, quieting his voice. "How do you see it, Cassie?"

She rubbed at her chin, drawing the hand across her mouth, her brow furrowed. "David was repeatedly stabbed. A number of blows, and by the look of the scene it was vicious. Aaron Bell received a single blow to the head and Tony Slater had a single stab wound to his chest. The attacker is giving in to their blood lust… getting excited and… bolder."

Tom frowned. "I'm not so sure." Cassie looked at him, then gestured for him to continue. He let out a low breath. "The violence is certainly escalating. Possibly the killer's anger or… blood lust, as you said, is ramping up."

"Exactly," Cassie said. "He started with a relatively quick kill, impulsive perhaps, then moved on to a stabbing, then a full-on frenzy."

"Or we're dealing with something else," Tom said. "Spree killers tend to adopt the same MO with every attack. That's one reason we are able to identify them and link the crimes together. Their MO can change over time, but usually that's over a period of months if not years."

"Right," Cassie said, "and so... what? Do you think we have a copycat here?"

"Copycat attacks are not unknown, especially in big cities, but... in a low-density population like that we have up here on the coast, it would be statistically unlikely."

"Tell that to Tamara," Cassie said.

"Or David," Eric added.

"It's possible," Tom said, "but I don't see it. Not here. Not like this." He exhaled, thinking hard. "You linked the first two because of what?"

Cassie arched her eyebrows. "Aaron and Tony knew one another. They argued recently, and have a shared history where they weren't keen on one another."

"Which gives us no reason why they should both wind up as victims of homicide," Tom said. "If one killed the other, then certainly. But they are both victims, and the only animosity between them was with each other. Right?"

Cassie shrugged. "Right. So, should we forget the fact they are seemingly in the same peer group, and treat the murders as random? That would destroy any motive or association to the killer we've been searching for."

"But these murders, and also I suspect the attack on David, are not random at all. There will be a reason," Tom said. "Even if the reason is... unreasonable."

"So why target David?" Eric asked.

"You tell me, Eric, why might he be a target for the killer?"

Eric considered the question. "He is a similar demographic to the previous victims. He's white, middle aged, but slightly older than the other two."

Tom nodded. "Go on."

Eric glanced towards the house as DC Danny Wilson came to stand with them. "But the attack was different—"

"More violent," Danny said, joining the conversation.

"More than that," Eric said. "Yes, he was in his home but the other two appeared to have let someone in or they were well inside the property. David opened the door."

"That's different," Cassie said. "And the level of violence pushed it further from our expected crime scene."

"So it could be a different attacker," Tom said, "or our attacker is evolving." He shook his head. "Like I said, I don't think there's been enough time for that to happen." He looked around the others, reading their faces. "What else?"

Cassie frowned. "David has been on television speaking to the motivations of the murderer."

"He thinks it's a personal thing," Eric said. "Maybe he attacked David because David annoyed him… made him angry by suggesting he knew what made the killer tick."

"Revenge?" Tom asked. Eric nodded. All eyes turned to Tom, waiting to see if he agreed. "It's possible. Unhinged, but certainly possible."

"What other reason could there be?" Cassie asked. "He might have drawn the killer's ire," Cassie said. "The *know-it-all* criminologist on the television calling it personal. Nutters have killed for far less in my experience."

"That would bring the motivation back to the peer group, then," Tom said. "And David is just a… what?"

"An escalation?" Danny asked.

"Or a distraction," Tom said. Cassie caught his eye, cocking her head.

"This is one hell of a distraction! What's wrong with a crank phone call to the hotline? This is... a distraction from what?" she asked. Tom was pensive, reluctant to say aloud the thoughts percolating in his head until such time as they made sense. Cassie's phone rang again, but this time she silenced it. "We can't see a direct link," she said. "Unless the killer's simply lashing out at everyone connected to the investigation. Could the DCI have been the intended target? David might have answered the door and he was the victim simply because Tamara was out."

"That's... a leap," Tom said doubtfully, though his mind whirled at the possibility. "It doesn't feel like the guy's MO. The others were singled out personally which suggests to me that David was too. Albeit, possibly for a different reason."

"Meaning?" Cassie asked.

"I'm working on it," he said quietly. Tom's gaze lingered on the porch, and his thoughts turned to picturing Tamara arriving back to this scene, and David dying in the hallway "I should go see her, Tamara I mean.

Cassie's eyes flicked to him, reading the tension in his expression. She nodded. "I'll keep you in the loop... though I suspect when DCI Talbot gets his feet under the table that will become difficult."

Tom gave a grim nod. "He can't stop me from visiting a friend though."

Cassie's phone buzzed once more. This time, she gave an exasperated sigh, lifting it to answer. Tom touched Cassie's arm lightly. "Keep in touch."

She managed a faint smile and nodded. Eric came alongside Tom as they walked back to his car on the other side of the cordon.

"I can drop you at the hospital," Eric said quietly. "Or take you home first if you need to change. You must be freezing in those running clothes."

Tom glanced down at his sweat-damp shirt, the early morning chill creeping under his skin. "Right," he said. "I'll get changed first. Then I'll head to the hospital."

Eric nodded. "No problem. Let's go."

CHAPTER TWENTY-FOUR

Tom arrived at the hospital during shift change, a notable point in the day when traffic queued both to get into and out of the hospital car park. Visiting hours began at the same time as patients arriving for their scheduled procedures. Despite the volume of people traversing the corridors, everything felt subdued. Staff, patients and visitors alike went about their business with hurried but purposeful strides.

He asked for help at the information desk and was directed to the relevant wing of the hospital moving at a brisk pace. On the second floor of the building, at the end of a corridor, Tom found a small waiting area furnished with plastic chairs and a humming vending machine. He found Tamara, pacing the area, her arms folded tightly. On a seat nearby, anxiously wringing her hands in her lap, was Francesca, Tamara's mum. Both turned as Tom approached.

"Tom," Francesca said, quickly rising and stepping forward to meet him. "Thank goodness you're here."

Tom offered her a brief nod, taking her hand in his and squeezing it gently. He looked at Tamara. "How's David?"

Tamara tried to speak, but emotion choked her. She had a

haunted look, and it was clear she'd been up all night. Francesca filled the silence. "He's still in surgery, Tom. Someone came to see us... oh, it must be hours ago now, and they said his injuries are severe. We don't know any more than that. It's very frustrating."

Tom laid a hand on Francesca's arm, gaze shifting to Tamara. "I'm sure he's in good hands and they'll let us know when they have something to tell us.

Francesca nodded, her shoulders sagging. She looked nervously at her daughter. Tamara appeared detached, lost in thought. "He's a good man – David. He doesn't deserve this."

"No," Tom agreed quietly. Tamara looked at her mum but didn't comment. Tom saw the strain in her expression. "No one deserves something like this."

"He should be strung up—"

"Mum, please," Tamara said, exhaling and turning to walk away.

"I'm just saying," Francesca argued. "Savages like this should be taken out of society for good!"

"That's not helping, mum," Tamara said quietly, moving to stand at the solitary window overlooking an internal courtyard below.

"I was only saying." Francesca's eyes latched onto Tom. "So you'll find whoever did it, won't you? Please say you will."

Tamara stirred; her tone subdued. "Mum, we've talked about this. Tom's... not officially on the job."

Francesca scowled. "Don't get me started. That's another ridiculous decision." She looked at Tom, supportively squeezing his forearm. "You've done nothing wrong, yet they punish you like you're... like you're a criminal." Tom inclined his head, forcing a smile. "You're the best detective Tamara has on her team. You should be out there catching this maniac and protecting decent people."

Tom kept his voice level. "I understand. I wish it were that simple, but it isn't." He hesitated, glancing at Tamara. "I'm here for you both, though. If there's anything I can do, then I will."

Francesca shook her head, upset, then stepped away to collect herself. "If you're here for a while, Tom, I'll go and get a cup of coffee from the cafeteria?" He nodded.

"I'll be here."

Francesca gathered her cardigan and her bag from a nearby chair, smiled at Tom and glanced at Tamara. "Can I get you anything, love?"

Tamara shook her head. When her mum walked away towards the stairwell, Tamara looked at Tom apologetically and gestured for him to join her.

"I'm sorry about mum. She is her usual insensitive self. She means nothing by it."

Tom smiled, glancing at where Francesca had last been seen before entering the stairwell. "She means well," he said. They were by the window and Tom looked out over the curated garden below. There was a bench in the centre of the courtyard with small trees all around. But for the brick building looming up on all sides, it would be quite a pleasant place to be. Tamara's stance was rigid, arms folded as though shielding herself from a cold only she could feel. "Thank you for coming," she said, her voice taut.

"That's okay."

"I feel... so powerless."

"How are you holding up?" Tom asked gently.

She attempted a tight, humourless smile. "I've had better nights." Then her voice caught. "We argued..."

"What happened?"

"The argument?" Tamara gathered herself, rubbing at her face with tired hands. "David was going on the BBC this morning to talk about the Bell and Slater murders. I wasn't happy about it, and I told him as much... in my usual, sledgehammer way."

"You get that from your mum," Tom said.

"Comments like that will not earn you favours, Tom." He smiled and she returned it, momentarily at least. She sighed. "It was when he got home. It was late..."

"David was where beforehand?"

Tamara's forehead creased in thought. "He was working late, at the faculty. Anyway, he came home, we argued and I stormed out." She inclined her head. "Like a child, I walked away. It's what adults do when someone doesn't say or do what you want them to."

"You wanted him to cancel the television appearance?"

"Damn right," she said. "I thought it would undermine me and make our investigation harder. I left... it must have been right before it happened. When I came back... he was on the floor."

Tom's brow furrowed. "You saw no one?"

Tamara was staring out of the window but not seemingly focussed on anything in particular. "I saw a vehicle in the street... a small van. It pulled away when I got to the drive, but I didn't get a look at the driver or the registration plate. I was... distracted, still ruminating on the argument."

"Do you remember anything about it?"

"One of the rear lights was broken," she said, thinking hard. "The driver turned the lights on as the van drove away and I saw the white light through the broken casing."

"The light worked but—"

"Yes, the casing must have been cracked or had a piece

missing. It should have been a red light, but I could see the white of the bulb."

Tom nodded. "Anything else?"

She shook her head, apparently disappointed in herself. "Some detective, huh? Someone tries to murder my boyfriend in our own home and I see and hear nothing. By the time I realised something was wrong, David was... bleeding out on the floor." Her voice was thick with emotion. "Tom, there was so much blood." She swallowed hard. "I keep thinking if I'd stayed, if I'd been there then maybe I could have stopped it."

Tom touched her shoulder. "Or you might both be in theatre fighting for your life."

"But even so, I—"

"I've been to your house," Tom said quietly. "Whoever did this was determined. Had you been there, I doubt it would have made much difference. The ferocity of the assault... is something I haven't seen many times. You're not to blame."

She nodded stiffly but tears threatened her composure. "That's easy to say. But it's harder to accept." After drawing a steadying breath, she shifted topics. "Any leads?"

"Cassie's working it," Tom said, conscious that they were all caught by surprise by the assault on David.

"There's little to work with," Tamara said.

"Cassie thinks it's the same attacker who killed Aaron Bell and Tony Slater."

Tamara glanced at him. "But you disagree?"

"I'm not sure," he said. "I wouldn't rule it out but I think there's more to it."

Tamara looked away, frustration simmering. "David had no involvement with either Aaron or Tony beyond his theories he talked about on television. Was that enough motive for some deranged person."

"Possibly." Tom didn't want to pass comment. The attack

on David could be construed as the act of a mad individual, but that didn't follow with the other two murders. They were missing something. "What about the rest of the investigation? Who is on your suspect list?"

She lifted a hand to rub her forehead. "You know the first two victims were ex-classmates, so we've been working that angle. The only people they fell out with was one another, so that's hampered us. Oh, and Noah Cook, but only because he had a brief spat at the reunion with Aaron. As far as we can tell, he has no contact at all with Tony Slater."

"Did you find out what the issue between Noah and Aaron was?" Tom asked.

"We haven't formally interviewed him yet," Tamara said, craning her neck to see down into the courtyard as a couple of people, a patient in a gown and a companion, came into view. "We've spoken to him on the phone, but he wasn't at home when Danny went to interview him and he cancelled the follow-up appointment." Tom was surprised to learn they hadn't followed it up yet. Tamara caught his eye and shook her head. "I'm not a fool, Tom. Charlotte Sears confirmed Noah took her home after the reunion finished and stayed for a drink at her place. They were together when Aaron was attacked." She arched her eyebrows. "And he has a cast iron alibi for the timeframe of Tony Slater's death."

"Who gave him that one?"

"CCTV," Tamara replied with a sigh. "Time and date stamped. Besides, he has never even appeared on our radar having lived in Sheringham all of his life. He's a fine upstanding member of the public. The man ticks no boxes for any of this."

Tom frowned. "Fair enough. Anyone else that you're looking at?"

She exhaled, pinching the bridge of her nose between

thumb and forefinger. "No. On the face of it, it seems like we should be looking for a stranger passing through... but David... is often right when he profiles these kinds of cases."

"He thinks it's personal, right?" Tom asked and she nodded. "Which means it's someone in their orbit."

"Yes, that's what he thinks."

"Do you agree?"

Tamara shook her head. "I do. But I haven't been able to move things forward, at all." She sighed. "Now it will be someone else's case."

"They're bringing someone in from Lynn," Tom said. "I was with Cassie when she got the call."

"Who?"

"Greg Talbot."

"Well... he's solid enough, I suppose," Tamara said but she didn't sound convinced.

"Cassie said otherwise, and to the Chief Super, too."

"I'm sure he took it well," Tamara said. "Greg is an experienced detective."

"He's not run many murder inquiries though," Tom said.

"No, he hasn't." Tamara sounded dejected, turning away from the window. A moment's silence thickened the air between them. Finally, Tom spoke.

"I'm sorry. I wish I could do more."

"I know," Tamara murmured. "Just..."

She seemed about to say more when brisk footsteps echoed down the corridor. A man in scrubs appeared, short hair sticking up from where he'd removed a surgical cap. He scanned the hallway, then approached them, his eyes flitting between Tom and Tamara.

"Mrs Greave?" he asked gently. She nodded. "I'm Dr Edwards. I'm sorry to have kept you waiting so long, but—"

"It's okay. Please, tell me—"

"He's out of surgery now," Dr Edwards replied, voice subdued but reassuring. "He lost a great deal of blood as a result of the number of injuries he sustained in the assault. We had to address internal injuries near the liver, heart and stomach. The most severe wound has caused one of his lungs to collapse." He looked between them, almost apologetic. "We've stabilised David, but his condition is critical." He hesitated momentarily. Tamara tilted her head and he winced. "I know this may sound odd, but he has been extremely lucky, when all is said and done."

"Lucky?" Tamara asked. "How is he lucky?"

"The wounds he has," Dr Edwards said, "could have been much worse. Clearly, he sustained a vicious assault on his person, but the knife wounds, in many places, are superficial. The attacker, I'm reluctant to say this, didn't seem to be very proficient with the weapon. I know that sounds odd but, in my experience with knife injuries, David should never have survived this." He shrugged apologetically. "I'm sorry. Perhaps I shouldn't have said anything."

"No, no. Not at all," Tamara said, her breath caught. "Is he awake?"

Dr Edwards shook his head. "He is heavily sedated. I believe this will help to give his body the best opportunity to heal. The next twenty-four to forty-eight hours will be crucial. If he remains stable, his chances of recovery improve significantly. But… I feel I must advise you that, despite what I've just said, his situation is very grave indeed. He is a very poorly man, and you should prepare yourselves for the reality of what that might entail."

Tamara's eyes flicked closed. "What are his chances?"

"I'm afraid I don't believe in giving out percentages," Dr Edwards said.

"Humour me," Tamara said, opening her eyes. "Please."

"Fifty-fifty," Dr Edwards replied. "I'm sorry, I can't say any more than that. Should his condition not deteriorate in the next twelve hours, then his chances will improve."

"Thank you," Tamara whispered. Francesca, arriving unnoticed behind them, let out a soft sob.

Dr Edwards gave them both a compassionate nod. "A nurse will come to take you down to ICU when you will be able to see him, as soon as we have him comfortable. It will need to be a brief visit, but you will be able to speak to him."

"Will he hear me?" Tamara asked.

"I believe he will, yes," Dr Edwards said.

"Thank you," Tamara repeated. The doctor excused himself, nodding to Tom as he backed away and turned on his heel, leaving the three of them together. Francesca turned her face away, wiping tears. Tamara took a trembling breath. "At least he's alive."

Tom placed a hand on her arm. "He's fighting, and he's in the best place."

She swallowed and turned to him; voice subdued. "I'll stay until they let me in. Then I'll probably stay here as long as they'll have me."

"Of course," Tom said. "And if you need anything, anything at all, call me, day or night."

She gave a shaky nod. "I will." Then her gaze sharpened slightly. "What are you going to do?"

"Me?" he asked innocently.

"Be careful, Tom. I'm sure all of this is connected, but I don't know what's caused this escalation. I don't know who's next—"

Tom was stern, focussed. "Noted." In a gentler tone, he added, "I'm more worried about you. You might still be a target, especially if this was about David being on the nail with his analysis."

She forced a smile. "Dave Marshall is here. We'll be safe enough."

Tom nodded. He wanted to say something more comforting but found no words that fit. Instead, he offered Francesca a reassuring squeeze of the hand in passing. "He'll pull through," Tom said quietly, though he couldn't promise any such thing. He looked into Tamara's eyes. "I'll be in touch."

Tom found himself replaying the conversation he had with the private investigator that Aaron Bell had hired, Shaun Whale. He was tasked with digging up information on Charlotte Sears and Noah Cook. Charlotte giving Noah an alibi for Aaron's death was convenient, although he was seemingly on camera elsewhere when Tony was murdered. Even so, he couldn't shift his thoughts away from that connection. It didn't tie Noah to either murder, but it was a link nonetheless.

Glancing at his watch, he then took out his mobile, dialling a number. The call was answered with a genuinely affectionate greeting.

"Tom. Janssen," Charlotte said. "What a pleasant surprise! What can I do for you?"

"Are you at home?"

"Yes, why?"

"I'm in town, and I thought I could stop by for a cup of tea."

"Um…" Charlotte said, hesitating. "Sure, why not."

CHAPTER TWENTY-FIVE

THE AVENUE, the road where Charlotte Sears lived in Sheringham, was on the eastern edge of the town and only a short walk away from the coastal path where they'd held the vigil for both Kristy and Aaron a few days before. Tom stood on the path looking at the house. It was a rendered 1930s semi-detached house set back from the road with a small garden to the front. It was a leafy road within walking distance of the town and Tom could hear the waves breaking due to the wind coming in his direction.

He made his way down the drive and a net curtain flicked aside in the nearest window, revealing a quick glimpse of someone inside. A moment later, before he could ring the doorbell, he heard a key turn in the lock and the door opened. He was met by Charlotte, a broad smile on her face as she raked a hand through her blonde hair. Sporting a set of bright blue-rimmed glasses today, her eyes lit up as she greeted him.

"Tom," she said. "This is a welcome surprise."

"Hello, Charlotte. I hope it's not a bad time," he said, keeping his voice warm, friendly. "I wanted to see how you were doing, after all that's been happening."

"How lovely of you." She hesitated, then stepped aside, beckoning him to enter. "Please, come in."

Inside, the hallway smelled faintly of coffee and felt chilly. It would probably warm up as the sun came around during the day. She led him into a modest dining room where the wall between it and the kitchen had been removed to open up the rear of the house. She gestured for him to sit.

"Would you like a cup of tea or maybe coffee?" she asked, moving through into the kitchen area. "I have a fancy coffee machine," she said, practising a slight curtsey before an impressive looking stainless-steel machine, as if presenting it as a competition win.

"A coffee would be great, thanks," Tom said, pulling out a chair at the dining table and sitting down. He looked out through the patio doors and into the garden beyond. It was landscaped, but clearly hadn't been maintained as intended. Charlotte glanced at him and followed his gaze.

"Noah designed all of that," she said, absently scratching the back of her neck as she kept an eye on the pressure gauge of the machine. "I must admit I don't have the time or the energy to keep it all going."

"I can imagine it's a fair bit of upkeep," Tom said.

"Yes, but Dean does a lot of it."

"Your son?"

"Yes," Charlotte said, slotting the filter head into the grinder. "Mind your ears," she said. "It's frighteningly harsh."

She was right. The machine began the grinding process with the fresh beans dropping down into the hopper. After what seemed like a ridiculously long time, the machine quietened as it pressed the ground coffee into the head. She withdrew it and snapped it into place, setting an empty cup beneath the filter head.

"How do you take it?"

"White, please," Tom said. "No sugar."

"A man after my own heart," Charlotte said, moving to the fridge and getting a bottle of milk. She poured the milk into a little stainless-steel jug and steamed it for a few seconds with the wand before adding it to the freshly extracted espresso. She put it down in front of Tom and went to begin the process again for herself. "So, what brings you here?"

Tom lifted his cup, smelling the aroma of the coffee. "I was in the area and thought I'd stop by. The last time I saw you it was all a bit emotional."

"You're so sweet," she said, coming to join him at the dining table and taking a seat opposite. Charlotte rested her elbows on the table. "It's very kind of you to check up on me." She reached across and gently patted the back of his hand resting on the surface of the table.

"I also wanted to speak to you about the night of the reunion."

"Oh?" she asked, tilting her head. "What was it you wanted to ask?"

"Noah brought you home, didn't he?"

She smiled. "Are we the talk of the town again? We used to be married. I think it's believable that we can still speak to one another, isn't it?"

Tom smiled too. "That's not why I'm asking. He brought you back here and... did he come in?"

Her gaze narrowed and she seemed uneasy with the question. "I thought you weren't with the police at the moment."

"I'm not, but they asked you the same question, I suppose?"

"They did," she said, her pleasant demeanour shifting slightly. "And I can tell you what I told them, if you like. I had to clear up after the reunion, along with other members of the organising committee and then Noah gave me a lift home."

She fixed him with a stern look. "And yes, he did come in for a bit. Is that okay with you... and the police?"

"Of course," Tom said. "It's just that Noah had words with Aaron on the night, and they wanted to establish his movements around the time of Aaron's death, that's all."

"And we did. He was with me," Charlotte said. "Not that it's any business of yours, Tom."

"Did anyone else see the two of you here, together?"

"Like who?"

Tom raised an eyebrow. "Your son, Dean... or your daughter, perhaps?"

"She stayed at a friend's house that night. I knew I'd be home late and so one of her friend's mums helped me out."

Tom nodded. "Right. And Dean?"

"With his girlfriend, at her place," Charlotte said, patience running thin. "What... why are you asking these questions?"

Tom smiled apologetically. "Sorry, it's a force of habit." He picked up his coffee cup and sipped at it. "It comes from being a policeman for so many years."

Charlotte seemed to relax a little, her posture less rigid. "I'm sorry too."

"What for?"

"For being so defensive!" She shook her head. "With everything happening recently, I guess I'm just on edge about it all."

"Aaron coming back to town?"

She snorted. "Yes, that was... a surprise."

"Were you surprised to find out he hired someone to look into you?" Tom asked. Her eyes darted to him and narrowed.

"Me?"

"Yes," Tom said, watching her intently. "And Noah."

"What... what for?"

"That's what I'd like to know," Tom said. He allowed the

silence to grow, still meeting her eye but she didn't flinch, nor did she look away. "So, no one came asking you questions?"

"Other than you... and your colleagues? No. What could he possibly want to do that for?"

Tom shrugged. "People do strange things. Oftentimes, it's the last thing you expect of them."

"That's weird!"

"I won't disagree. But you can't think of a reason why Aaron did that?"

"No," she said firmly. "Why don't you ask... whoever it was he paid to stick his nose into my life. Ask him what he was doing."

"I did."

"And?"

"He wouldn't tell me either. Or he didn't know which I think is the truth. Aaron never told him."

"Weird," Charlotte repeated, only this time barely above a whisper. She was absently biting the nail of her thumb, staring thoughtfully straight ahead.

"Tell me, were you and Noah... on good terms that night?"

"As good as ever, yes. Why do you ask?"

"I gather the two of you haven't been seeing eye to eye recently, that's all."

"Who fed you that nonsense?"

"Noah.' Her eyes drifted up to meet his but she looked away quickly.

"Did he?"

"Something about the two of you disagreeing about Dean's future."

"Oh right," she said, nodding. "That's true. We have argued about that. I think Dean should go to university but Noah wants to keep him here at his side."

"Working with him?"

"Yes, I think so. Noah has a grand *Cook and Son* business idea. It's daft."

"Is it?"

She scoffed. "That landscaping business barely pays enough for Noah to live on, let alone support two full-time employees. It's stupid. Dean can do so much better."

"It's honest work," Tom said.

"And seasonal, for the most part. A lot like most jobs in these parts."

"But you're getting on?"

Charlotte shifted, a slight flush touching her cheeks. "Yes, we've been getting along better lately. Even though we're divorced, we still share a son." She brushed her hair away from her eyes. "Actually, we're closer now than we've been in years."

"That's good," Tom said, keeping his expression neutral. "Glad to hear it. So, no tension?"

Charlotte looked away briefly. "Nothing unusual." She smiled and glanced away but when she turned back, the smile was more guarded than before. He let the silence stretch for a moment, and was about to ask another question when the door to the kitchen opened and a young man entered. He had long brown hair that hung almost to his shoulders. He was slim and Tom would have suggested he had a grunge-thing going on with his clothing choices. That is, if it was the nineties, and grunge was still a thing. He had no idea what this look was called these days. He dreaded what choices Saffy would make when she entered her late teens.

"Hey," the young man said, then paused as he saw Tom.

"Dean, this is Tom," Charlotte said. "I used to go to school with him, along with your father."

Dean nodded briefly towards Tom who smiled. There was something familiar about the teenager, but Tom couldn't place it. He was confident that he'd never come across him in a professional capacity, but the sense that he knew him lingered.

"All right," Dean said to Tom. He was chewing gum, loudly. His mum disapproved.

"I wish you'd keep your mouth closed when you're eating, Dean."

"I'm not eating," he said. "I'm chewing. It's different."

"It's very uncouth," Charlotte said, looking apologetically towards Tom, who smiled.

"Sorry," Dean said, taking the gum from his mouth and depositing it in the knock box Charlotte used to knock out the ground coffee from the filter head.

"And that should go in the bin," she told him as the boy made his way towards the hall.

"Next time," Dean said over his shoulder. He turned and smiled at her, walking into the hallway backwards. "Sorry, Mum. Nice to meet you, Tom."

"Yes, it was nice to meet you too, Dean," Tom said, watching the lad turn and walk away. The familiarity was still there, only now Tom thought he knew where he'd seen Dean before. He looked at Charlotte. "A handsome lad."

She smiled proudly, looking into the hall where her son had been. "Yes, he is. If only he had a bit more get up and go about him, he'd be almost unstoppable."

"Teenagers," Tom said. "He'll find his way."

"I hope so," she said, exhaling. She turned back to Tom. "So, why did you really come here today?"

"You don't believe me?" Tom asked, feigning offence.

"I do, but there's more, isn't there?" She stared at him. "You want to ask about Noah, don't you? Do you think he could hurt Aaron? I mean, do you really think that?"

"People do all sorts of things you don't expect," Tom said. He met her eye. "All you need is the right trigger."

"Not Noah. He was with me when Aaron died... and he was in a garden centre when Tony was attacked."

Tom cocked his head. He hadn't asked her anything about Tony, let alone Noah's link to it, if there even was one. "Right, yes," he said. "He couldn't have been involved."

"That's right."

"What time did he leave you?" Tom asked. "On the night of the reunion, I mean?"

She seemed exasperated with him. "Are you going back there again?" Tom waited silently. She gave in. "It was probably around four in the morning."

"Four? That's quite late—"

"Or early," she said, "depending on how you look at it." She rolled her eyes as Tom maintained his gaze. "All right, we... got to talking about old times, and one thing led to another. You know how it is?"

Tom smiled awkwardly. "I see, of course."

"We're grown adults," she said. "And we have a shared history—"

"And a child," Tom said. She nodded.

"But... I don't want it common knowledge, if you don't mind? I've had the label of being a slapper since I was at school."

"You were never thought of like that."

"Really?" Charlotte said. "How many other girls gave birth to a child in the fifth form?"

Tom scratched the back of his neck. "I never heard anyone talking about you like that."

"Thank you, Tom." She reached across the table and touched his hand. "You are kind, even if you are a very bad liar."

He laughed. She glanced at the clock on the wall. "Do you have to be somewhere?" he asked.

"I do. Work," she said, looking up at the ceiling. "It's been difficult recently because my car's been off the road. Fortunately, Noah has let me borrow his to get around when I've needed it."

"You have it fixed now?"

"Yes," she said. "I picked it up from the garage yesterday. It makes life so much easier. One of us in this house has to go to work to pay for things!" she said, raising her voice and looking up at the ceiling. She smiled at Tom. "It's only part-time but it means I'm around to collect my daughter from school. Not that she'll need me much soon enough."

"How old is she?"

"Going on twenty-one with the attitude she has about her!" Charlotte got up from the table and went in search of her things, gathering her bag and car keys then looked for her mobile phone. "I think I left my mobile in the front room." She pointed at Tom's coffee cup as he made to stand. "You finish your coffee, and then we can walk out together."

He nodded, picking up his cup as she hastened through into the hallway and disappeared into the front room of the house. Tom rose and quickly tore off a sheet of kitchen roll he found on the counter beside the hob. Using it, he retrieved the chewing gum that Dean had left in the knock box, folding it quickly and slipping it into his pocket before Charlotte reappeared, mobile held aloft triumphantly in her hand.

"You found it?" Tom asked with a smile.

She nodded. "Always where you left it!" she said, smiling.

Tom drained his cup and put it down on the counter next to the sink. He joined Charlotte and they left the house via the back door. The garage was at the end of the driveway which ran along the side of the house. Charlotte grasped Tom's forearm gently and leaned in to give him a kiss on the cheek.

"It was lovely to see you again, Tom."

"Same," he said, smiling. She set off to the garage where her car was parked and he made his way along the side of the house and back into the street. He had the sense that he was being watched and when he looked around, his eyes lifted to an upstairs window and he saw Dean looking down at him. Tom smiled, but as soon as he did, Dean disappeared from view. Tom rubbed at his chin, turned and began the short walk back into town.

Moments later, Charlotte drove past him in her little hatchback. She tapped the horn as she passed and Tom waved to her. As he walked, he took out his mobile and called Cassie. She answered immediately.

"Cassie, did you follow up with Noah Cook?"

"Cook?" she asked, surprised. "I tried but couldn't get hold of him. I set Danny onto him. I figured that was something he could manage without screwing it up." She sighed. "I was wrong, obviously."

"So you haven't interviewed him?"

"No, but there's no real need. He has an—"

"An alibi for both murders, right. Listen, I have a favour to ask," Tom said. "But it will probably take some doing."

"I know you've been away from things for a while, sir," Cassie said, lowering her voice. Tom could hear activity in the background. "But there is a double homicide inquiry up and running plus the matter of a third attempted—"

"I know, but it's important," Tom said, "and, as it happens, probably relevant."

"Name it."

"Can you meet me?"

"No chance," Cassie said. "I'm about to brief DCI Dinosaurus on the case. I'll be tied up here for a while... possibly the next sixty-five million years or so."

"Then send someone you trust to meet me. I've got something for you," he said quietly, stopping as the sun broke through the clouds and he felt the warmth of it on his face.

"Sounds intriguing," Cassie said. "What is it?"

Tom felt the folded-up piece of kitchen towel in his pocket. "Something and nothing, or it could be everything."

CHAPTER TWENTY-SIX

A STIFF BREEZE ruffled Tom's hair as he leaned on the rail, staring down at the incoming tide lapping at the slipway of Sheringham's old harbour. The sun was sitting low in the sky but this area of town was now in shadow and the temperature was rapidly dropping away. He'd been thinking all day whilst walking around the old haunts of his youth, the promenade, the high street, although it had changed a lot over the years. At least, it wasn't as he remembered it. It seemed smaller now somehow. Maybe it was just that his world had grown whereas his childhood town had remained much as it always had been.

What if he was wrong? He had never been labelled an arrogant man. He knew he was fallible. He was human. However, he felt confident in his theory. He simply needed some evidence to back it up.

"Fancy bumping into you here."

He turned just as Cassie appeared at his side, leaning her back against the rail and casting an eye around their immediate area. The small café at the edge of the harbour was closed, undergoing some kind of refurbishment before the main tourist season kicked in. This late in the day, there were only a few people passing by and no one was close or paying them any attention.

"Hi, Cassie. How did it go with Greg?"

Cassie took a deep breath, reaching into her shoulder bag as she spoke. "I misspoke earlier."

"You did?"

"I did," she said, producing a folder and bending her knees to gently place her bag at her feet. "DCI Talbot is not a buffoon. He's way, way worse than that. I would go so far as to label him a cretin." Her brow creased and then she shrugged. "But that's harsh on cretins. It is what it is."

"Did you manage to get what I asked for?"

"Aye," she said, passing the folder to him. "But you're not looking at that, right?"

"Scout's honour," Tom said. "I didn't see anything." He opened the folder and scanned the index documenting the contents, listed on the first page.

"You know, you could tell me what you're looking for," Cassie said. "That way, I could have just looked rather than go through this cloak and dagger, Scarlet Pimpernel routine this afternoon." She turned around, seemingly comfortable they were alone and not observed. She leaned on the rail, looking out at the darkening horizon, interlocking her fingers before her.

"That would take away the sense of trepidation, of living dangerously," Tom said, without looking at her. He was busy reading through the pathologist's post-mortem. He slipped past it having not found what he was looking for. "I know how much you enjoy pushing boundaries."

"It's true," Cassie said. "I do like that aspect of my character."

"Yes, it's why you get on so well with Saffy. Although, I would expect her to grow out of it when she matures."

"Aye, me too," Cassie said. "So… are you going to tell me whose DNA you had us map at such short notice?"

Tom stopped reading the document he'd been searching for. His eyes flicked to Cassie. "Do you have the results already?"

"I do," she said. "Have you any idea the number of favours I had to call in to get that turned around in a working day? It's unprecedented."

"I didn't think anyone owed you any favours," Tom said thoughtfully.

Cassie shrugged. "True. I'll rephrase it. Have you any idea how many favours I owe people because I had them turn this around in a working day?"

"That's more like it." He held her gaze, waiting. She gave in first.

"The DNA shows a familial match to—"

"Aaron Bell," Tom said. Cassie's mouth fell open.

"You knew?"

"I guessed," Tom said, inclining his head. "But I needed you to run the test to be sure."

"So… who is it?" Cassie asked. "Who's the mystery man? The DNA shows it's a man, and a close match. The lab says they are almost certainly father and son."

"Dean Cook," Tom said, biting his bottom lip. Cassie's eyes narrowed.

"Charlotte Sears's son?"

Tom nodded.

"How did you know?"

"I didn't," Tom said, raising his gaze and looking out to sea. "I only met him myself for the first time this morning. When he walked in… it was like looking back in time. He has a lot of his mother in him, but the way he walks, carries himself and the smile." Tom shook his head. "He's Aaron all day long."

Cassie rolled her tongue around the inside of her cheek, then frowned. "Do you think Noah is aware?"

Tom exhaled. "I saw it right away, but he's grown up with him. He's raised him." Tom shrugged. "Does he see it? I don't know. It answered the question of why Aaron hired a private detective to look into Charlotte and Noah."

"You think Aaron found out or he knew all along?"

"I don't know—"

"Hang on," Cassie said. "I thought Aaron dated Charlotte's sister, Kristy?"

"He did, yes," Tom said. "And Charlotte was pregnant going into the fifth form, the year after we all graduated."

"There must have been an overlap," Cassie said. Tom remained tight-lipped and simply nodded.

"The DNA proves it," Tom said. "Aaron broke up with Kristy but, unless my maths is off and I don't think it is, he was also having some relationship with his girlfriend's little sister at the same time."

"Do you think she knew as well?" Cassie asked. "Do you think Kristy knew or found out?"

"Careful, we're getting deep into the realms of speculation there."

"Still…" Cassie blew out her cheeks. "Finding out my boyfriend was a nonce, and noncing my little sister while he was at it might be enough to see me jump off a cliff too."

Tom winced. "It's… awful."

Cassie arched her eyebrows, then pointed at the folder in Tom's hand. He was struggling to stop the breeze from blowing sheets of paper around the harbour. "What are you looking for in the file then?"

"This," Tom said, pointing to the document he was reading. It was Aaron Bell's medical history, covering the years he was living in and under the care of NHS practitioners anyway. "Aaron suffered from mumps when he was in his early twenties."

"I thought there was a vaccine for that?" Cassie said, her eyes moving from the paperwork to Tom.

"His parents were outliers back in the day," Tom said. "They had a big focus on nutrition and wellbeing... natural immunology and all of that."

"Decades ahead of their time," Cassie mused sarcastically. "They could get a channel on the internet these days. Make a fortune."

"Yes, quite," Tom said. "It says here that the illness had a knock-on effect to Aaron's fertility." Tom met Cassie's quizzical eye. "He couldn't have children."

Cassie looked hard at him. "And so... he comes back home and seeks out the child he never claimed—"

"Or bumps into the child he never knew he had," Tom said. "Then hires a private investigator to try and figure out whether Dean is his son."

"That could cause a few ructions among the local wildlife," Cassie said softly. Tom couldn't disagree. Tom closed the medical folder. It was firm background evidence, but still circumstantial when it came to tying it to either murder.

"Tell me, have you got Tony Slater's personal records back yet?"

"Aye," Cassie said. "Which one, specifically, are you referring to?"

"Mobile phone records."

Cassie took out her mobile and called Eric, putting the call onto speaker so Tom could hear as well. "Eric, it's Cassie. Can you pull up Tony Slater's mobile phone records, please."

"One second," Eric said.

"Has the new DCI missed me?" she asked.

"Not yet. He's still in with the chief. I think they're planning a fresh appeal at a press conference." Eric cleared his throat. "Right, I'm in. What am I looking for?"

Cassie looked at Tom who had his mobile phone in hand. "Can you check to see if this number comes up?"

"Hi, sir, sorry I didn't know you were there," Eric said, his tone lightening as he recognised Tom's voice.

"The number, Eric. Quick as you can," Cassie said. Tom read out the mobile number and Eric took it down.

"Right… ah..," Eric said. "That's interesting." They waited whilst he carried out his search. "Okay, this number has repeatedly called, and been called by Tony's number on multiple occasions over the past six months. And… notably, on the morning of his murder. An incoming phone call that lasted four minutes and sixteen seconds. Whose number is it anyway?"

Cassie looked at Tom. "Yes, Tom. Whose number is it?"

Tom took a deep breath, lowering his gaze. He hadn't wanted it to be true, but somehow he'd known all day that they were approaching this point. He'd wanted to be wrong.

Eric continued. "There was also a 999 call made from Tony Slater's mobile at 10:34, but the handler never communicated with the caller before the call ended. That would have been around the time of the attack, wouldn't it?"

"Tom?" she asked, looking up at him. "Who was it?"

Tom was pensive. "We're going to need a few more bodies to come with us."

CHAPTER TWENTY-SEVEN

Tom sat on the bench, his hands in his coat pockets, staring out over the sea. This was the perfect location to capture the beauty of the Norfolk coast. Only a few metres from where Kristy Sears lost her life, the bench sat just off the coastal trail on the clifftop, hemmed in by long grasses growing to either side, swaying in the breeze.

"Tom?"

He looked to his left, seeing Charlotte approaching. The breeze blew hair across her face and she tried to shift it away from her eyes but the attempt was futile. Beside her, his expression cast iron stone, was her ex-husband Noah. Unexpectedly, Dean was also with them. A pang of guilt struck Tom, but he was committed now. This was how it had to be. He took his hands from his pockets and rose from the bench, turning side on to the view as they climbed the gentle slope towards him.

"Hey," Tom said. "Thanks for coming."

"You made it sound important,' she said, tilting her head and smiling as she came to stand before him. "What's this about?"

Tom looked at Dean and then Noah, offering him a nod which was returned in a curt fashion. "Noah. Thanks for coming."

Noah glanced at Charlotte. "I wasn't given much of a choice in it. What do you want, Tom. Me and the boy have a job to get into."

"Dean's working with you, is he?"

Noah smiled, elbowing his son gently in the arm. "I thought it'd be good for him to spend a bit of time outside. Much better than being inside playing around on that game station thing."

"Play Station," Dean corrected him. It would appear that Dean couldn't muster the same enthusiasm as his father.

"Maybe Dean could wait for you in the van," Tom said. Noah baulked at the suggestion and Tom noted the smile fade from Charlotte's face. Noah sneered at him.

"Anything you have to say to me can be said in front of the lad," Noah said. Tom stared at him.

"I think it would be for the best," Tom said. Noah held Tom's eye for a moment, then turned to his son.

"Maybe you should give us a bit of space, son. I'm sure it won't take a minute." He handed his keys to Dean who accepted them, glanced at his mum and turned to walk away. Noah reached out and caught him by the forearm. Dean was surprised, but Noah pulled him into a quick hug. "We'll not be long, lad." Dean nodded and walked back down the slope towards the car park. He glanced at Tom as he left, but said nothing. Noah sighed, watching him go for a moment, then turned back to Tom. "Out with it then, Tom. Why did you summon us here?"

"To find out why you killed Aaron," Tom said to both of them. Charlotte scoffed, shaking her head in disbelief. Noah held Tom's eye though, working his jaw ever so slightly. "Are you going to even bother denying it?"

"Of course we'll deny it!" Charlotte said. "Why would—"

Tom took a piece of paper from his pocket, unfolding it and handing it to Charlotte. She looked at it, flapping in her hands as she tried in vain to hold it steady. She looked up at Tom. "What's this?"

"It's proof that Dean isn't your son, Noah," Tom said flatly. Noah was unfazed. "But you already knew that, didn't you?" He looked between them. "You both knew. Has it always been so, or did you also learn it recently? Perhaps at the same time as Aaron found out."

Noah's brow furrowed, but his expression was one of resignation above all else. He met Tom's gaze. "I knew," he said quietly. Charlotte glanced at him. He looked at her, lips pursed. "I always knew, if I'm honest."

"You never said," she replied and Tom could hear the surprise and the emotion in her voice.

"I just lied to myself, Charlotte," Noah said. "And I kept it going."

"Why?"

"Because you gave me everything I'd always been looking for. You gave me someone to love, a family to care for… a purpose. I'd never experienced that, not in any meaningful sense anyway. You knew what my homelife was all about. The arguments… the drinking." Noah shrugged. "All I ever wanted was the stability of a loving family. You offered me a chance for that… and I took it willingly."

The realisation that Noah had kept the secret without her knowing, saw Charlotte choke on her words. She tentatively reached out to her ex, gently touching his hand. He reflexively moved towards her, but she let the touch linger only for a moment before she withdrew. Looking at Tom with a firm stare, her eyes gleamed defiantly.

"Where did you get this information?"

"Does it matter?" he asked. "What matters is that two men are dead. Was Aaron's life worth keeping your secret?"

"He was going to ruin everything!" Charlotte snapped. "He didn't care about who he hurt, as long as he got what he wanted. The same old Aaron. Nothing had changed in him at all over the years. He was still the selfish bastard he always was."

"But you fell for him," Tom said.

"I was a child!" Charlotte retorted. "He coerced and manipulated me into doing what he wanted. And then... when he'd had his fill he cast me aside like a piece of rubbish!"

Tom had to consider that that may well be true. Charlotte had been only fourteen, coming fifteen, when Aaron had had the affair with her behind Kristy's back. Aaron himself was only fifteen at that time, and so it was hardly akin to the predatory affections of a grown man. Embarking on a relationship with Kristy's sister like that was morally dubious, without doubt, but teenagers did stupid things the world over. It was also quite easy to shift all of the blame onto a dead man who couldn't defend himself.

"You kept his secret," Tom said, not wishing to cast any judgement. All he wanted was the truth.

"How could I not?" Charlotte said, her eyes glazing. Was that anger, frustration or genuine upset at the memory. "I was in pain, grieving. My parents were shattered at the loss of their precious daughter—"

"Their favourite," Tom said quietly.

Charlotte bristled. It was well known at the time how Kristy was the perceived golden child in her family. She was the sports star at school. She was top set in every subject and had been voted Head Girl by her peers in her final year, accepting the coveted *Person Most Likely to Succeed Award* at the graduation ball. Charlotte, barely a year younger than her older sister had never managed to hit the same heights. She was intelligent, beautiful, and well liked among her own peers, but was always in the shadow of her sister, no matter what she achieved.

Studying people for much of his adult life, Tom could see how Charlotte could have pursued what her sister had, if only to prove she was equally capable. He could see that determination reflected in her expression now, glowering at him.

"I was just as good as she was!" Charlotte said. "But they never saw it."

"Your parents loved you," Tom said. "We all knew that. And so did your sister."

"Don't you dare bring her into this," Charlotte said. Tom glanced to his right, hearing the waves crashing against the groynes and the cliff face far below them.

"Did she know?" Tom asked. Charlotte blinked at him, her angry defiance dissipating. "Did she know what you and Aaron had been doing?"

"Don't—"

"Did she find out?" Tom persisted. "And that's why she came up here."

Charlotte choked on her words, her head bowing, reluctant to meet Tom's gaze. "I... I..."

"Kristy was your greatest advocate," Tom said. "She cheered you on from the sidelines at every sporting match she could make. I saw her. I remember it. But she couldn't bear your betrayal, could she? She found out—"

"Aaron told her!" Charlotte screamed at him, her head snapping up, tears in her eyes. "He told her. Not through guilt, but because he wanted to hurt her. She finished with him and he wanted to get back at her."

Tom pursed his lips. Up until this point, he hadn't wanted to explore this angle. It would be impossible to prove but he had to unsettle Charlotte. It was the only way that he was going to draw the truth from her. From both of them. Noah, who had remained pretty much silent up until this point, stepped forward. Tom instinctively took a step back, unsure of what Noah was thinking.

"Whatever she did back then, Charlotte didn't deserve what Aaron planned to do when he came back," Noah said. "And I'm damned sure that I didn't."

"He was planning to claim his son, wasn't he?"

Noah nodded.

"What happened? Did he bump into you in the street and clock the resemblance with Dean? I have to admit, it struck me as soon as I saw him."

"He told me some nonsense that he couldn't have children," Charlotte said. "That Dean was his only chance at being a father—"

"It's true," Tom said. "Aaron couldn't have any more children."

"Dean was my son!" Noah said bitterly. "Not Aaron's. I raised him. It was me who picked him up when he was crying, changed his nappy when he was dirty. I taught him to ride a bike... bought him his first razor when he needed to learn to shave. Me! Where was Aaron?"

Tom shook his head. "I don't know."

"Exactly," Noah said. "I raised him. Dean's my boy. And that son of a bitch wasn't going to take him away from me. Not if I had anything to do with it."

"So... you killed him?" Tom asked. "Does that sound like the proper course of action to take?"

"No... it wasn't like that," Noah said, dragging a hand through his dishevelled hair. "That's not how it happened. We went there to talk to him. To reason with him—"

"Noah, be quiet!" Charlotte snapped. Noah looked at her, his eyes narrowing. "Don't say anything. He's fishing, that's all. He doesn't know anything."

"They have trace evidence that can prove you were there," Tom said, glancing at Noah's boots and recalling the castings that were taken at the scene. "Plus, they have mobile phone data. Did you leave your mobiles at home when you went to see Aaron that night after the reunion? Because the GPS signal given off will put you right at the scene." They glanced awkwardly at one another. "What did happen that night?" Charlotte closed her eyes and Noah looked crestfallen. "Tell me," Tom said.

"We only went there to talk to him," Noah said. "I swear... he was going to confront Dean. He was going to tell him."

"And you couldn't let that happen," Tom said.

"No..." Noah replied. "We wanted to reason with him. To explain that it wasn't in Dean's best interests at the moment. Charlotte and I are getting back together. We are going to be a family again, the three of us... and your daughter, right love? Maybe, in the future, then Dean could learn the truth—"

"No!" Charlotte said. "Not now, not in the future. Not ever!"

"Charlotte, we can explain—"

"Never!" she bit back. She stared at Tom. "He laughed at us. You didn't know him like I did. Aaron... he laughed at us. At me. It was like our lives, Dean's life, meant *nothing* to him. The same old Aaron. It was all about himself."

"Who hit him?" Tom asked, glancing between them. "Was it you?" he asked Noah, who almost imperceptibly shook his head.

"I did," Charlotte said. "I hit him."

"What with?"

She shrugged. "Some stupid ornament he had on the table." Noah lowered his gaze to the ground at his feet.

"An ornament?" Tom asked. She nodded but avoided his gaze.

"Yes," she said. "I just… reacted on impulse, in anger. I couldn't believe how belligerent he was. I hit him… and… he fell." She looked away. "I threw the ornament in the bushes when we left. I didn't even realise it was still in my hand until Noah pointed it out as we got back to his van."

Tom watched her closely. She still wouldn't meet his eye. "Noah," he said, and the man looked up at him. "What did you do then?"

"We left," he said. "I pulled Charlotte away and, like she said, we got back into my van and I drove her home. Aaron was on the floor… groaning, but he was alive. I swear he was alive. He wasn't badly hurt." Noah was certain. "I would never have left him if I thought he… he… was going to crawl away and fall into the pool and drown. I would never."

"You didn't think to help him?" Tom asked. "You could have called an ambulance."

"I thought," Noah said, his brow creased, "that if he got up, he might attack Charlotte or me, because he was sure to be angry that she'd hit him like that. I thought it best that we just go. So, I got us out of there as quickly as we could." He looked sheepishly at Tom. "It was an accident. Fights happen all the time. That's all it was. Just a stupid fight."

"That cost a man his life," Tom said. Noah's gaze lowered again, and he nodded. "And Tony?"

"That's nothing to do with us!" Noah said. He looked furtively at Charlotte. "I was buying some bits and pieces for work. The police checked. I couldn't have done it."

"No, you couldn't," Tom said, looking to Charlotte. "But she could."

"No, she—"

"Phoned Tony on the day he died," Tom said. Noah glanced at her. "You were in regular contact with him, weren't you, Charlotte?" She lifted her head, but she looked past Tom, out towards the horizon, emotionless.

"Why would you be calling Tony?" Noah asked. She didn't answer. "Charlotte? Why would you be calling him?"

"Because she's been having an affair with him for months," Tom said. Noah's head snapped round to glare at Tom.

"No, that can't be right," Noah said. 'Tell him, Charlotte."

"Calling each other at odd hours of the day and night," Tom said. "Stealing moments when you could."

"C-Charlotte?" Noah asked, turning to face her, his mouth open. "Tell him it's not true." He glanced between her and Tom with a confused expression. "He's got it wrong… tell him —" he glared at Tom. "You've got it wrong, Tom."

"I haven't though," Tom said. "What happened, Charlotte? Did you go to see Tony expecting a sympathetic ear after telling him what had happened? Did you tell him what you'd done hoping he'd help you, offload some of the guilt, maybe?"

"You have *no idea*," she said through gritted teeth. "No idea what I've had to deal with—"

"Tony made a 999 call," Tom said. "He never got the chance to ask for help before the call ended. And I suspect the call ended when you stabbed him, Charlotte."

She stared at Tom, pure rage in her eyes. "He said he wanted a life with me. That he was going to leave her, that… that plastic-fantastic, orange painted, biscuit of a wife of his. He lied to me… he was the same as all the others."

"Another accident?" Tom asked. "Tony just fell onto that kitchen knife, did he?"

"Charlotte…" Noah asked, imploring her to deny it. To deny all of it. But she didn't.

"Just another pathetic little man," she said, almost spitting the words. "A spineless, self-serving, pathetic little man… out for what he could take from me." Noah reached out and tried to take her hand, but she snatched it away from him, hissing as she did so. "Don't touch me!" Noah recoiled, visibly shaken.

"You… didn't do that," Noah said. "Not you. You couldn't do something like that. It's not who you are…"

"And what would you know?" Charlotte sneered at him. "You tinker around with plants and hedge cuttings. You're happy to just get by."

"I'm happy to be with you," Noah said, crestfallen.

"Then you are settling for less than you deserve," she said. "And I need *more than* settling in my life."

"I… I don't understand," Noah said.

"It's quite simple really, Noah," Tom said. "Charlotte saw her life as she knew it coming to an end. Aaron was going to tell everyone about what happened all those years ago. He was going to lay parental claim to Dean… and in doing so, probably ruin Charlotte's life in the process. I don't doubt he didn't care about that. Aaron was self-centred. Charlotte couldn't allow that to happen."

"No," Noah said. "It wasn't like that. We're starting again. We were going there to convince Aaron, not to attack him. You should look at the security footage. He has so many cameras—"

"You *really* are a fool, Noah!" Charlotte said, viciously chiding him. "You married me despite knowing that my child wasn't yours. You're pathetic."

Noah visibly shrank before them, shoulders sagging. Tom kept his eyes on Charlotte, but addressed Noah. "You've been lending Charlotte your van when she needed it, while her car has been off the road, haven't you?"

"Yeah," Noah said. "So what?"

"Did you lend it to her last night by any chance?"

Noah looked at him. "Yes, why?"

Charlotte lifted her chin and straightened her back, taking a deep breath. "You'll never make any of it stick," she said. Tom inclined his head, looking past her. Charlotte turned, following his gaze over to the end of the footpath where Cassie stood, Eric alongside her and Dean beside him. Cassie lifted a transparent evidence bag in the air. Inside it was a hammer. The handle was long, thin with a ball-peen head. They approached slowly, Dean hesitant beside Eric.

"Dad," Dean said, "they searched your van. I couldn't stop them."

Noah was agitated but it didn't appear to Tom that he was concerned by the search of his van. He was more confused than anything. "It's okay, son. I'm sure it's..." He looked at Tom questioningly.

"You stayed the night with Charlotte after you both visited Aaron, didn't you?"

"Yes," Noah said. He glanced nervously at Dean. "We... spent the night together. I... er... left before Dean woke up."

"And in that time, Charlotte returned to see Aaron... and attacked him with the hammer, your hammer."

"You can't prove any of this,' Charlotte hissed.

"And you used Noah's van to drive to the home of Professor David White last night, didn't you?" Tom asked. Charlotte remained tight-lipped. "You followed him home, probably from his office, and then you attacked him and left him for dead." Tom looked at Noah. "Using your vehicle again even though hers was back from the garage. She was setting you up, Noah. Setting you up to take the fall if it went wrong."

"Don't believe him, Noah," Charlotte said. "He's making things up as he goes along—"

"Really?" Tom asked. "Well, seeing as I'm on a roll. Let's see what else I can think of. I do wonder about what drove your sister, Kristy, to jump to her death from these cliffs… or did someone ensure that she did? It would take a cold, jealous person with an incredibly violent temper to do something like that, wouldn't it?"

Charlotte seethed, but before she could reply, Eric stepped forward and grasped her left arm. He pulled it behind her back, followed quickly by the other arm. She didn't resist. He secured her in handcuffs. Cassie came to stand in front of her.

"Charlotte Sears, I am arresting you on suspicion of the murder of Aaron Bell, the murder of Anthony Slater and the attempted murder of David White…"

Tom stepped away, steering Noah to come with him. Dean, gobsmacked and clearly in shock came with them although he was unable to tear his eyes away from his mother.

"Baby?" Charlotte said, in the first moment of genuine emotion that Tom witnessed, as she looked at her son. "I love you. Whatever anyone says, I love you and I did all of this to keep you safe. I love you…"

Cassie and Eric guided her back along the path. Dean was openly crying now and Noah was struggling to take it all in. He looked at Tom.

"I don't understand… it was an accident—"

CHAPTER TWENTY-EIGHT

TOM LED Noah away from Dean, ensuring they were out of earshot.

"After you left and went back to her place, Charlotte must have returned to Blakeney while you were asleep and she finished the job..." Noah looked towards Dean who seemed utterly overwhelmed. "I suspect that was when the final blow came from the hammer. A hammer Charlotte took from your van. Aaron wasn't simply struck once by accident in a fit of pique. He was murdered. Afterwards, she must have cleared away the hard drive to get rid of all the camera footage from the second visit showing what she'd done."

"David?" Noah asked. "What has that attack to do with anything?"

"David White is the criminologist who went on television, explaining how he thought the two murders, Aaron and Tony's, were crimes of a personal nature. I think – and it is only my theory – that Charlotte believed attacking David might draw attention away from her, away from the personal nature motivating the crime. That was David's theory. If the police thought it was a random killer rather than someone close to Aaron and Tony, then she might get away with it. And, if not..." he winced, "your van will have been spotted at the scene, thereby placing you there. You would have been present at the scene of Aaron's death and the attack on David White."

"By Charlotte," Noah said. Tom nodded solemnly. "No. S-She wouldn't do that to me," Noah said, but his tone was less than convincing. Tom placed a supportive hand on his shoulder.

"I'm sorry, Noah. I really am." Tom took a deep breath. "She wanted me around, thinking I might be able to glean information about the case from my colleagues. She was trying to stay in the loop and keep ahead of the investigation."

"What about Tony?"

Tom was unsure. "Maybe she confided in him, I don't know. I think that was an impulsive act of self-preservation rather than a premeditated act."

"That'll be no comfort to his family," Noah said bitterly. Dean walked over to them, still clearly upset. Noah forced a smile but he was also on the verge of breaking down.

"What are we going to do now, Dad?" Dean asked. Noah put an arm around his son and pulled him into a hug. He kissed him on the top of his head and held him tightly.

"We stick together, son. No matter what happens, we stick together."

Tom left the two of them alone. Noah would need to give a detailed statement regarding the events of their visit to Blakeney but that could be done later. When he and Cassie hatched this plan, he hadn't been sure as to the extent of each of their involvement in the crimes. In a way, he was pleased that it fell on Charlotte and not Noah, too. Dean was about to face a truly traumatic series of events in his life, learning about both the past and the present. At least he would still have Noah, his father, by his side. It wouldn't matter that they were not biological blood relatives. Tom knew that from his own experience with Saffy. He couldn't love her any more than he did.

Glancing back at Noah and Dean, still embracing one another, he felt they would survive this. Somehow.

At the end of the path he came to the car park. Officers had already sealed off the van belonging to Noah Cook. Tom walked close to the rear, spying the damage he'd noticed on the night of the vigil and now he spied the broken rear light, the one Tamara described. He was met by DCI Greg Talbot, who raised his chin as Tom approached.

"Hello, sir," Tom said, unsure of the reception he was likely to receive.

"Tom," Talbot said with a curt nod.

"I'm sorry to have stumbled into the case—"

"Forget it, Tom," the DCI said holding up a hand. "What other DCI can take over a double murder inquiry and get a result on the same day?" He smiled, his slightly pink, rounded cheeks lifting together. Tom smiled back.

"It's quite a result, sir."

"They'll call me Super Copper back at the nick," Talbot said. The smile faded. "They won't. I know what they call me, but a result is a result, either way!"

"I'm pleased for you, sir," Tom said.

"I've spoken to the Chief Superintendent, Tom. I felt I had to, once it was clear what we were going to do this afternoon." Tom felt a knot tighten in his chest. "He's in complete agreement that it's a job well done, all round."

"Thank you, sir."

Talbot offered Tom his hand and he accepted it. "Now," the DCI said, glancing around them to make sure they wouldn't be overheard, and touching the tip of his forefinger to his nose in a telling gesture, "we've also had a nudge from the coroner.

That little matter you got yourself caught up in a while back... the unofficial word through back channels is that it's going to be ruled as a justifiable homicide." He winked at Tom. "The disciplinary panel have always been likely to follow the same ruling. You'll be in the clear, son. Don't worry."

Tom felt a sudden release of pressure. Although not official, that was the best case he could have hoped for. The nightmare of the past few months was coming to an end.

"Thank you, sir."

Cassie bounded over to him, looking between the two men. "Sorry, am I interrupting?"

"Not at all, DS Knight," Talbot said, excusing himself. "I need to call this in."

"What is it, Cassie?" Tom asked once they were alone.

"I just heard from Dave Marshall at the hospital. It's good news. They think David is out of the woods. He's showing strong signs of recovery. It's still early days, but... it's positive. It would appear that Charlotte isn't great at wielding a knife. She may be cold-hearted as well as cold-blooded, but she's not much of an assassin."

Tom exhaled heavily. "A good result all round then," he said. Noah and Dean came into view up the slope, a dozen metres or so away from them and walking slowly. Noah had an arm around his son's shoulder. Tom's pleasure was tempered slightly. "For some anyway."

"They have each other," Cassie said softly. "And that's something."

"I hope it's enough," he said quietly. "I suppose I should contact Aaron's wife and set her mind at ease about what Aaron was up to. I wouldn't want her to hear it on the evening news."

"Elena?" Cassie asked, snorting. Tom looked at her. "She left me a voicemail this morning from Stansted. She was about to board a private jet and fly out to Switzerland. Something tells me she won't care all that much. She's an odd one for sure."

Tom arched his eyebrows. "The world would be a dull place if we were all the same, wouldn't it?"

"And we would likely be out of business," Cassie said. "The way society works, there will always be criminals."

"And people needed to chase them," Tom said. "If they can stomach it."

"I'll need to take a formal statement from you soon. Maybe you'll be back at work before I do that."

"The jungle drums are still working then?" Tom asked, picking up that Cassie had also heard word of what verdict the coroner was planning to announce. She cocked her head with a knowing look. Tom shook his head. "Does anyone know how to keep a secret these days?"

"It will be good to have you back, sir," Cassie said. He was pensive and she must have picked up on it, reading his expression. "You are coming back, aren't you?"

"I'll be around," Tom said.

"I'll need that statement," she said after him as he made to walk away.

"You know where to find me," he said without looking back.

FREE BOOK GIVEAWAY

Visit the author's website at **www.jmdalgliesh.com** and sign up to the VIP Club and be the first to receive news and previews of forthcoming works.

Here you can download a FREE eBook novella exclusive to club members;

Life & Death - A Hidden Norfolk novella

Never miss a new release.

No spam, ever, guaranteed. You can unsubscribe at any time.

Enjoy this book? You could make a real difference.

Because reviews are critical to the success of an author's career, if you have enjoyed this novel, please do me a massive favour by entering one onto Amazon.

Type the following link into your internet search bar to go to the Amazon page and leave a review;

https://geni.us/JMD-WDC

If you prefer not to follow the link please visit the sales page where you purchased the title in order to leave a review.

Reviews increase visibility. Your help in leaving one would make a massive difference to this author and I would be very grateful.

ALSO BY THE AUTHOR

In the Misty Isle Series
A Long Time Dead
The Dead Man of Storr
The Talisker Dead
The Cuillin Dead
A Dead Man on Staffin Beach
Death at Neist Point

In the Hidden Norfolk Series
One Lost Soul
Bury Your Past
Bury Your Past
Kill Our Sins
Tell No Tales
Hear No Evil
The Dead Call
Kill Them Cold
A Dark Sin
To Die For
Fool Me Twice
The Raven Song
Angel of Death
Dead To Me
Blood Runs Cold
Watch and Prey
When Death Calls

Life and Death**
**FREE ebook - visit jmdalgliesh.com

ALSO BY THE AUTHOR

In the Dark Yorkshire Series

Divided House
Blacklight
The Dogs in the Street
Blood Money
Fear the Past
The Sixth Precept

Psychological Thrillers

Home Wrecker
Family Doctor

Audiobooks

In the Hidden Norfolk Series

One Lost Soul
Bury Your Past
Kill Our Sins
Tell No Tales
Hear No Evil
The Dead Call
Kill Them Cold
A Dark Sin
To Die For
Fool Me Twice
The Raven Song
Angel of Death
Dead To Me
Blood Runs Cold

Collections

Hidden Norfolk Books 1-3

Audiobooks

In the Dark Yorkshire Series
Read by Greg Patmore

Divided House
Blacklight
The Dogs in the Street
Blood Money
Fear the Past
The Sixth Precept

Collections
Dark Yorkshire Books 1-3
Dark Yorkshire Books 4-6

In the Misty Isle Series
Read by Angus King

A Long Time Dead
The Dead Man of Storr
The Talisker Dead
The Cuillin Dead
A Dead Man on Staffin Beach

Printed in Dunstable, United Kingdom